The Slow
Release

The Slow Release

STORIES ABOUT

Death

FROM THE
FLANNERY O'CONNOR AWARD
FOR SHORT FICTION

EDITED BY
ETHAN LAUGHMAN

THE UNIVERSITY OF GEORGIA PRESS
ATHENS

Published in part with the generous
support of Mrs. Lorraine Williams

© 2019 by the University of Georgia Press
Athens, Georgia 30602
www.ugapress.org
All rights reserved
Designed by Kaelin Chappell Broaddus
Set in 9/13.5 Walbaum 12pt

Most University of Georgia Press titles are
available from popular e-book vendors.

Printed digitally

Library of Congress Control Number: 2019933147
ISBN: 9780820355313 (pbk: alk. paper)
ISBN 9780820355306 (ebook)

CONTENTS

ACKNOWLEDGMENTS

The stories in this collection are from the following award-winning collections published by the University of Georgia Press:

Molly Giles, *Rough Translations* (1985), © 1985 by Molly Giles; "Rough Translations" first appeared in *Ascent*

Melissa Pritchard, *Spirit Seizures* (1987), © 1987 by Melissa Pritchard; "Taking Hold of Renee" first appeared in *Other Voices*

Nancy Zafris, *The People I Know* (1990), © 1990 by Nancy Zafris

Dianne Nelson Oberhansly, *A Brief History of Male Nudes in America* (1993), © 1993 by Dianne Nelson; "Evolution of Words" first appeared in the *Iowa Review*

Mary Clyde, *Survival Rates* (1999), © 1999 by Mary Clyde; "Jumping" first appeared in the *Georgia Review*

Robert Anderson, *Ice Age* (2000), © 2000 by Robert Anderson; "Death and the Maid" first appeared in *American Writing: A Magazine*

Gina Ochsner, *The Necessary Grace to Fall* (2002), © 2002 by Gina Ochsner

Ed Allen, *Ate It Anyway* (2003), © 2003 by Ed Allen; "Ralph Goes to Mexico" first appeared in *Gentleman's Quarterly*

Barbara Sutton, *The Send-Away Girl* (2004), © 2004 by Barbara Sutton

Anne Panning, *Super America* (2007), © 2007 by Anne Panning

Jacquelin Gorman, *The Viewing Room* (2013), © 2013 by Jacquelin Gorman; "Passerby" first appeared in *TheScreamOnline*

Monica McFawn, *Bright Shards of Someplace Else* (2014), © 2014 by the University of Georgia Press; "Snippet and the Rainbow Bridge" first appeared in *Bellingham Review*

Toni Graham, *The Suicide Club* (2015), © 2015 by the University of Georgia Press, "The Suicide Club" first appeared in *Jabberwock Review*

Anne Raeff, *The Jungle around Us* (2016), © 2016 by the University of Georgia Press; "Chinese Opera" first appeared in the *New England Review*

Lisa Graley, *The Current That Carries* (2016), © 2016 by the University of Georgia Press

A thank you also goes to the University of Georgia Main Library staff for technical support in preparing these stories for publication.

INTRODUCTION

The Flannery O'Connor Award for Short Fiction was established in 1981 by Paul Zimmer, then the director of the University of Georgia Press, and press acquisitions editor Charles East. East would serve as the first series editor, judging the competition and selecting two collections to publish each year. The inaugural volumes in the series, *Evening Out* by David Walton and *From the Bottom Up* by Leigh Allison Wilson, appeared in 1983 to critical acclaim. Nancy Zafris (herself a Flannery O'Connor Award–winner for the 1990 collection *The People I Know*) was the second series editor, serving in the role from 2008 to 2015. Zafris was succeeded by Lee K. Abbott in 2016, and the press has just announced that Roxane Gay will be the next to assume the role, choosing award winners beginning in 2019. Competition for the award has since become an important proving ground for writers, and the press has published seventy-four volumes to date, helping to showcase talent and sustain interest in the short story form. These volumes together feature at total of approximately eight hundred stories by authors who are based in all regions of the country and even internationally. It has been my pleasure to have read each and every one.

The idea of undertaking a project that could honor the diversity of the series' stories but also present them in a unified way had been hanging around the press for a few years. What occurred to us first, and what remained the most appealing approach, was to pull the hundreds of stories out of their current packages—volumes of collected stories by individual authors—and regroup them by common themes or subjects. After finishing my editorial internship at the press, I was brought on to the project and began to sort the stories into specific thematic categories. What followed was a deep dive into the award and its history and a gratifying acquaintance with the many authors whose works constitute the award's legacy.

Anthologies are not new to the series. A tenth-anniversary collection, published in 1993, showcased one story from each of the volumes published in the award's first decade. A similar collection appeared in 1998, the fifteenth year of the series. In 2013, the year of the series' thirtieth anniversary, the press published two volumes modeled after the tenth- and fifteenth-anniversary volumes. These anthologies together included one story from each of the fifty-five collections published up to that point. One of the 2013 volumes represented the series' early years, under the editorship of Charles East. The other showcased the editorship of Nancy Zafris. In a nod to the times, both thirtieth-anniversary anthologies appeared in e-book form only.

The present project is wholly different in both concept and scale. The press plans to republish more than five hundred stories in more than forty volumes, each focusing on a specific theme—from love to food to homecoming and homesickness. Each volume will aim to collect exemplary treatments of its theme, but with enough variety to give an overview of what the series is about. The stories inside paint a colorful picture that includes the varied perspectives multiple authors can have on a single theme.

Each volume, no matter its focus, includes the work of authors whose stories celebrate the variety of short fiction styles and subjects to be found across the history of the award. Just as Flannery O'Connor is more than just a southern writer, the University of Georgia Press, by any number of measures, has been more than a regional publisher for some time. As the first series editor, Charles East, happily reported in his anthology of the O'Connor Award stories, the award "managed to escape [the] pitfall" of becoming a regional stereotype. When Paul Zimmer established the award he named it after Flannery O'Connor as the writer who best embodied the possibilities of the short-story form. In addition, O'Connor, with her connections to the South and readership across the globe, spoke to the ambitions of the press at a time when it was poised to ramp up both the number and scope of its annual title output. The O'Connor name has always been a help in keeping the series a place where writers strive to be published and where readers and critics look for quality short fiction.

The award has indeed become an internationally recognized institution. The seventy-four (and counting) Flannery O'Connor Award authors come from all parts of the United States and abroad. They have lived in Arizona, Arkansas, California, Colorado, Georgia, Indiana, Maryland, Massachusetts, Texas, Utah, Washington, Canada, Iran, England, and elsewhere. Some have written novels. Most have published stories in a variety of literary quarterlies and popular magazines. They have been awarded numerous fellowships and prizes. They are world-travelers, lecturers, poets, columnists, editors, and screenwriters.

There are risks in the thematic approach we are taking with these anthologies, and we hope that readers will not take our editorial approach as an attempt to draw a circle around certain aspects of a story or in any way close off possibilities for interpretation. Great stories don't have to resolve anything, be set any particular time nor place, or be written in any one way. Great stories don't have to be anything. Still, when a story resonates with enough readers in a certain way, it is safe to say that it has spoken to us meaningfully about, for instance, love, death, and certain concerns, issues, pleasures, or life events.

We at the press had our own ideas about how the stories

might be gathered, but we were careful to get author input on the process. The process of categorizing their work was not easy for any of them. Some truly agonized. Having their input was invaluable; having their trust was humbling. The goal of this project is to faithfully represent these stories despite the fact that they have been pulled from their original collections and are now bedmates with stories from a range of authors taken from diverse contexts.

Also, just because a single story is included in a particular volume does not mean that that volume is the only place that story could have comfortably been placed. For example, "Sawtelle," from Dennis Hathaway's *The Consequences of Desire*, tells the story of a subcontractor in duress when he finds out his partner is the victim of an extramarital affair. We have included it in the volume of stories about love, but it could have been included in those on work, friends, and immigration without seeming out of place.

The stories in this volume reflect on death in diverse ways, including the following: as a subject of our macabre fascination, as an event we prepare for, as something that so easily overcomes all other thoughts, as it relates to forgiveness, as it initiates a process of mourning, and as an occasion for a bittersweet celebration of a life. The included stories are ordered roughly in sequence according to these preoccupations, although admittedly with some overlap. This volume will show how fifteen Flannery O'Connor Award–winning authors conceptualized death and how the characters within their stories process the myriad emotions that accompany the loss of someone or something dear.

Anne Panning's "What Happened"—the absence of a question mark in the title signaling that Panning's piece is a briefing rather than an interrogation—attacks our fascination with bereavement head-on, asking, "Why, then, do we seek blood, tragedy, horror?" This question can be asked of television and film centered on crime, fictional or not, as well as literature. Panning, as well as the other contributors, does not seek to satisfy our appetite for "blood, tragedy, horror" but instead recenters our attention on the connection that is the antidote for loss. Each story adds to our collective understanding of and reaction to death. "What Happened" is not only a fascinating diversion in form and tone from the other Flannery O'Connor Award stories but also an indictment of our infatuation with violent tragedy. Anne Raeff's "Chinese Opera" is a different kind of exploration of mortality, this time told through the eyes of a child hearing of the murder of her neighbor and former baby sitter. The adults in young Simone's life—from her own father to the mother of the deceased—introduce her to different customs and rituals associated with death—from the Zoroastrian custom of exposing the dead to the elements to the traditional customs and rituals inherent in a Roman Catholic funeral. Robert Anderson's "Death and the Maid" features characters who make a living off of dead bodies, as the story follows a farmer's wife who inters bodies for the city on her Texas property. The wife's relationship with her interred (she often has "conversations" with them) turns from simply unsettling to supernatural when one urges the other to reveal dark secrets.

Four stories in this volume depict characters as they prepare for the death of a loved one. An ailing grandmother prepares for her own funeral in Molly Giles's "Rough Translations." After her death, the focus then shifts to her children as they process the loss of their mother. Monica McFawn's "Snippet and the Rainbow Bridge" relates the story of two animal rescuers who must decide the best course of action for an invalid horse. Barbara Sutton's "The Brotherhood of Healing" follows a sickly yet unstressed Mrs. Rodgers as she is matter-of-factly told that an upcoming surgery has unfavorable odds of survival. Ed Allen's

"Ralph Goes to Mexico" recounts a road trip taken by the lonely Lydia, her leukemia-stricken feline in tow, so that he can see Mexico before he dies. Lydia's relationship with her pet and the companionship he provides is the centerpiece of the narrative, and Allen uses the piece to explore how we all need an anchor to tie us to others.

Much of this volume concerns the process of mourning the death of a loved one. At times such a process finds resolution, as in Gina Ochsner's "How the Dead Live," in which we are treated to the final days of a father's time on earth as he lovingly watches over his pregnant daughter as a ghost, from beyond the grave. Undead protagonists stalk a handful of other Flannery O'Connor Award stories not included in this volume, musing on their life in retrospect, or, in one particular case, watching detectives solve the case of the their (the deceased's) own murder—but Ochsner's story is unique in offering a note of hope and encouragement to continue despite tremendous loss. In other stories, such as Melissa Pritchard's "Taking Hold of Renee" and Nancy Zafris's "Grace's Reply," characters find it nigh impossible to function after a loss. The death of a loved one—especially a child—is never fully overcome, but Renee is exceptionally debilitated even two years after her child's death. Zafris's Grace begins to accept the loss of her son after she finds another person to pour herself into. Dianne Nelson Oberhansly's "Evolution of Words"—atmospheric as it is brief and heartbreaking—reads like a prose poem, rendering a melancholy San Francisco in exquisite, rainy detail: the city "a miracle of light, the rain-wet streets opening from Battery to Sansome and finally down to Grant." As the narrator re-creates a hypothetical vision of a lost family member walking through "the world in rags," the story meditates on the lingering effects of suicide and shows how survivors fashion situations in their heads to find peace after the death of a loved one.

One story in particular covers a topic that—until compiling

this volume—I had previously not connected with the concept of death: forgiveness. Jacquelin Gorman's "Passerby" offers a unique take on the need for forgiveness following a death as an important aspect of death's aftermath. Those at fault, for whom guilt weighs just as heavily as grief weighs on the bereaved, stand to benefit from the peace of mind that comes when those who have been wronged make their peace with the one responsible for their pain. Forgiveness catalyzes the sense of community necessary to overcome tragedy and cycles of guilt.

Communities, which in these stories are made up of people bound together by similar experiences and losses, play a crucial role in the process of healing. In Mary Clyde's "Jumping," young Joan recounts a tragic skiing accident and the lasting impact it made in their community. "Jumping" is a story about the impossibility of escaping from memories, about how one experience forever changes a person's outlook, and about (as in many other stories in Clyde's collection) the importance of the bonds found in community and friendship. Toni Graham's "The Suicide Club" is the title story of a collection that shows how people cope (or refuse to cope) with a loss. Though the death of Holly's fiancé is the inciting narrative incident, "The Suicide Club" is more a story of Holly's reaction and recovery and of the hope that can be found amid anguish. Holly attends a weekly "suicide survivor's workshop," glibly rebranded "the suicide club" by a brash New York City transplant who, like Holly, also lost someone to suicide.

At times, the loss of a loved one occasions more of a celebration than a lament. Such is the case with this volume's final story, Lisa Graley's "Burying Ground." In it, a group of old friends, standing graveside, discover the deceased had one last trick to pull. The (nonliteral) band of brothers then spend the day reminiscing, introducing levity to the funeral—a levity that runs through all of Graley's collection. A shared history binds these men together, and they realize that death and life both have their place in the world, choosing to celebrate life rather than mourn its loss.

In *Creating Flannery O'Connor*, Daniel Moran writes that O'Connor first mentioned her infatuation with peacocks in her essay "Living with a Peacock" (later republished as "King of the Birds"). Since the essay's appearance, O'Connor has been linked with imagery derived from the bird's distinctive feathers and silhouette by a proliferation of critics and admirers, and one can now hardly find a publication about O'Connor that does not depict or refer to her "favorite fowl" and its association with immortality and layers of symbolic and personal meaning. As Moran notes, "Combining elements of her life on a farm, her religious themes, personal eccentricities, and outsider status, the peacock has proved the perfect icon for O'Connor's readers, critics, and biographers, a form of reputation-shorthand that has only grown more ubiquitous over time."

We are pleased to offer these anthologies as another way of continuing Flannery O'Connor's legacy. Since its conception, thirty-seven years' worth of enthralling, imaginative, and thought-provoking fiction has been published under the name of the Flannery O'Connor Award. The award is just one way that we hope to continue the conversation about O'Connor and her legacy while also circulating and sharing recent authors' work among readers throughout the world.

It is perhaps unprecedented for such a long-standing short fiction award series to republish its works in the manner we are going about it. The idea for the project may be unconventional, but it draws on an established institution—the horn-of-plenty that constitutes the Flannery O'Connor Award series backlist— that is still going strong at the threshold of its fortieth year. I am in equal parts intimidated and honored to present you with what I consider to be these exemplars of the Flannery O'Connor Award. Each story speaks to the theme uniquely. Some of these stories were chosen for their experimental nature, others for their unique take on the theme, and still others for exhibiting matchlessness in voice, character, place, time, plot, relevance, humor, timelessness, perspective, or any of the thousand other metrics by which one may measure a piece of literature.

But enough from me. Let the stories speak for themselves.

ETHAN LAUGHMAN

The Slow
Release

How the Dead Live

GINA OCHSNER

From *The Necessary Grace to Fall* (2002)

The Dead Man walks slowly up and down the staircase of his daughter's house. His tread is soundless and he is glad the ordinary creaks of the fifth and seventh steps do not report his presence for he does not wish to disturb his daughter. He walks the stairs hoping for a sliver in his foot, something to startle his awareness. He can't quite remember what his feet used to feel like, should feel like, but now they are heavy and it is with effort that he picks them up and slides them onto the steps.

Another problem: he is always dropping and losing his glasses on the staircase where his son-in-law, Neil, steps on them. The Dead Man depends upon Karen, his daughter, to find his glasses and to unbend the frames. Later, he'll discover his glasses atop the refrigerator, wiped so clean he believes he can see inside her head and read her thoughts.

At night his daughter's and son-in-law's dreams tumble like lint to the low point of their sloping room, under the door's sweep to the top of the stairs where the Dead Man sits and cards Karen's dreams from Neil's. Her dreams are of artichokes and loam, the sad sound of the geese honking, and the smell of clay. Neil's dreams reek of leather, the exhaust of crotch-rocket street bikes and of a woman named Marla. The Dead Man marvels at the colorless quality of Neil's dreams that unspool in shades of gray. The Dead Man calmly sorts their dreams and imagines he is playing a round of poker with the stars, while beside him at the top of the stairs Shura, his daughter's Siberian Husky, snores softly. Looking at the dog, he thinks he would trade everything he has ever had or known for a single night's sleep.

Only Shura senses his presence. Shura follows him to the swing on the back porch where the Dead Man measures slow arcs through the nights, which seem to him to be getting longer and longer. On the porch Shura sleeps at the Dead Man's feet and chases birds in his dreams, running the crows off into a mud-fish sky. The Dead Man has never envied a dog so much as now. He envies all the night animals that curl up like the ends of paper, fold up in darkness and go to sleep in the quiet. He considers the ceaseless movement of the sea, wonders if, like him, the sea is jealous and, given a last wish, would want to hold still within its tremulous boundaries and slumber.

Some nights, the Dead Man studies the moon and thinks in the calm of darkness where he would want to sleep, if he could sleep. But thinking this way wears on him and he licks his finger and holds it out, testing the pitch of the earth's trembling. In those moments he wonders if there are other walking, breathing dead summoned from trampled memory. He might like to get together a game of poker, bet the pale dreams of his son-in-law against the dreams of someone else's in-law.

The Dead Man counts his shallow breaths and phlegmless coughs as he swings and smokes Neil's cigarettes, enjoying those cigarettes even more, knowing that dead men shouldn't be able to smoke. A collection of his daughter's memories, the Dead Man is held together by his faulty suspenders and his dentist's bridgework. He knows that mourning can afford a clarity of vision. He suspects that each day in the hour before dawn when most people are dreaming his daughter is fishing through memories of him, panning for the different parts. A camping trip in Minnesota reveals his hands, cracked by wind and water. A Christmas long past yields the handkerchief she gave him, now folded and refolded so many times it is an exercise in geometry. Her fifth birthday brings back the cleft in his chin, and the best, a prewar memory, two legs—count them: one, two. The Dead Man rubs his hands along the muscles in his thighs, marvels at the wonder of them, aware that he had never done this in life.

This piecemeal restoration amazes him for what she remembers and how she remembers, and even more important, what she forgets. Parts of him are missing, little lapses between the bones. His daughter's memory, though good, has skipped over some essential ingredients like water and blood and the dark bodies of his internal organs. He would like to lay his hand on the darkness inside himself, to touch it, to name it, for in between his ribs are endless openings, each rib another vaguely phrased question. Sometimes when the wind picks up, the Dead Man thinks that if he could stretch his arms out wide enough he could be borne by the wind, his hollow bones singing like lyres.

The Dead Man wonders how long his daughter will keep him in her house. He wonders what will happen when she lets go. Will he be caught and carried away by the wind as a balloon accidentally released by a child? Will he be catapulted to the moon? Will he go to hell? Is he in it already? These thoughts tire the Dead Man, reminding him that even in death there is desire and the state of being wearied by desire. He wishes she could hear him, held fast in her house. He wishes he could grab her by the shoulders and give her a hard shake. "Let me go," he'd demand. "Please," he'd say, a word he'd used sparingly all his life. After all, he had his reasons for diving headlong from the ninth floor of the Providence Center Parking Garage and he wishes his daughter could understand this.

For now, the Dead Man spends his days in his daughter's front yard where Neil has collected battered and broken-down vw bugs and buses. He runs his hands lovingly over their rusting shells and bent frames. He is walking in a graveyard of used cars and feels he is on holy ground, and wishes, once again, that he could feel his feet.

The Dead Man had lost a lot of things in life: his hair, his temper, his patience, and a few teeth. In death the catalogue continues: the sense of taste, his voice, and these losses never fail to surprise him; he never figured these sensations could simply vanish like the last of a pen's ink. He can't recall how things should feel against the skin, under the fingers. He can't discern changes in temperature (though when Karen catches Neil in an outrageous lie, he can still hear the mercury drop in her voice). He knows that soon all he'll be left with is weight, with knowing what is light and what is heavy.

Hungry to touch and be touched, a kiss and a stinging slap are one and the same to the Dead Man, who treasures both. Unable to shrug himself free of itches, the Dead Man thinks the flies have returned. He looks at the ants and sees only teeth, at the grass, which yields only blades.

The Dead Man can smell sugar going to grain long before it does. He can smell food going bad in the refrigerator days before it spoils. Owing to the powers of his nose, the Dead Man thinks he is becoming a dog. He is also an expert on shit. In the droppings left like miniature core samples over the yard by the wintering geese, he detects the presence of clover and other grasses.

In his son-in-law's shit, which looks and smells like hard-boiled eggs going bad, he smells red meat and knows Neil has been eating meals without his daughter, who does not cook red meat. The Dead Man can smell his son-in-law's infidelities and he hopes Neil is nursing a small colon cancer.

The Dead Man is conscious of his daughter's pregnancy before she is. Her skin smells differently, more metallic, and he feels a kick at the place where his heart used to be, an echo. The Dead Man is also aware that his daughter is unhappy and that her first thought upon discovering her pregnancy will be one of hope. She will pray that a child is just the thing that is missing in her marriage, the thing to make a quick mend. But in his newly acquired prescience and the amazing faculties of his nose, the Dead Man is sure that just the opposite will be true, that Neil is on his way out the door, and that this child, as beautiful as he knows it will be, will only hasten Neil's departure.

The Dead Man waits at the top of the stairs. In the bathroom, his daughter holds a plastic wand in her urine stream. The Dead Man knows it's a boy and wishes he could tell her so, and that it won't matter: her husband will leave anyway, but, like having a baby, it will be a good thing. Still, he is sorry that she will soon learn that being left is its own kind of deadness.

He counts the seconds along with his daughter, waiting for the pink stripes to emerge on the test strip. When the lines appear, Karen opens the bathroom and hunts out Neil, her mouth flattened into a tight grimace and her eyes watering. It is an old and familiar look, one the Dead Man recognizes instantly: Karen is both happy and sad at the same time and will check her elation and fear to match Neil's, will wait on him to decide what will win out, smiles or tears.

Confronted with the litmus strip, Neil is speechless. The Dead Man bites his bottom lip hard enough to have drawn blood had he been alive.

"It's OK, Hon." Neil breathes and blinks. "It's better than OK. It's wonderful." Neil holds Karen's hands in his as if they were two cold, small fish. The nervous blinking gives Neil away. Blink. Blink, blink, blink. The Dead Man hears each damn blink.

But for the wind shouldering through him, rattling his bones, nothing would make sense. The Dead Man especially likes the rush of wind sweeping up at nightfall. It reminds him of the bending elephant grass from his days on Hill 881 South in Khe Sanh, of being one of the few who survived (minus a leg). The wind reminds him of breathing, tells him that though he is dead, somehow through the regenerative powers of will, or perhaps loneliness, he is still alive. In the wind, the Dead Man thinks he can hear the voices of all those he once loved: his platoon commander Jerry Shiporsky—St. Jerry of the Overbite—picked off while crapping in a latrine. He remembers his wife, Ray Lynn, who left him because she was tired, she said, of nursing a man who couldn't heal. In the wind held aloft by the cold currents of nighttime blasts, the Dead Man hears them calling him, urging him, Jump, they say, and the sound filling his ears is beautiful music.

Karen spends most of her time eating and sleeping and dashing to the bathroom where it is a fifty-fifty guessing game: Will she empty her bladder or her stomach? Today it's her stomach, and when she emerges from the bathroom to sit on the edge of her bed the Dead Man considers mopping her brow with his overfolded handkerchief. He shuffles toward her, but stops when he sees her fingering an old picture of him just returned home from the war. He always hated that picture of himself. In it his eyes are hollow, like the sound of laughter in an empty room. In this moment, he feels remorse and almost wishes he hadn't jumped. He remembers how carefully he propped his crutches up against the cement ledge. But if he were honest with himself (and now it's hard not to be anything else) he feels remorse in fractions, two parts regret to one part relief. And he is sorry for this. He knows Karen is angry. But thankfully, not punitive. After all, she's recalled the prewar image of him and lucky dog, he's got both his legs back now. But then the Dead Man sees a strange look settling over Karen's face and she rips the photo, violently and into tiny pieces. Watching this stops him cold, like the shock of ice water, and he has no idea what to do next.

When he was alive, he contemplated all the ways a man might die. Now that he is dead, the Dead Man watches his son-in-law and counts the ways a man might live. He finds Neil contemptible, hates him, in fact, and has enough hate in his empty chest for three men. He despises Neil's stories and his nervous blinks. When Neil tells Karen a lie, the Dead Man can see it in Neil's eyes, which go blinkity, blink, blink.

Neil is a thirty-year younger version of the Dead Man and this revelation comes as a kick in the hollows of the Dead Man's chest. The discovery should make him more sympathetic toward Neil, but it doesn't. He hates Neil more for it, for what he is doing and will do to Karen. The Dead Man notes the gathering lines around his daughter's mouth and eyes. As he studies her, his remorse solidifies into a single hardened image, the face of his wife. And the Dead Man puts a finger on a true sorrow from his younger years, when, like Neil, he was full of shit.

7

If he concentrates, the Dead Man can recall the fatal flaws of his personality that haunted him in life. He carries his shame like buttons on the gig line of a shirt. He was an ass, he thinks, in spite of his pain meds. He recalls dead-end arguments with Ray Lynn, arguments she never could have won, for his point in arguing was not to be right or to prove anything, but to deliver sharp, angry words that felt good to shout and that he would forget having said before nightfall.

His son-in-law is careless with his daughter's heart: he no longer opens doors for her, and one evening, when Karen trips over Neil's feet, he does not try to catch her. Seeing this hurts the Dead Man in the hollowed cavity of his chest where his heart was. He considers the pain in his empty chest, astonished at the power the living have over the dead. He thinks he would like to stay here a while longer to take care of his daughter. On the other hand, he notes that all his feeble parlor tricks—all his attempts to spur his daughter to a just anger so that she will say the words that will make Neil go—have failed.

Each night after he is done sorting, the Dead Man places the dusty lumps of Neil's nighttime dreams next to his daughter's hairbrush, hoping she will detect what he can: the red strands of Marla's hair, the smell of gasoline and polished chrome, the scent of quick and easy lies and sure departures. But each morning Karen sweeps the tufts into her palm, flushes them down the toilet, scolds Shura for shedding so much, and walks to the staircase where she will discover again, with renewed amazement, the Dead Man's bent glasses.

Time haunts the Dead Man. He knows that since it takes at least nine months to bring in a life, it will take about nine months for his daughter to finish mourning his. If he has calibrated the clocks correctly, he should go about the same time the baby is born. With only so much space for each person in another's sphere of love and attention, the Dead Man takes delight in knowing that his daughter, despite her unswerving nostalgia, will have to slowly release him.

To help him count the wait, the Dead Man collects clocks, watches, egg timers, bedside alarms—even a sorry metronome belonging to Ray Lynn—depending upon those tiny clicks and ticks to sing out the thousands of seconds of every day. They become ridiculous, melodramatic in their reverberations, measuring Saturdays, which follow Wednesdays and Thursdays and Fridays, each of which are equal to their value. He has never been good with time, he thinks, each tick another small suffering. He remembers the VA hospital, the absence of clocks, but time heavy in the fold of the curtains, drawn and undrawn. The clanking of the food cart, which wasn't a bell, but might just as well have been. The throb of each wound, carrying its own separate heartbeat, and Ray Lynn holding his hand counting aloud: One, two, three. In spite of all manner of measuring, he is beginning to think that time occupies only as much space as is felt in the bones. He notes, with an unerring sense that defies those ticking household clocks, how a short time, these months of climbing his daughter's stairs, bear stretch marks lengthening to years, to decades of memories.

Now the Dead Man marks time by the wags of Shura's tail, Neil's snoring, and the buzz of a lawnmower trimming grass in an unseen yard beyond the hedge. He thinks about math, negative numbers in particular, and the infinite march of numbers in two directions at once. The similarities between integers and time is not lost on the Dead Man, who noted just the other day that his good watch was running backward.

The days are lengthening, a ribbon of light stretching a little longer through the afternoon. The Dead Man can't wait for the dark, thinks it is in the cool of the dark when a numbered beauty marks the wind that he can feel thrumming in his bones. As the sky darkens, exposing tiny stars, distant toothaches every last one of them, he thinks again of playing poker, and of the transparent dreams—both his and Neil's—he'd gladly gamble away. Next door, the old ladies are arguing with a game show host, and the sound of friction grates the air, in the clacking of the geese's bills, in the bristled movement of the laurel hedge. With envy he watches the geese beat at the air and take labored flight over the hedge, their hollow bones catching the wind while his bones bear years of weight, a lifetime of gravity.

It's February now, the month of iron, and he feels his daughter's hold on him slipping. Early one evening Karen goes into labor. With each contraction, a little more of the Dead Man fades, as if a fine dust of the photographer's silver has settled over him. As her labor progresses, the empty spaces inside his chest and between his bones expand. By the time Neil stuffs an old gray travel bag with Karen's toiletries, the Dead Man can no longer see his shoes. He imagines he is upping the ante with the constellations. The two old men huddled in the sky have two-of-a-kind and a full house. But the Dead Man doesn't hesitate. He'll bet Neil and meat-eating Marla will marry before the year is out, that Karen will name her boy after her father.

Six hours after Neil and Karen leave for the hospital, a thin rain taps against the rusting hulks of the vw frames in the yard. The Dead Man has never felt so good, but it is a fragile feeling. With each passing minute he feels weaker and makes his way to the

back porch. He is disappearing bits at a time, particle by particle, memory by memory. He had heard that 30 percent of ordinary house dust was actually dead skin cells. Now he knows this
is true and he can feel himself flaking to dust. And he was right
about light and heavy, too—he has no sensation of either. With
care he wipes his glasses to better study the changing boundaries of his body.

He can't hear the clocks anymore. The plucks of the rain
sound the same to him now as the ticks of Neil's blinks. The geese
are still bickering in the backyard, fighting over the sweet spots
to roost. They sound like the neighbor ladies quarreling and at
first the Dead Man can't tell—is it the geese or the old women he
hears? The noise wears him out and suddenly he is tired, as tired
as an ocean, and thinks if he could drift to sleep, his sleep would
fill a cosmos.

The wind picks up and pins the neighbor ladies' trash against
the laurel hedge. The Dead Man lifts what is left of his arms and
imagines that wind lifting him into a similar, weightless flight.
He feels himself unraveling, one rib at a time, and he has never
been so happy to be forgotten. He is glad, too, that Karen is not
here, for he would have felt compelled to say goodbye, and he
couldn't imagine a task any harder. So many things the Dead
Man would have wanted to tell his daughter. So many things
he would clarify so that she would not have to know them the
way he does. But he knows that even if he still had his voice, she
would not hear it, as she has never heard it, preferring instead to
own each ache for herself, each wound another scar.

The Dead Man tilts his head back and counts out his last seconds among the stars. It's here, he thinks. And with a quick and
exquisite pain he pulls a short breath through his nose, feeling
the last of his lungs go. He closes his eyes, giving himself over to
the settling darkness within and the darkness without, happy at
last, and happy that he can know it.

The Suicide Club

TONI GRAHAM

From *The Suicide Club* (2015)

> If you would have a thing shrink,
> You must first stretch it.
>
> TOO TE CHING

Holly learned the Vicks VapoRub trick from a long-ago boy-friend, a fire fighter. When firefighters need to perform cadaver removal from an accident site, they goop up their upper lips with the ointment, as it does a fine job of masking the odor of decomposing corpses. She stands in front of the bathroom medicine cabinet, rubbing a thick glob of VapoRub underneath her nose. The burn of the menthol fumes rising in her nostrils furnishes blessed relief, even if the smell clashes with the sandalwood incense she has lit. Until she remembered the factoid about Vicks, she had not been sleeping well, because of the stench.

Her cadavers are those of rodents, poisoned mice that died in the crawl space beneath her house. Friends warned her not to put poison in the basement, that the vermin would die on her property and smell up the house, but what else could she do? She was not about to set out traps and then be faced with the pungent remains of squashed mice. One needs a husband to dispose of trapped rodents. Or a fiancé, but Reed is as dead as the mice.

After she slips into bed, she remembers that she has not yet checked the Web for today's prospects. Does she care enough to get up and log on, or should she let the search wait until morning? She thinks she hears a rustling—is it Teddy; is he okay? But then she remembers her eight-year-old son is in California with his dad for the summer. Oh gosh, what if the sound is a mouse? She is sitting up now, not having really intended to, just like stories she has heard about dead bodies flipping up into a sitting position in a particularly vigorous case of rigor mortis.

She listens awhile, hears nothing. She beams a flashlight around the room and into the closet, sees nothing. Now she is hyper-alert. She may as well go online.

Her group therapist, Dr. Jane, suggested the online dating service, an idea that at first mortified Holly. Never in her life did she imagine that she would have to troll for dates; she has never been hard up for men. Until now. And though she would never say this to anyone, she has always felt that matchmaking, like Broadway musicals, is something more in the purview of Jewish folks than of WASPs. But, as Dr. Jane told the members of the suicide survivors group Holly attends, one needs to be proactive if one expects to move into the final stage of grief. One needs to integrate the loss and move on.

Holly brings her laptop into bed and logs on to e-Luv. She has chosen as her screen name Sandy_Agow, a subliminal nod to her birthplace, San Diego. The first two weeks she was a member of e-Luv, she was thrilled every morning to check for potential dates, hoping that just the right man would pop up on the screen, a man who could make her let go of Reed—"integrate" the loss. But the progression of men has included a long queue of undesirables. She has been sent men with no hair, men with poor grammar, men named Les and Ralph and Wally, men who have personal relationships with Jesus, men who read Ayn Rand, men who bowl.

Tonight Divorcé #1 at first looks like an actual possibility: he has thick dark hair, intense brown eyes, and at first glance nothing seems wrong with him. But as she reads his profile, disappointment washes over her. He is named Sandor, and he reveals he has never been married (at age forty-nine). In the space where one is asked to reply to "What secret about you do only your best friends know?" he states that he cries very easily. She zooms on his posted photo to increase its size, and she now sees that the poor man has a weak chin. Sure, answering a question like that can be tough; her own answer was "Find out, Mister!"

The boxes to check to indicate religion include Christian, Jewish, spiritual but not affiliated with any particular religion, atheist, and other. He has checked "other." What is he, a male Wiccan? No, those people are usually tremendously obese. Maybe he's a full-bore Satanist, a weeping Satanist.

E-Luv enables its clients to click on a box that says, "Close match now." She clicks this box at the bottom of weepy Sandor's page. His face vaporizes into cyberspace.

The odor of sandalwood is beginning to ease her into a better frame of mind. She has lit incense in every room in the house, and sandalwood-ginger scented-oil candles burn in the bedroom, and the fragrance has broken through the VapoRub. Maybe the aromatherapy concept is not hokum, after all.

Divorcé #2 is named Cliff. He would not be so bad if he had known enough to shave off the mustache that gives him that seventies look. But she cannot really post on the e-Luv Contact Board a message advising Cliff that he needs to lose the mustache if he expects to get a woman. She does not wish to sound as shallow as some of the men on e-Luv do. One of them, a very handsome guy with a full head of hair and a cleft chin, specified exactly what kind of woman he wanted: "A wholesome, Monica Potter type," he stated. He had added, just in case, "Look her up." Holly had, against her better judgment, googled Monica Potter. She learned the woman was a young blond actress. Potter's shoulder-length hair blew in the wind in one of the photos on the Web. From the looks of her, she was probably twenty years younger than the bachelor. Holly remembered a Randy Newman song from when she was a kid, in which Newman sang, "Jesus, what a jerk."

Holly is happy to be at work; the shop smells like books. Sometimes she thinks the real reason she decided to open a bookstore was so she could breathe in the scent of books all day, six days a week—the ink, the paper, the cloth of the hardbounds—as heady as an aphrodisiac. *H. Hemenway, Booksellers*, reads the sign on the shop's facade. The "s" forming the plural "booksellers" represents a bit of a pose, as she is sole owner and the only real salesperson, unless you count Cadon, the college student she employs part-time, who is a desultory salesperson at best. Using what was left of her divorce settlement to pull up stakes in Los Angeles and open her own bookstore in a college town in Oklahoma was a very bad choice in today's business climate, with independent bookstores falling like dominos. And the fact is, she had never so much as taken a business course in college, nor had she ever worked as a shopgirl when she was still a student. Her job history consists of only two places of employment: an editorial position at Houghton Mifflin after she graduated and a tech writing job in L.A. with the Motion Picture Academy's film archives.

Reed had been given a great opportunity with a start-up in Oklahoma City, or so he claimed. Holly had been so crazy about him that she could not bear to stay behind in California when he decided to move to OKC. The past few months have made it clear that one might be advised not to buy a bookstore just because one likes to read and has worked in the publishing end of the book business. She has begun to realize that she may be like the fat guy who loves to eat and to cook but who goes belly-up when he opens a restaurant.

The shop is empty this morning, save for her and Cadon. She has opened up only moments before and is rearranging some greeting cards on a rack before the walk-in traffic begins. The bar mitzvah cards are not selling and are beginning to look dusty and faded—she should have known not to order ethnic or non-Christian cards in a place like Hope Springs. She assumed the state university campus in town would include a sufficient number of Jewish faculty, but apparently either she guessed incorrectly or the Jewish faculty are keeping a very low profile in Hope Springs. The Christian bookstore a few blocks away from Hemenway's does a thriving business in didactic tomes, "inspirational" fiction, the *Left Behind* series, and greeting cards that feature images of angels or of Jesus.

Cadon has put on a Sade CD, which hits just the right note today. She wonders how Cadon even knows about Sade—her fame was before his time. The twenty-somethings of today—the Cadons and Jadons and Aidens and Braedens—are not likely to know who Sade is. Holly has found that, often as not, young adults are ignorant of Bhopal, do not know who Gorbachev was, and have never heard of *The Satanic Verses*. And as for the old black-and-white Hollywood films she learned to love when she was working at the Academy archives: not a chance. The younger generation wants action films, movies with computer-generated images like that *Silver Surfer* thing.

She is of the Matt and Steve and Jeff generation, those who listened not only to Guns N' Roses but also to Sade. *Is it a crime?* Oh dear, the CD playing reminds her of a weekend on Padre Island with Reed—the little bistro in the hotel played a lot of Sade. Don't think about sex, she tells herself. The bell over the door tinkles and she looks up.

The man who enters the shop is Dave, an older guy from Dr.

Jane's suicide survival group. He's from New York, and Holly found him brassy, even abrasive, until she began to know him better.

Dave approaches the card rack where she stands. "Interesting that you would name a bookstore Hemingway's," he says.

She has become accustomed to the fact that Dave seldom offers salutations or greetings, just jumps into conversation in medias res.

"Good morning, Dave," she says. "Actually, it's Hemenway's, not Hemingway's—Hemenway is my last name."

He expels a short laugh. "Funny, I never knew your last name. I guess the Suicide Club is like A.A.—we're all supposed to be anonymous."

For a moment Holly draws a blank. Oh my gosh, he calls the grief support group the Suicide Club? She is not sure if he is being cynical or just making an offbeat joke, so she wills her expression to remain impassive.

"Do you have the last Chris Hitchens book?" he says.

"You mean *God Is Not Great?*" she says, keeping her voice fairly low. A couple has just come in, and they are more likely to be looking for *The Purpose Driven Life* than the Hitchens. As the man and woman come closer, Holly hopes they did not hear her say, "God is not great." She goes to the back of the store and fetches the Hitchens for Dave, who has followed her to the shelves. She hands him the volume, asking if he needs anything further.

"This ought to do it," he says. "My wife and I saw someone last night on the Hair Network railing against this book," Dave adds. "We figure if they hate it, we'll love it."

"The Hair Network?" Dave always makes her feel slow, the way most New Yorkers do. What is the Hair Network, she wonders—something like the Hair Club for Men? Dave does have a significant bald spot.

"You know," Dave says. "One of those Trinity Broadcasting

stations—the ones where they preach the ol' fire-and-brimstone and all the televangelists wear pompadours," he says. "Lot of black hair dye."

She cannot help but smile, then turns to wait on the couple, directing Dave to Cadon at the register.

"Going tomorrow night?" Dave says. The Suicide Club. Yes, she is.

As she drives home from the shop, Holly decides about dinner. She will have what she thinks of as "the modified Atkins"—a porterhouse accompanied by half a bottle of Cabernet. She wishes Teddy would be home to have dinner with her, but, per the joint custody agreement, he is in L.A. with her ex until school starts in the fall. During the year since Reed killed himself, Holly has grown increasingly anxious over custody transfers. Theo now questions her suitability as a parent. Although Teddy was not in the house at the time Reed pulled the trigger, the suicide has made the premises, in Theo's eyes, a charnel house—far too unsavory an environment for his little boy. When her ex learned of Reed's suicide, all he said was "It was always clear to me the son-of-a-bitch was no gentleman." She did not point out to Theo that some of his own consorts have not exactly been cotillion material.

She sneezes sharply and her eyes involuntarily close; the car swerves out of its lane. As she sneezes again, she nearly sideswipes a car with a bumper sticker saying, "A dusty Bible means a dirty life." She spent some time this afternoon in the stockroom at the shop and is likely sneezing from that particular dust.

Holly has to wonder if Theo might not be correct—maybe Reed's death has warped Teddy in some way, especially since Reed and her son were buddies from the get-go. She should check into whether there is a suicide survivors group in Hope Springs for children but figures she instead might need to take him to a child psychologist in Tulsa. She has not told Theo about this, but this spring when she took their son to see the film *Bambi*, Teddy was the only person in the theater—child or adult—who did not shed a tear when Bambi's mother died. Holly was shaken by his stoicism, which seemed unnatural. But was it the death of a mother that failed to move her child, or was he showing signs of emotional blunting due to the trauma of Reed's death? She hardly knows which is worse.

Maybe having a whole bottle of wine on hand for tonight might be advisable, she figures—the modified-modified Atkins. But thanks to the nutty blue laws in Oklahoma, she will not be able to pick up a bottle of wine at the grocery store when she buys the porterhouse. She sneezes again, then turns left at the Christian bookstore, parks the car in front of the tribal tobacco outlet, and walks over to the liquor store.

When Holly arrives at Bethel Baptist, where Dr. Jane McAllister holds the Wednesday night suicide-survivors workshop, she sees that she is the last person to arrive and that Dave is already talking. She missed last week's session, as the sneezing fit after work turned out to be the first sign of a brutal cold. Dr. Jane wears a pale yellow linen suit and is nodding at whatever Dave has just said, and she gives a wink of acknowledgment as Holly enters the room.

"And then my sister was on my case like stank on a monkey," Dave says.

SueAnn, a forty-something lady whose teenage son killed himself, offers a few examples of her own tussles with relatives after her son's death, and Dr. Jane reminds everyone that in the wake of tragedy, often the worst comes out in people, and that this is understandable. When the room goes silent, Holly apologizes for being late, and for missing last week's session.

Dr. Jane inquires, "Are you okay now?"

"My cold's gone," Holly says. But she hears her voice crack on the word "gone," and to her embarrassment, tears form and cling to her lower lashes.

"Is there something wrong, Holly?" Dr. Jane says.

Can she really tell them what has upset her? Almost certainly they will find her narcissistic, and what is bothering her is hardly grief.

"I went to the urgent-care clinic to get some medicine for my sore throat," she says. "And to make sure I didn't have bronchitis." She pauses and watches everyone look inquisitively at her. "The doctor, a man, when he took my history asked me if I were still menstruating."

"And your age is only . . . ?" SueAnn says.

"Thirty-six." She instantly feels as if she has Tourette's, impulsively blurting out, "The dumb bastard."

"Perhaps that wasn't very judicious of him," Dr. Jane says. "When I was in grad school, we were taught never to ask that question—even if the patient were in her seventies. We were told to ask, 'When was your last period?'"

"I don't get it," Dave says, looking genuinely puzzled.

SueAnn says, "Holly don't look old enough for menopause. And no gal likes being thought of as a dried-up ol' thing—sure she's upset!"

Holly feels shamed, not only because the doctor assumed she was old, but also because her reproductive functions are being discussed in a group setting. She uses a longtime coping device, a little internal mantra that she taught herself in elementary school: I'm-not-here-now, I'm-not-here-now, I, am, not, here, now. She focuses intently on Dr. Jane's shoes, channeling all her energy into studying them, homing in on the visual and tuning out the aural. Dr. Jane always looks as if she is dressed for Major Metropolitan, not Hope Springs, Oklahoma. Holly has never seen her wear jeans or polyester blouses or matronly shoes. She suspects Dr. Jane would not ever be caught wearing Birkenstocks as Holly does tonight. Jane is wearing bone T-straps with a three-inch heel and acutely pointed toes.

Only this morning, Holly noticed a Dillard's shoe-sale advertisement in the newspaper and found herself lingering over the ad. The shoes pictured all had women's names assigned to the respective styles: high-heeled mules named Rochelle, sandals named Jill, wedges named Norma. Who decided to give shoes women's names? she wonders. She considers whether a shoe called Holly would be a Birki or a stiletto or a loafer.

She brings herself back into the room and sees that Dave is again speaking. "Yeah, my wife slapped me in the face once when I told her she was acting menopausal."

Holly arrives home from the shop, carrying groceries into the kitchen. She and Reed bought the house only six months before his death, and though she can no longer sleep in the bedroom that was hers and Reed's, she does not wish to sell the house.

She and Teddy and Reed's Irish setter, Joyce, stayed with her mother in the immediate aftermath, and a few days later, when the yellow police tape came down and Holly began to regain some of her equilibrium, she numbly thumbed through the classifieds until she found the heading Crime Scene Restoration. The ad that caught her attention was the one that contained, in large block letters, the promise LIKE IT NEVER HAPPENED!

When she came home from work that terrible day, she had called out the ironic "Honey, I'm home!" that was Reed's and her habitual greeting, but there was no response, except that Joyce jumped up on her as he always did when Holly came home. "Down, Joyce. Reed?" she called. Nothing. Not seeing Reed in the kitchen or the study where he usually worked, she climbed the stairs to the bedroom.

She now knows that most often it is men who shoot themselves. Statistics indicate that women rarely choose a gunshot to the head as their mode of suicide. There is conjecture that most women find the idea of mutilating their faces the most undesirable way to go. Women usually swallow pills, or sometimes sit in their cars and breathe in carbon monoxide. Holly had always imagined, though, that one tiny gunshot to the temple would not be all that bad and certainly would be quicker than taking pills and having to lie down and wait to die. She had imagined a tiny, bullet-sized indentation in the temple, bleeding slightly at the entrance site, and envisioned perhaps a slightly larger exit wound somewhere else in the head. Neat, practical, effective. It was not as if one needed to ram a shotgun into her mouth and blow off her face. No, what Nancy Reagan had once termed "a tiny little gun" placed strategically at one temple did not seem too grotesque.

But when she entered the bedroom, though it took several moments for what she was seeing to actually seem real, all she could think of in her dumb horror was photos she had seen of Jackie Kennedy in a pink suit splattered gruesomely with crimson-brown blood. Reed lay on the floor, his face obscured by gore, an evil scarlet halo on the carpet beneath his head. The amount of blood on the walls and ceiling shocked Holly to the core.

She wishes she could say that she had run to Reed, stooped to take his pulse or to perform CPR, or even knelt to pray. But the fact is, she did exactly what that sixties comedian Lenny Bruce claimed Mrs. Kennedy did when her husband was shot: "hauled ass."

To be accurate, Holly *crawled* ass. She sank to her knees as if she were a plastic blow-up doll with a slow leak, a slow descent to the formerly eggshell carpet. She scooted along on her belly down the hall to the phone, crawling like a blindworm with Joyce creeping along with her, whimpering.

The crime-scene-restoration company had done wonders with the bedroom. After they were finished, Holly could find no trace of the blood that had punctuated the room. The workers asked her permission to discard the black-and-white movie posters that dressed up the walls. Fred and Ginger and Clark and Claudette were blood spattered, which morbidly called to mind the old riddle from elementary school: What's black and white and red all over? She did not even see the gun until after the police arrived—a 12-gauge shotgun. The fact that Reed owned a shotgun came as a total surprise to her. She cannot imagine where he must have been hiding the thing.

What used to be the bedroom is now the guest room and vice versa. Though the former guest room is smaller than Holly and Reed's bedroom, it does not feel as spooked. But of course Reed is still dead, and she is now a bombed-out hull and thus a member of the Suicide Club. As with the crime-scene-fixing company, she found Dr. Jane's grief support group in the Yellow Pages, in this case online.

Her laptop sits on the kitchen table where she left it this morning. She logs on to e-Luv. A man has e-mailed her: "Damn your cute Sandy." She immediately zaps him, then clicks on the profile of a decent-looking bearded man named Larry. As she reads his profile, nothing about him strikes her one way or the other; he seems fairly generic. But as Holly reads over Larry's responses to the list of e-Luv-provided questions, she is stopped short by one of these. The question is "Name four things you cannot live without." When perusing some of the past male responses, she has noticed that the answers seem to run the gamut from "my boat" to "my kids" to "good wine" to "excitement" to inappropriate statements about sex. But poor Larry has answered "air, water, food, sleep." She looks back to the top of the page and sees that he has listed his occupation as civil engineer.

But her late fiancé, Reed, had plenty of imagination, along with good looks, bedroom skills, intelligence, and wit. Only fly in that VapoRub was that he also shot himself in their bedroom; probably Larry would not do such a thing.

She snaps shut the computer's lid, opens the bottle of Cab-ernet, and pours herself a glass. When Joyce nuzzles her, begging, she dips her finger into the glass and lets the dog lick off the wine. Holly lowers her face to Joyce's furry head, breathes in the familiar musky smell. That was the worst thing in the days following Reed's death: she could smell his hair everywhere she went, as if the scent clung to the inside of her nose like a fragrant mist. Her hands, too, had tingled, nearly vibrated, with the phantom pain of feeling Reed's curly hair. She sits at the kitchen table, staring at nothing. Her hips, seeming heavy as a sandbag, moor her to the chair. The dead-mouse smell creeps up through the floorboards, eradicating any yearnings for dinner. She should get up and light some candles and incense. Maybe she ought to call back the restoration company and see if they can find the bodies and haul them out. *I'm not here now, I'm not here.*

"I'm alive in the moment, present here and now," Holly recites, then repeats the affirmation several times. She is sitting in a chair across from Dr. Jane in the psychologist's office on the university campus. Holly has scheduled a private session, having begun to feel mildly alienated by the group meetings. Her usual mantra is deemed by Jane a "dissociative reaction" and something of which she should divest herself. Jane herself has suggested the replacement mantra "I'm alive in the moment, present here and now." Holly feels like a talking computer, as she does not for a moment feel alive in the moment, present here and now. If she wanted to sabotage the session, all she would need to do is voice for Dr. Jane the as yet unspoken mantra, the one that comes closest to the truth: *I'm dead every moment, world without end, amen.*

Instead Holly says, "Reed might still be alive if it weren't for me. It's all my fault." She cannot forget what he left as a suicide note: *Goodbye, cruel world!* He even remembered the comma between "goodbye" and "cruel." She did not know then, nor does she now, whether the message demonstrated mordant humor or whether Reed actually meant *Goodbye, cruel Holly*.

She conjectures again that Reed's gambling might not have escalated so ferociously if they had stayed in L.A. The combination of being cut off from his friends and family and spending too much time online had driven Reed deep into Internet poker and then Indian gambling casinos—"gaming" casinos as they are euphemistically phrased. He had slid right off the edge and gone down quickly. She does not need to tell Dr. Jane about the quarrel the night before Reed died.

"What about the money he stole from you, though?" Jane says.

"He took it, more than stole it," Holly says.

Jane says, "Where's your rage? Are you intent on making a saint out of him just because he's dead?"

I don't have any rage, Holly thinks but says nothing. Poor Reed—how can she rage against someone desperate enough to take his own life?

It has begun suddenly to rain. Holly is still not accustomed to the summer storms in Oklahoma, which come quickly out of nowhere and rumble overhead like the Heartland Flyer train. The rainwater pounds the windows and skylight in Dr. Jane's office, and Holly mercifully cannot hear what Jane is saying. She sits inert, watching Jane's lips move like an actor's on TV when the sound is turned off. In the weeks before Reed's death, he often sat in front of the TV smoking Camels and staring at the screen with the sound muted. When Holly entered the room, he would turn to her with the look of dull glass in his eyes. The rain escalates as Dr. Jane's lips offer subaudible counsel.

As Holly walks across campus from Dr. Jane's office to the lot where she parked her car, the sun bearing down on the back of her neck makes her feel like a burger under a broiler. She has left Cadon in charge of the shop, so when she spots an on-campus café called Kampus Koffee she decides to stop for an iced tea. She pulls open the glass door and immediately spots Dave from the suicide survivors group. Her impulse is to push the door closed and go elsewhere.

But Dave has seen her. She gives him a small wave, and he stands and makes a "sit here" gesture, pointing to the chair across from him. Holly complies as Dave nudges aside the spiral notebook he was writing in.

Once Holly has ordered and she and Dave exchange a few pleasantries, silence sets in and she feels as if she should get the conversational ball in the air. She knows he is a professor of architecture at the university, so she says the first thing that comes to mind, "Sketching out a building?" and points to the notebook near his cup. She instantly regrets the moronic inquiry, but heck, is she expected to begin a dialogue about Buckminster Fuller or something?

Dave comes as close to looking flustered as she has ever seen him. His hand moves to shield what he has written, and color rises in his face. "It's just a list," he tells her. "Sometimes when I'm idle I make lists—it's nothing, really."

"Let me see," she says.

Just as Holly complied when he indicated she sit with him, Dave passively hands over the notebook. "Things That Look Like Other Things" is the scrawled heading. She reads the list:

1: Men named Buck or Rowdy who look like accountants
2: Women named Joy who might better have been named Dolores, or even Oleander
3: Zucchini, which look like cucumbers
4: Penguins

My gosh, what a strange little man he is, Holly thinks. Before she looks up from the list, she attempts to keep her face deadpan. "I don't understand about the penguins," she says.

Dave says, "Did you see that movie about the marching penguins?"

When Holly nods, Dave continues, still appearing a bit embarrassed. "The film depressed the hell out of me," he says. "The damn birds do nothing but suffer from birth to death. Even the act of conception seems grim."

Not knowing what to say, Holly only shrugs.

"I'm a Jew, you know," Dave says, "but in school I studied Eastern religions, and something from the *Tibetan Book of the Dead* always stuck with me."

Holly nods again, waiting.

"I'm not saying I believe this," Dave says, "but the *Book of the Dead* says that if you wreck your karma, you get stuck on the karmic wheel and are likely to be reincarnated—transmigrated they call it—as an animal. I don't want to be a fuckin' penguin."

Holly is nonplussed. Dave has heretofore seemed like a fairly pragmatic guy. "And you feel as if you've damaged your karma?" she says.

The volume of Dave's voice decreases to just above a whisper. "I wasn't there for my dad."

She reminds Dave that Dr. Jane says all suicide survivors feel guilty.

"Maybe so, but Poppy had cancer and I was so self-involved I didn't even know it. Truth be told, I hadn't even called him in half a year." Dave looks so aggrieved that Holly feels compelled to share her own guilt.

"I can top that," she says. "The night before Reed shot himself, he said to me in a really quiet voice, 'I'm no good.' You know what I said to him?"

Dave shakes his head.

"I said, 'Darling, I've been telling you that for months!'"

They hold each other's gaze, words unnecessary. Only a suicide survivor really knows another; that much Holly has learned. Dave reaches across the small round table and places his hand paternally over hers, patting her as if she were an infant. Dave's face across the table is mournful and kind. From the crown of her head, Holly feels an inchoate glow of warm radiance, luminance. The feeling disperses through her body, as if she were being filled like a balloon and might rise up from the wrought-iron chair and hover at the ceiling like the floating Little Mermaid in the Macy's parade.

Dave offers to walk Holly to her car, but she declines and trudges back to the lot where she parked the Mustang. She has not told anyone other than Dave, not even Dr. Jane, about the terrible thing she said to Reed the night before he committed suicide. She cannot fathom what made her cough it up to Dave. Maybe she saw evidence in his stricken countenance that he too carried a corpse on his back. His transgression seems to Holly so much less malignant then her own. *He hadn't phoned his father in months*—in her view, no huge malfeasance. She, however, had answered Reed as if she were Nora Charles tossing off a sassy line of dialogue in a 1930s *Thin Man* movie.

But she was no Myrna Loy, no glamour-girl comedic leading

lady. She was the person who hauled ass, leaving her beloved face up in a pool of congealing blood. Dave's point about karma has hit home with her, and she knows she would be getting off easy if she came back as a penguin.

Teddy telephones just after Holly finishes dinner. He and his father went to the beach today, Teddy says, and he is still giddy with the thrill of sand, breaking waves, and Sno-Cones. Theo took Teddy to Santa Monica Pier, and Teddy is effusive about riding the bumper cars. She asks to speak to Daddy, ready to ask Theo if she can have Teddy back a couple of weeks early.

In response to her query, Theo says, "What the hell would he do there—go to Jesus camp?"

"There are other activities," she says, knowing that Theo is correct: summer for children in Hope Springs consists of Vacation Bible Camp, and even the woods are beset by deer flies and chiggers. Holly caves more easily than she would normally, not wishing to be overly selfish. She cannot deprive Teddy of California beaches and subject him to a parched summer in a landlocked state so backward it does not even have a major league baseball team. "We'll stick to what we planned," she says, then speaks briefly again to Teddy before she hangs up.

She is still somewhat unsettled by her session with Dr. Jane, and by the odd interlude with Dave in the café. She roots in a kitchen drawer for matches so she can spark up some calming candles and incense, but as she lights a white lotus candle, she realizes that the mouse cadaver smell has notably abated. Maybe the downpour of rain somehow purged the odor from the basement and purified the air. Or maybe the smell at last simply dissipated. By the time Teddy comes home, the house will probably smell fine.

She has brought home from the shop a copy of the *Tao Te*

Ching, recommended by Dave, which she sets down on the table and will begin reading while she eats dinner. Dave claims the book helps him deal with the loss of his father. But before Holly starts dinner, she checks e-Luv. The matches she has been sent today are all either ugly as gargoyles or Pentecostal or Republican. She dispenses with the "matches" and scrolls through photos of non-matches, looking for someone appealing. When she gets to page 10, like a "Yes!" floating up in the fluid in a Magic 8-Ball, a photo of a man closely resembling Reed becomes visible. For one exquisite, awful moment, she thinks the man actually is Reed—that the promise has been magically fulfilled, *like it never happened.*

Waiting4U is the man's screen name, allowing Holly to continue to think of him as Reed. The most unlikely thing is that the man's hair is the same shade as Reed's: dark red, not the carrot-top red one most often sees, but a rare deep burnt carmine. Like Reed, the man has black eyebrows and slightly swarthy skin. What is even more improbable is the sole dimple on one side of his mouth, exactly like Reed's. She indulges in a momentary fantasy, the sort of unlikely scenario one encounters in soap operas: Reed has a twin they never knew about, and she has now found him. She knows such things can actually happen. Only a few months ago she read in the *Tulsa World* that in Ecuador a chance meeting had reunited twin sisters who never knew of the other's existence.

Holly sees that Waiting states the last "good book" he read was (but of course!) *The Purpose Driven Life.* She thinks of Dave's list from earlier today—things that look like other things—and is reminded of Lauren Bacall. The actress once married Jason Robards, and the consensus was that she did so only because the actor resembled Humphrey Bogart. Bogie had been the love of Bacall's life; evidently, when she saw Robards, she felt that through some sort of necromancy she could again be made love to by Bogart. The marriage had not worked out.

Now Holly sees that Waiting is not a divorced man but a widower. She scrutinizes the rest of his profile, scrolling doggedly up and down, looking for signs of Reed-kinship. Waiting was born in Texas, where he still resides, whereas Reed was born in Colorado. That does not mean they might not still be twins, though—if Waiting was adopted out, his actual place of birth might have been "revised." But he claims to be thirty-five and a Taurus, whereas Reed was thirty-eight and a Pisces.

Under "Favorite Things to Do" Waiting has written: "Watch sports on my widescreen, ride my Harley, watch movies (favorite: all James Bond), dance at C&W clubs, and especially—cheer on the Cowboys. But none of those since my wife passed away. I don't really have any favorite things to do, anymore. Maybe I signed up for e-Luv too soon, sorry."

Holly's guts whirlpool, and she feels sweat bead on her upper lip. Grief trumps country-and-western bars, even trumps that awful book. She sits staring at the pulsing cursor on the screen, her hands motionless on the keyboard, but Joyce begins to whine to go outside. She writes: "Dear Waiting4U, I lost someone, too." She sits a few moments more, then impulsively reaches across the table for the Tao Te Ching. She has always believed that a book can help just about anything. She opens randomly to a page and chooses what she will send to Waiting4U:

> *A man is supple and weak when living, but petrified*
> *and immutable when dead.*
> *Grass and trees are fragile and pliant when living, but*
> *dried and shriveled when dead.*
> *Thus, the steely and the strong are the comrades of*
> *death;*
> *The supple and the weak are the comrades of life.*

She types the verses carefully, then adds "(from Lao Tzu)" and "If you feel like e-mailing me, my real name is Holly."

Before she can change her mind, she clicks Send. Something

surges inside her. Who ever knows what might happen, anyway? With a roll of the dice, the universe can transmute. Faster than a speeding bullet.

She flings open the kitchen's French doors to let the dog outside and Joyce vaults out to the yard. Inhaling deeply, Holly smells the rain-washed air. The Oklahoma red-clay soil seems to glow in the dusk like smoldering coals. In the distance stands a water tower, the painted-on words visible from her yard: Hope Springs. She stands motionless at the threshold, thinking she hears something. Can it be someone whispering, something slithering? She sees nothing out of the ordinary, so she listens intently. There is a barely perceptible buzzing sibilance, and Holly senses an invisible presence. Beyond her is the known world, the mountainless vastness of the plains.

Jumping

MARY CLYDE

From *Survival Rates* (1999)

This is what never happened.

Kelly and Veronica and I are standing in front of the church waiting for rides home. The boys are chasing each other with their jackets open, even though their faces are red and roughened by the cold. Then childhood's most exuberant exclamation: "You're going to die!" One boy to another, completely true and completely not.

"Yeah, yeah," Kelly says, with a mittened shooing motion, feigning magnificent indifference to hide the awful excitement of girls turning thirteen.

"I think he likes you," I say to Veronica. (Notice, please, my generous compliment. What is more kind than a recognition of someone else's love?)

"Who? Brent?" she says, acting surprised, but I see she's already thought it.

The mothers' car tires slurp through wet snow.

Kelly says, "You'll make a cute couple." Coming from Kelly, this means something. Coming from Kelly, it means you're in.

Veronica's smile always made her look stupid, so when I invent this scene, I can't let her mess it up by smiling. I allow her a

33

contended nod. I want everything to be perfect. When Veronica climbs in her mother's car, cold but happy, I know that it is.

It would have happened thirty-three years ago. It would have helped if it—or something like it—had. *If only*. I see it all the time in my work, how small events can change history. I study names, nomenclature: place names, given names, family names, ethnic names, nicknames. A time or two I've been an expert witness. Once I was interviewed on network news. I turn up forgotten information about why baby girls are named Artemisia; why some place was called Maybe. I know the name Wendy first appeared in *Peter Pan*, and the most common name in the world is Mohammed. I've learned the flukiness of names and namegiving. I've seen how a name's viability can be lost because of a bad-apple Judas or Benedict.

I think of Veronica, the ski lift accident, and the time that came after as I've thought of names and naming—a freakish thing that has made all the difference, though I'm still trying to identify what that difference is.

Recently the accident's details started coming back to me—a return like comets or geese. A reentry, an insistent one, like a birth. Parts of what happened then interrupt my day now, insisting I think about it, somehow respect it, understand it matters—I don't know all what. I find myself explaining to my husband Dave a particularity of the ambulance ride—that the sirens were off—or recalling the sky, how the air was truly clear.

"Joan?" he says, curious but patient. "Joan, why are you talking about it now?"

They fell from ski lift chairs, and we thought it was just someone throwing garbage.

"What the heck?" Kelly said. We had been taught littering was a crime.

But then we saw: too big, too heavy. They were actually being thrown themselves, launched from their seats, bucked like rodeo riders, tumbled like dice. They fell gracefully downward. Floated on a summer day in tragedy's own slow time.

I said, "Kelly, what should we do?" I rubbed my eyes behind my eyeglasses, a pantomime of disbelief, but how could this be true?

We had been camping with our church group lower on the mountain, and this afternoon we were riding the ski lift to enjoy the view. But now beneath us, ahead and thirty yards farther down the hill, we could see our companions, three girls and our camp leader, lying on the ground. They moved, but it was only a leg or two, lethargic, ineffectual efforts, as if they had all stumbled while drunk.

"Jump," Kelly commanded, "before they start it up again, before it throws us out."

One of the ski lift chairs was wrapped crazily around a huge support beam. The ski lift was disabled. It wouldn't have started, couldn't. I saw that, knew it exactly.

Kelly jumped first, landed in a crouch, steady as a gymnast.

I hung from a footrest twenty-five feet above the ground, looking at aspen trees. Their leaves fluttered encouragingly. The beauty of the day would be remarked on—how it was shattered by tragedy—when our story was reported later on the ten o'clock news. But of course, nothing was shattered. It was an "America-the-Beautiful" sky: noble and particularly blue.

I later said how I felt it in my stomach, the wind that blew my body slightly just before I let go, but I have no confidence in that now. It may be just part of the story and not part of the truth. I know I counted to five, twice. I remember the hurt and relief of landing.

I called to Kelly. "Wait for me. I'm bleeding." I had fallen forward and scraped my face and bent my glasses. I was desperately afraid of what might happen next—what *did* happen—that she would run down the hill for help. That would leave me to follow, doing ... but what *would* I do when I got to our companions? I might have counted again before I ran, but I didn't hesitate long. This impresses me, that as a child I faced this, went forward into the mayhem, recognizing there was no way out.

I felt the hot and cold sting of the scrapes on my face. Rocks made the path uneven. I recall the stubby milkweed pods and fragile Queen Anne's lace. There was a Utah summer's own dusty, bitter, green smell. But then as I got to where they lay, there was no picture and only sound. It came when one of them called my name. Linda spoke to me, but I was too frightened to understand her.

Later, in the hospital, I asked her what she'd said. She was in an immense cast, traction like a cartoon strip. She had disappeared and become someone new. Her eyes were blackened, and she sucked water from an accordion-hinged straw. She said, "I guess I told you to get help." Her jaw was wired shut, but that wasn't why what she'd said hadn't sounded true. I felt that on the mountain she'd asked me something important, but also not obvious. Some secret available only to someone surprised and crushed after falling through the summer sky.

But besides the empty sound of her question, I recall nothing. In those moments on the hill there was shifting color; there was shape; but it tumbled without form or meaning, kaleidoscopic, as if I too were falling. The victims seemed dismantled by the plunge, not just injured but unformed. I ran again after Linda spoke to me, blindly following Kelly. Down, down, down. A flight over a quiet ski run, pursued by demons I would have years to get to know. Stopping to check my bleeding, I looked up at the bottom of another girl's shoes. We were spaced irregularly on the lift. Hers was probably the next occupied chair.

"What's going on?" she said. She was peevish. She swung her legs and chomped her gum. "Why aren't we going?"

It strikes me even now, as it did then, that what I was about to tell her would change her life. I felt the messenger's importance, a power I wouldn't feel again for many years until I was the one who had to tell my father his sister had died.

"They're hurt," I said. "It's bad."

She chewed her gum slowly, readjusted her headband, and tried to look back.

Then I heard a voice behind me say, "Lie down." I recognized a woman from the church camp. "Look, see," she said, "you're bleeding." She thought I was why Kelly had been so excited.

My glasses were sitting crookedly on my face. I feared they might cause her not to take me seriously, and I had something important to say. "It's not me who's hurt." Appearing worried then, she handed me a wrinkled tissue and trotted up the hill.

I realized my glasses' lenses were scratched. I'm extremely nearsighted, and damaged glasses pose a frightening threat. "Kelly," I whispered below the ski lift, willing her return and my rescue, wishing I had gone with her, thinking how she'd escaped.

"Sh," the girl above me said. "I think I can hear them bawling."

I could hear the abrupt *tda-tda-tda* of winged grasshoppers and the purr of a few clover-seeking bees. The aspen trees seemed to tremble, and I wanted Kelly—and the old life she represented—more than I've ever wanted anyone in my life.

Three years before, on the way to see the school nurse in fifth grade, Kelly had said, "I have a secret." Though Kelly called herself a tomboy, Kelly and her mother bought her dresses at J.C. Penney. They had attached petticoats that made a stiff elegant sound. While the rest of us wore saddle shoes, Kelly wore black patent-leather slip-ons, which she rubbed with Vaseline.

That day I suspected she loved Stephen Edison, and I presumed she was about to confess, maybe even tell me what it was like to be kissed. Instead she confided, "I have to wear deodorant."

"Deodorant?" This was exciting, because I'd already started wearing deodorant and I hadn't thought to tell her first.

Kelly said, "You're so lucky not to have to." She combed her hair with her fingers and tossed it over her shoulders in the cold, world-weary that girls with long hair learn. "What are you going to be when you grow up?"

"Teacher," I said, feeling doomed and lowly.

"I'm going to be a nurse in an operating room because my mom says I can think on my feet. Possibly I'll marry a doctor." Then pitying me, she turned me toward her. "You'll be a great teacher because you remember all those things no one else cares about."

When I told my sister that Kelly was my best friend, she said, "Yeah, but are you hers?"

My mother and our neighbor took me home from the hospital where I hadn't needed treatment. My father had been called to the ski resort because he was the Mormon bishop. He found me on a stretcher in the back of the ambulance but stayed when it left because Sister Bennett, our camp leader, was being given blood and was not transportable. Everyone realized she was dying.

My mother had a car, but we rode home from the hospital in the neighbor's. I believe my mother accepted his offer because it seemed her part in what was expected: that she must be too distressed to trust herself to drive. Tragedy is about playing roles.

I was already suffering the guilt of survival when she saw me in the emergency room and said, "Oh, Joan!" What was probably an expression of concern seemed to me an accusation.

The neighbor turned the car radio knob and the radio needle glided through the numbers. He didn't say a word. Finally I asked, because no one volunteered it, "Who died?" My voice sounded strange and empty.

Maybe this is why my mother took the ride, so she wouldn't have to be alone with me and the question. She touched her throat. "Veronica," she said. "And Sister Bennett is very badly hurt."

The burden I assumed in asking was not what I'd expected, not the pain of loss but the difficulty of an appropriate response. The fact was, I didn't feel like crying. I felt raw as my scrapped face, but also stoppered. As my mother looked at me, most of all I wanted to be alone.

That night in my dreams white sheets hung from a clothesline. They floated, then dropped suddenly and became the humps of ghosts who chased me.

My mother's idea of comfort was to say, "Sh, sh, sh."

The year I was born the top five names for girls were: K(C)atherine, Susan, Deborah, Karen, and Mary. Her name was Veronica Fuke. She never had a chance, you see. The first name was too exotic, the second blunt or angry or obscene. She licked her lips tentatively just before she spoke, and when she talked you noticed moist breathing. Asthma, I now guess. Her nose wasn't so much fat as flabby.

She was in 4-H. She grew vegetables with ignoble shapes or names: banana squash and rutabaga. Her family ate dehydrated fruit and were glad to show you their dehydrator—proud as though it were a new care. The boys at church teased her, which she took with such a diffuse lack of interest they were forced to stop. She had a blue mole by her eye; her little finger curved slightly inward.

I can't recall a single unkind, impatient, or angry thing she ever did. And I didn't like her. Worse, I didn't care about her. I don't know if I smiled at her, ever. There are bonds stronger than love. And what I know is that, if she'd lived, I'd have completely forgotten her. My behavior toward her then would not seem to matter now. So this is it: in her death I was caught, frozen in my indifference, an indifference nothing will ever help.

Her mother was pudding—soft with small, swollen feet. Later, she died of a tumor so big the whole congregation would watch it grow. It tugged at the shape of her formless dresses. She did not seek medical intervention and was patient in her suffering. Apparently the alternative—survival—seemed too perplexing or complicated to undertake. The elders gave her blessings and prayed for her return to health. But her daughter had been thrown from a ski lift. That might have proved something to her, or left her less susceptible to religion, more available to fate.

I want to believe Veronica died as calmly as her mother. If patience in death isn't courage, it's certainly the next best thing. I imagine Veronica surprised and then done with it, down with living on a day too beautiful to have given any warning. Perhaps she slipped out of life with simple grace.

The newspaper caption under her picture said, *Fell to her death.* I remember when I first read it, for some reason I thought it was *fell through* her death. And it seemed for a moment— though I knew better—as if she'd miraculously survived.

The morning after the accident my mother made me go with her to see Veronica's mother. It didn't occur to me to protest.

"Sister Fuke," my mother said, "we want you to have this." She shoved something draped by a dishcloth. It takes on a bread shape as I see myself standing on that narrow porch, but it also reminds me of Veronica's own covered form beneath the ski life. Veronica's mother wrapped her arms around it, hugged it. She had other children: a boy who later grew a straggly black beard to cover acne scars when he was only fifteen, a young daughter who would take to her stepmother with tenacious goodwill. But they were not around that day.

Veronica's mother bent toward me; her face was a haggard wilderness of suffering. I was young, still thought the worst pain was physical. Fascinated, I didn't know enough to look away. I wondered if this was what had turned Lot's wife into the pillar of salt.

Then I realized Veronica's mother was speaking to me. Too late, I saw her need. She said, "Honey, did Veronica say anything before she died?"

Grief, I saw, is shameless.

I looked to my mother, but she had slipped into her survival mode, becoming something firm and carefully closed. Behind Veronica's mother, I could see the clutter, newspapers scattered by the broken-down sofa. I knew where they kept some of their belongings: that there was a picture of Jesus ascending to glory in the living room, that a large yellow cat balanced on the edge of the kitchen sink and swatted at a spider plant. I saw how knowing those things hadn't stopped anything from happening, any more than the horseshoe that hung by the backdoor.

"Dear?" Veronica's mother whispered.

I knew I must lie. Such responses are instinctive, but I didn't know what to say.

"She just cried," I said. I spoke the lie humbly, knowing I'd failed her. Veronica's mother moved back into the room and suddenly she blurred, seemed to expand. It scared me until I realized that she'd moved into line with the scratched part of my lenses. She put the bread on the sofa and then slumped down herself.

When I called Kelly on the phone she said, "We must shut our eyes and promise to never even walk down their street again."

My father spoke to the families with radiant conviction about life being eternal, which is, after all, a paltry comfort when there is still the whole of mortality to be somehow gotten through. At the funeral, he read Veronica's poem because her young cousin broke down, and he handed Sister Bennett's daughter his handkerchief. Then, right there, he raised money for a flagpole. Something had to be done, something to help us all sleep and eat and live. The flagpole was tangible, a solution. Its erection was an action, a counteraction to the falling. Something of an exchange.

It stood in front of the church with a stone wall behind it. Sister Bennett had died for something, giving service to her camper girls. But of Veronica Fuke, what might be said? How do you make her noble? How do you make it feel as sad as it should when she wasn't particularly likable?

By Thanksgiving I was washing my hands between thirty and forty times a day. First my knuckles, then my fingertips became fiery and etched like Martian canals. They blend in the tender crusty valleys between my fingers. My mother took me to the doctor, who held them gently, as if touch could injure them more. "How are you sleeping?" he said, turning them over, and I knew he'd guessed.

Sometimes leaves blew off aspen trees in my dreams. Or newspapers fluttered from wire cages and then turned vicious as they flew toward me. *Sh, sh, sh,* I'd tell myself.

"Fine," I said. "I sleep OK." I knew better than to be found out.

On the remaining Fourth of Julys of my youth, we raised the flag at the church in a sunrise service. Then the deaths seemed patriotic.

"Can you believe it?" the invitation crows, under a picture of a geriatric bulldog. "We've been out of high school twenty-five years!" I show it to Dave the way you show people your driver's license—hoping they won't laugh, but ready to join them when they do.

"You going?" he asks, pinching cilantro into Mexican salsa—his own recipe, of which he's overly proud. He's got a baseball cap on backward, which proves the seriousness of his chore.

"High school," I say, "is like a party where you drank too much. You hope you didn't embarrass yourself in ways you can't entirely recall."

"That, you see, just might be the fun of it—the amnesia factor, the wait and see." He plugs his mouth with a finger dipped in salsa.

"Needs more onion," I say of his recipe.

He wipes a hand on his apron. "You should go. They'll be glad to see you." He angles the knife in my direction in an unintentionally dangerous way. "Though they won't know you without your cat's-eye glasses." He growls and tries to nip at my ear.

I'm indignant. "In high school I wore contact lenses." We reserve our tenderest vanity for the least significant things.

Two weeks later I'm waiting my turn in Optical Boutique. Suddenly this pops into my head: They bounced when they landed. No floating, none at all. Why is this revelation so amazing to me? Why does it seem so relevant?

The spectacles for sale are lined up in lighted glass cases. They look like Hollywood or synchronized swimming. I'll feel intrusive and clumsy when I take one from its place.

This: I have fallen from innocence. Fallen in love. On my face. Also into line. But this must be said: I *jumped* from the ski lift.

Two other girls were hurt, injuries that changed their bodies as well as their minds, bones crushed in uncompromising ways. Linda would wear forever the appearance of an invalid—a shriveled arm, one leg shorter. But she also wore an expansive calmness, as if the accident had freed her of the worry of too much good fortune. I've heard she is an excellent mother, that she teaches business ethics and even plays the guitar.

The other girl, Kathy, became obese. She was addicted to pain medication, but also apparently to pain. She spoke about both with authority as well as awe, like a serious art collector. She'd been adopted as a baby, and in late adolescence went on a quest to find her birth father. When she found him in a big Eastern city, she slept with him, in what must have seemed a brilliant, definitive revenge.

It was called The Accident, as if there was or would only be one. There was occasional need for clarification about what exactly had happened, and so I was asked. It amazed me how I'd become an expert on this: the how of how people died.

The summer before I started high school, I gave up washing my hands. I weened myself slowly, using Jergens hand lotion as a crutch (its smell still makes me feel vulnerable). Then I painted my nails the color the seniors were wearing, a pearly white—drama and sophistication both. My disgraceful hands became glory. Isn't it so often so? I was known for having beautiful nails. Confidence is built on such small things.

Kelly and I went to the same high school, but she became dramatically out of date. Her rebellions were quaint and naïve. She wrote toothless letters to the school newspaper's editors. Her popularity plummeted, and—I confess—I wasn't sorry. I had moved on. I had the stuff of high school success: nice legs, a smart mouth. Teenagers are merciless, a bit sadistic. What did I care that her petticoats no longer rustled? What did it matter when the world was exploding, blooming with forbidden pleasures—sinewy boys and smudgy-edged sins.

Kelly still had that sense of purpose. When the rest of us were painting on thick eyeliner and conscientiously cursing our parents, Kelly had school spirit and a quiet, too-tall boyfriend. You would see them on the school lawn, laughing or walking hand in hand into the dance. She had no need for subversion. She simply lacked outrage.

When my mother said, "I haven't seen Kelly in so long," I shrugged. "Yeah?"

My mother narrowed her eyes and said what she often did, "Is that any way to talk?"

"We don't have anything in common," I whined, because what can you have in common with someone after you've watched people die? We passed in school halls with only a "Hi there." Embarrassed like former lovers. Knowing we shared a guilty knowledge—the how of how people died. Or maybe she was shy because we were no longer friends. But our past connection was an impossible attachment, severed by an event of unbearable significance and terrible discovery. Mortality is not a subject a teenager should dwell on. And how can you be friends with someone who knows a secret as big as all that?

Only once do I remember talking. I was at a church dance, sending a confused message to my nonmember boyfriend. She approached me while her boyfriend was outside to tell me her brother had received his mission call to Australia that her mother had been praying for. I thought how Kelly could do more with her appearance. For one thing, she should cut her hair. And I wondered how the accident had changed her. Had it taught her to be good or just unaware? Then suddenly I feared she'd talk about it, and I had no idea what I would say. But instead, she said, "You know, you have really pretty eyes," and I remember thinking how I wished she'd said that back when it would have counted, back when it would have done me some good.

In the yearbook under her picture, it said, "Girl most likely to stay out of jail."

Years ago, at the end of trying to have a baby and getting to where it stopped hurting so much, Dave floated on our water bed and diagnosed me. "Obsessive-compulsive disorder," he said in an accent he claimed was Viennese.

"Getting up in the morning?"

"*Having* to get up in the morning. Stay," he said. "Let's eat brie and crackers and make crumbs and love. We'll send Queenie for the newspaper. We won't get up until we've renamed all the major cities in America."

The bed rocked as if it were keeping time. The clock radio was regrettably still. I said, "Is that any way to face life?"

"Aha!" he said, as if he'd caught me. "You don't *face* life, You *live* it." He was prone to mottoes of treacly optimism.

"I could stay in bed if I wanted." But I had to grip the blankets when I said it to keep from throwing them off.

"Couldn't," he said.

"Could." It seemed hard to breathe, though the blankets weren't at all close to my face. Concentrating, I counted but only got to five. "Long enough," I said. The cold air and being upright made it feel as if I'd won.

"Admit it," he yelled. He leapt to his feet on the bed, causing waves that he convincingly surfed in plaid boxers. "You *do* things. You fold every towel long, then short. You wipe off the table left to right. You floss!"

"To clean my teach," I said, too primly, but then remembered suddenly the long-ago pleasure of washing my hands, knowing how important it was to keep moving. How could I explain it? The awful phrase: like a sitting duck.

Sometimes I dream of snowfalls that are sucked back up into the sky. Once I dreamed of four waterbirds diving toward the earth, then suddenly swooping upward, sunlight glittering from the sequined eyeglasses they wore.

Sister Bennett had a nasally laugh I can no longer quire remember. She once told us, "For Pete's sake, drop the 'Sister Bennett.' You girls can call me Louise"—which we did, but only until she died. We loved her. Maybe that's why I don't speak of her. Maybe in loving her I've more successfully put her to rest. Or perhaps she doesn't haunt me because she was not my age and even though she died, she couldn't have been me.

Veronica means "true likeness."

I wish I'd been friendly to Veronica Fuke.

I wish Kelly had come back for me, so that I wouldn't have had to go back up the hill and hear Sister Bennett moan or ride down the canyon alone in an ambulance.

Kelly sang "The Impossible Dream" in a chorus at graduation. Kelly didn't die.

Quickly, before I can think what I'm doing, I get on a plane to go to my high school reunion. "Obsessive-compulsive disorder," I explain to Dave, who smiled in agreeable acceptance as he kisses me goodbye.

The reunion is at a water-slide park I didn't know existed, situated next to what we used to call the State Mental Hospital. Surely they've let all those folks go.

Can any place look as foreign as the place where you were born?

A man barks my name and embraces me. I have no idea who he is.

"Look at you," people keep demanding. "Will you just look at who's here?"

There's a man on the fringe of the group, left out of the hugs and squeals of enchantment, missing front teeth—old, surely not our age. Then someone places him. A boy who was left out back then or laughed at, still not included. But here he is, present, because it is *his* class, too.

Dependables of a high school reunion: only the people who were too skinny in high school are skinny at all. But also: the nice kids all became nice adults.

"Kelly's looking for you," my classmates tell me, as if we were best friends, as if I should even be here.

They show pictures of their children, who look more like themselves than they do. A classmate has died of an ominously initialed disease. "Didn't you know?" the others say to me. It occurs to me I did, but I've forgotten. Forgotten too how his widow married his best friend and for many that eased the pain.

Then Kelly's arms around me. She holds me like—of course, a long-lost friend—but also possessively. For a moment I think she holds me like her own child.

She whispers in my ear, "I'm sorry I made you jump."

"You didn't," I say.

"We *had* to jump," she says looking for something in my face.

"Yes." It's an insignificant enough concession—and suddenly, possibly even true.

She has small blue eyes. When I notice the beak of her nose, I realize she resembles some kind of waterfowl. She is a hand-shaker, a woman who refers to herself by her last name. She doesn't put up with regrets or last chances or grudges. Before she tells me about how she became a school principal, or asks me how my father is, we have to talk about the accident. This is what reunion means, I think: the effort to make something whole.

She says they screamed as they fell.

"Yes," I say, "now I remember."

She says she lowered the footrest.

"You told me to roll when I landed," I say.

She shakes her head, "I must have gotten that from movies."

She tells me she spoke to each of them. Linda asked for help. Veronica didn't answer. And I felt a sick confirmation, all these years later, of how she'd already died. Kelly says she slept with her mother that night and dreamed she would raise a retarded child. She awoke knowing that would be her life. "It has been," she says simply, explaining her brain-damaged daughter.

I slap at a mosquito, wondering what causes what. Kelly tugs restlessly at her bangs, a mannerism so startlingly familiar I can't believe I'd forgotten it. She tells me her husband fell off scaffolding when they were dating, was impaled on rebar from two stories up.

"No—*fell?*" Are lives prone to motifs?

Her smile is rueful, as if the joke's on her. "But really, now he's fine."

When I don't say anything, she says, "Look. We jumped to save them." And I can see her going down the path below the ski lift, sure-footed, even wise. I think, though I do not tell her, that in jumping we saved ourselves. In the action, we exercised an option; we made an exclamation. We said, *We have survived.*

I can ask my classmates about Linda and Kathy, but I don't. It just feels like too much to know. Kelly sips the drink she's holding as she stands in front of the illuminated contortions of a water slide. I tell her about how lately I keep thinking about it.

She says, "That happens. What else would you expect?" Then, "You know, some good came of it." She means something spiritual. Mormons hope tragedy improves the soul. But for me, what I'd like is for the accident not just to have mattered but to surrender some kind of meaning. But it merely teases. The only thing that *feels* as if it is significant is that Sister Bennett was the same age as we are now.

The park lights flicker.

I imagine the four of them, a grotesque sculpture garden in the moonlight, still lying beneath the ski lift, ten miles up the canyon at a ski resort a movie star now owns. They are stone blocks of ancient ruins, worn and weary of their work. And if we hadn't jumped? Would I then imagine us sitting there as well? Still? Action won't always save you, but it at least allows you to imagine you can be saved.

Here is the difference, I think suddenly: They fell to their deaths. We jumped to life. Instead of meaning, there is only that fact.

When the management locks us out of the water park, we stand under the unsteady lights of the parking lot and continue to tell our stories. "Fun as a blue M&M," I hear someone say. Kelly looks at me fondly. She bends to tie her Reeboks—now she's the one wearing sensible shoes. Then there are only a few of us remaining. Rhonda, still well-groomed and placid, talks about her book about monster trucks. Patty touches my arm, says, "You always had beautiful fingernails."

Suddenly it's just the two of us. Kelly puts her hands on my shoulders and turns me toward her. What I see in her face is not the child she was but, like a ghost, the grandmother she will shortly be.

I know what she'll say before she says it. "I'm sorry I didn't come back for you."

My grandmother said, "Dreams are better than real, they're true." In mine, Dave and I go into a redwood forest. In a gift-shop cabin we buy a packet of seeds. On the back is this earnest plea: *The mighty sequoia is endangered. Please, kind traveler, germinate these seeds. Helps us save our trees.*

I plant them in my backyard. First one, then thirty or forty. Oh, the pleasure of planting those trees! The delight of giving them names: Larkin (from the songbird), Ulysses (the cunning hero), Gabriel (with his Judgment Day horn). Names for the children we never had. But they grow like Jack's magic beans into shocking and unkempt adolescents. I tend them and try to talk them out of such unruly heights, but they slump and act disrespectful. They do forest wheelies, wear mirrored sunglasses, and smoke cigarettes.

I say, "I think I'll call California, see if they want them back."

Dave of course, smiles and sings, "Let them be."

But in the background they're shoving each other. They've begun to leave messy fingerprints as they scrape the bottoms of clouds. Then suddenly I see a pattern. My trees are thick as a logjam, plugging up the summer air. You could step securely from one to another, like Towers of Babel. Everywhere you could walk up and down in the summer sky.

Chinese Opera

ANNE RAEFF

From *The Jungle around Us* (2016)

The Buchovskys were at the Chinese opera the night Danny McSwene was murdered. The three of them—Simone, her sister Juliet, and their father—had been there all day, from nine in the morning, to be precise, and were not released from the performance until ten that night. The coroner's report said that he had died somewhere between eight and midnight, so his death might not have occurred during the performance but, rather, when they were eating dinner later. The exact time was not crucial. Still, Simone would always think of the actors' endless wailing and excruciatingly slow movements and their white, painted faces whenever she thought of Danny McSwene's last moments.

Their father had a long tradition of dragging them to such events. When they were small Simone was sure he searched carefully for the most tedious and difficult performances to bring them to. She thought he was trying to teach them something—patience perhaps, or tolerance—but now that she was twelve, her older self realized that he simply had had no idea what torture these outings were for young children, and she was convinced that he thought she and Juliet enjoyed them as much as he did. He liked to refer to the three of them as a trio. Simone always imagined them as a trio of flute, violin, and piano, though she could not say who was which instrument, but as she got older she could not think why her imagination had settled on such shrill and plucky instruments. They were really much more like bassoons and violas—unassuming and hardworking.

It was especially cold the day they went to see the Chinese Opera, the day that Danny McSwene died, and it was cold in the theater too. Simone kept her coat and gloves on the whole time. She imagined, however, that the actors were warm enough. They were heavily clad, and their movements, as slow as they were, seemed to require a lot of effort—each placement of the foot, each slow swoop of the hand, even the eyes labored, prowling slowly, meeting the gaze of the enemy or a lover. At first she enjoyed the performance. She liked the feel of the gong reverberating in her legs and in her heart and was amused by the costumes and the stories, the details of which were outlined in the program. She fell into a sort of trance, concentrating on color, sound, and movement without thinking about the plot or the cacophony, but after the one intermission, during which the three of them ate black bread with butter and honey that their father had prepared at home, she grew increasingly bored.

Their father had promised to take them to their favorite diner after the performance for a late dinner. Their father was able to get them to do just about anything—sit through a lecture about the diary of a foot soldier in Napoleon's army or the uncut version of a movie about the Russian icon painter Andrei Rublev— if he promised that they would have dinner at a diner afterward. Though each had their favorite form of eggs, all three of them always ordered eggs. Eggs and milkshakes.

During the second half of the opera, it had grown even colder, and all Simone could think about was that she was cold, though she never would have dreamed of excusing herself, of asking permission to take a walk or go to the Coliseum Bookstore, which was just a stone's throw away from Lincoln Center, where the marathon Chinese opera festival was being held. So she sat through the rest of the performance, rubbing her hands and dreaming of the oily warmth of the diner. Later, after hearing the awful news about Danny McSwene, Simone felt that she should have been using this time more wisely instead of wasting it, thinking about the cold and wondering whether she should order a mushroom or cheese omelet.

Danny McSwene was their favorite of their neighbors' seven sons. There was quite a difference in age between the oldest sons, who were twins and lived together in South America, where they worked for a philanthropic organization, and the youngest, who had graduated from high school the year before. Danny was right in the middle and the quietest of all the McSwene boys, although Simone did not really know the twins or Alan, who was next in line and had been shot in the lung in Vietnam and then married a Japanese woman he had met when he was on leave. When Alan came home, he and his wife lived with the McSwenes until they could get settled. It was summer, and Simone remembered them lying on lounge chairs in the backyard for hours at a time until they both were very brown. With the two youngest boys, Simone and Juliet played catch, but though both girls were athletically inclined, they were no match for the McSwene boys who included the two of them in their games nonetheless, perhaps, Simone thought, because they secretly longed for sisters.

But what they really looked forward to were the nights when Danny McSwene babysat. As soon as their father was out the door, the excitement would begin. The first step was to clear the living room, move everything—the couch, the chairs, tables, rugs—through the kitchen and into the family room. They did this efficiently and carefully, making sure not to scrape the walls or scuff the wooden floors.

"You don't know how lucky you are to have wooden floors," Danny McSwene said every time. "Carpeting is the scourge of the modern world. How on earth is anyone supposed to dance on carpeting?"

When all the living room furniture was piled into the family room, they changed into their dance clothes. Danny McSwene wore special shoes and wonderful black pants with pleats. He had a collection of silk shirts—pink and purple and green. Simone and Juliet put on their good school shoes. One night Simone got to wear pants and lead while Juliet wore a dress and followed and the next time they switched roles.

Danny McSwene had a collection of records that he carried in a green, patent leather satchel he had bought in New York specifically for that purpose. They always started with waltzes and ended with the cha-cha, their favorite. His favorite was the tango, which Simone found a little embarrassing, especially when he insisted on more passion. "Where's the passion?" he would call over the music. "More passion, more passion!"

At the end of the dance sessions, they had always put the furniture back exactly right, so their father wouldn't notice, though he would not have minded, would have been happy to know that they were having such a good time with Danny McSwene. Still, Danny had made them promise not to tell anyone, and they never did, not even after he was dead.

They did not learn about Danny's death until two days after it happened because they were not in the McSwenes' inner circle.

Though they were all fond of one another and happy to be neighbors, the Buchovskys kept their distance as good neighbors do, and the McSwenes kept theirs. And so they learned about his death from the local newspaper, the *Suburbanite*. On the front page there was a photo of Danny McSwene in his chef's uniform. He had just graduated from the Culinary Institute of America the spring before and had moved to New York, where he had gotten a job at a restaurant with stars. The newspaper said that he had been found in his apartment in Greenwich Village—shot in the back of the head. *Execution style*, they called it.

They did not go to the funeral. Their father avoided religious ceremonies of any kind, even weddings, and tried to have as little as possible to do with all things religious, though they sometimes went to concerts at Riverside Church in New York because he was a great admirer of liturgical music, especially Russian Orthodox, which he played at full volume while they cleaned the house every Sunday morning. Despite his appreciation for religious music, it was a matter of principle with him to fight against what he called the forces of unreason in his own, quiet way, as he did when he was drafted into the army and refused to declare a religion on the official paperwork. Even when the superior officer explained that they needed a religion so that they would know how to dispose of his body if he died, their father was unbending.

"You can just leave me there for the vultures, like the Zoroastrians do," her father had said. Every time he told the story, Simone could not help but imagine her father dead, the vultures pecking at his flesh, his eyes, and when he came to that part she always laughed so as not to let on that she was frightened.

"Like who?" the officer had said.

"The Zoroastrians," her father had answered.

"Is that a religion?"

"Yes," her father had said. "They leave their dead exposed to the elements and the vultures in what they call the tower of silence."

"How do you spell that?" the officer had asked.

Her father had spelled it out for him.

The man had grabbed the form, crossed out *none*, and written *Zoroastrian*. "There, now you have a religion. Now you can die."

Still, even though Simone was afraid to see it, she felt they should be there to watch Danny McSwene's body be let down into the earth, to throw a clump of dirt onto the coffin as she had seen mourners do in movies. "Don't you think we should go?" she asked her father just an hour before the funeral was to begin.

"It's much more important to pay our respects afterward," he explained. "They won't even notice who's at the church."

"But for Danny," Simone said.

"Do you think he was a believer?" he asked.

"I don't know. We never talked about it," Simone said.

"Well, if he wasn't, he would have preferred us not to go," he said.

"But we don't know whether he was or wasn't," she argued.

"No, we don't," he said, leaving her with nothing to argue against, for one cannot argue with incertitude.

"What if it were a Zoroastrian funeral?" Simone asked. "Would we go then?"

"Maybe," he said. "At least then it would be all out in the open."

"What would be out in the open?" she asked.

"Everything," he said. "Everything we don't want to see."

"Like the wound?" she asked.

"Like the wound," he replied, taking her in his arms, for she had begun to cry.

When they saw the mourners arriving back at the McSwenes' house after the funeral, Simone, Juliet, and their father went over to pay their respects. They dressed all in black. The girls wore Danskin tops and had made a special visit to the Tenafly Department Store to buy black skirts and tights. Their father wore his funeral suit. They brought a bottle of vodka and baklava because their father said they should bring something not too elaborate. At the McSwenes' house, there were plenty of black scarves and black ties and black shoes, but they were the only ones all in black. They stood awkwardly in front of the picture window that looked out onto the McSwenes' backyard where, just the summer before, Simone and Juliet had played catch and flipped baseball cards.

Their father made his way around the room, shaking hands with Mr. McSwene and all the remaining McSwene boys. When he had finished conveying his condolences to the men of the family, he joined his daughters at the window. "Mrs. McSwene is upstairs in the bedroom," he said. "I think you should go see her."

They climbed the stairs to the second floor slowly. They had never been upstairs before. The McSwene boys had been outdoor companions, and it never would have occurred to them to visit their rooms, look through their books, listen to their records. Mrs. McSwene, all in black also, was lying on top of a cream-colored bedspread like a giant felled chess piece. Surrounding her, on both sides of the bed, were women of all ages, the two oldest seated near her head holding her hands and the younger women closer to Mrs. McSwene's feet, kneeling on the floor, clasping her legs.

No one noticed Simone and Juliet as they stood in the doorway watching. Simone wanted to flee, but she knew they could not simply turn around, descend the stairs, and tell their father that they had not known how to approach Mrs. McSwene. He would not have understood about the barrier of women. And they could not have lied and said they had spoken to her when they hadn't. It would have made them sad to lie to their father about such a thing. Juliet pulled on the sleeve of Simone's black shirt, but Simone ignored it. She was focused on Mrs. McSwene's grief. She moved toward Mrs. McSwene and, as if she were Moses and the women the Dead Sea, they parted before her.

"I would like to extend my condolences," she said, but all Mrs. McSwene did was tilt her head without looking in her direction, as if she were blind and trying to hear more clearly. "Of all your boys, Danny was my favorite," Simone said, and Mrs. McSwene began to weep. She twitched on the bed and gasped, and the women ran back to hold her hands and wipe her brow. Someone brought a glass of water, and the older women pulled the weeping Mrs. McSwene up on her pillows and held it to her lips, and when she would not drink, they tried pouring it into her mouth, but the water ran down her chin and onto her black dress.

"She doesn't want to drink anything," Simone said quietly, and all the women turned and stared at her. Juliet ran out of the room.

"Come closer, Simone," Mrs. McSwene demanded in her raspy, smoker's voice that was raspier still from crying. "Sit down."

Simone sat down and closed her eyes. Mrs. McSwene pulled her closer and whispered directly into her ear, "He was my favorite too." Then she turned away and started to weep again.

When Simone returned to the living room, the mourners were looking out the picture window, watching the bright pink winter sun setting. They were standing, holding their drinks as if poised, waiting for that last burst of pink to disappear so that darkness could fall. Her father was not one of the sunset watchers. He was leaning against the wall looking at a large art book, which he was holding up with one hand.

"Simone," he said as if he had been worried that she was lost.

"It's getting dark," Simone said.

"I suppose we should be going. Where's Juliet?"

"I don't know," Simone said.

"We must find her, then," her father said. He returned his book to the shelf. The sun had set and the mourners had dispersed from the window and formed small clusters around the living room, talking quietly, more quietly, it seemed, because it was dark. Someone turned on the overhead light and everyone looked up, as if they had been caught in a searchlight. A woman began weeping. "Should I turn it off?" the man who had switched it on asked.

"No, it's getting dark," someone answered for all of them.

They walked silently back home. Their father wanted to make scrambled eggs for dinner, but no one was hungry, so they had chamomile tea and zwieback, which is what they ate when they were sick. That night Simone could not sleep. She tried reading, forcing herself to read what she called the *pretty poems*, the ones she usually skipped over—Wordsworth and Cummings, Houseman. She hoped, for some not-very-well-thought-out reason, that flowers and love and small hands would cheer her up, but she could not rid herself of the image of Danny McSwene sitting at his desk with a bullet hole in the back of his head. She tried to imagine what kind of person would feel compelled to execute Danny McSwene, who had always been so polite and had a dimple in his left cheek.

Simone closed her eyes and pretended she was sleeping in a house overlooking the ocean. The house was humble—a small, whitewashed cottage with a fireplace and stone floors. She tried listening for the crashing of the surf on rocks and the sound the wind makes on water. But Danny McSwene entered her cottage by the sea, sat in her simple wooden chair in her simple kitchen with cast-iron pans and earthenware pitchers. He sat down and said that he was very, very tired and asked for a glass of water. "Please," he said, and blood was pouring out of his head and onto his shirt, and a puddle of blood formed on the stone floor at his feet.

Simone got up then, walked quietly down the stairs, put on her coat and gloves and scarf. She stood in the backyard looking at the back of the McSwenes' house. She had expected it to be dark, but to her surprise, the house was totally illuminated, and she could see clearly into the empty living room and kitchen. She saw the furniture and the bookshelves and the fireplace.

She walked toward the house, and when she reached it, she stood in the flower bed underneath the living room picture window, her breath clouding the glass. She stood there waiting for someone to come down the stairs, but no one appeared, so she stayed put, stood there in the dark and cold until dawn. She wanted, then, to turn around and walk back to her warm house, get under the covers, sleep finally, but she remembered Danny and how he could feel neither heat nor cold, nor long for sleep, so she stayed.

Finally, just when dawn was turning to day, she saw Mrs. McSwene descending the stairs, pausing on each step as if to make sure it was strong enough to take her weight.

Mrs. McSwene stepped off the last step and walked into the living room. She paused in the middle of the room. Her lips were moving, and then they stopped, as if waiting for a reply. Mrs. McSwene was wearing a robe, and Simone imagined the women helping Mrs. McSwene change out of her black funeral dress. She wondered whether she would have preferred to keep it on. Something seemed to startle Mrs. McSwene, and she swung around, and before Simone could drop to the ground or run, Mrs. McSwene saw her. Because Simone did not know what else to do, she waved. Mrs. McSwene walked to the window and pressed her face to it, and her faced seemed like some separate thing trying to push its way through the glass.

Finally, Mrs. McSwene opened the back door and Simone entered. "Sit," Mrs. McSwene said, pointing to the sofa, and Simone sat down. Immediately, Simone began shaking. "How long have you been standing out in the cold?" Mrs. McSwene asked.

"A long time," Simone said.

"I'll bring some whiskey," Mrs. McSwene said and walked over to the liquor cabinet. She carried two very full glasses of whiskey back to the sofa and sat down next to Simone. Her robe had come undone, and Simone could see Mrs. McSwene's thighs, so she averted her eyes. Mrs. McSwene noticed that her thighs were exposed and stood up to adjust her robe, then sat down again, farther away from Simone. She reached into her pocket for a pack of Newports, tipped a cigarette out, and lit it, inhaling deeply. Simone took a sip of whiskey.

"I need your help," Mrs. McSwene said.

Simone leaned in toward Mrs. McSwene.

"I want you to tell them to go away," Mrs. McSwene said.

"Tell whom to go away?" Simone asked.

"All of them—my sons and sisters and the cousins and friends and in-laws. I don't even know who they all are, but they seem to know me, know that what I need to do is eat soup and rest and cry. They keep telling me that I should cry, that crying will do me good."

"But, I . . ." Simone's hands began to tremble, so she put them under her thighs, and pressed down hard upon them. "But I don't know them," she said.

"What?" Mrs. McSwene asked.

"I don't know them," Simone repeated.

"Of course, you can't tell them," Mrs. McSwene agreed. "You're just a child." She pulled out another cigarette and held it gently in the palm of her hand as if it were a baby bird.

"I didn't say I couldn't tell them," Simone said. She thought of Danny and how he would have known how to get them all out of the house without making anyone feel bad.

"So you'll do it?" Mrs. McSwene took her hand.

"Yes," Simone said. "Where are they?"

"They're everywhere. You'll just have to start opening up doors," she said.

Simone climbed the stairs slowly, thinking that the only thing she wanted now was a plate of her father's heavy, hot kasha, thinking that if she ate enough of it, she could finally fall asleep, sleep way into the afternoon until it was dark. She sat down on the stairs and tried to muster the courage to open the doors to the rooms where the sleeping mourners lay. She knew that Danny would have wanted her to help his mother, who had loved him more than she had loved her other six children. But Simone couldn't do it. Back down the stairs she went, softly, so as not to make the floorboards creak. She turned the latch and opened the front door and stepped outside where the sun was now bright and ricocheted off the remaining patches of snow, catching her right in the eye as if she were the killer.

In the days that followed, Simone avoided the McSwenes' house, so she did not know whether the flock of cars that stood in their driveway had thinned slowly or whether they had all disappeared at once like geese from a lake. Once they were all gone, she wondered whether Mrs. McSwene missed having them all there, trying to get her to eat and drink and cry and bathe. She imagined Mrs. McSwene lying on the living room couch and Mr. McSwene standing in front of the fireplace playing the bagpipe that always stood in the corner near the sofa. But maybe he stopped playing the bagpipe after Danny's death. Maybe all they wanted was quiet, but this is something she would never know. The Buchovskys did not talk to the McSwenes much after Danny's death. They waved from their side of the fence and left them bags of apples from their apple tree on their back porch.

But sometimes at night before she fell asleep, Simone would imagine herself finding Danny McSwene's killer, cornering him in a dark alley, smashing his head against the wall while he begged for mercy and leaving him there, bleeding on the street. It was always raining in her presleep fantasies, and in the distance she could hear cymbals crashing like at the Chinese opera, and she moved in rhythm with them until they ceased completely and all she could hear was Danny's executioner calling out for her help: "Don't leave me here, don't leave me. Have some mercy, for God's sake, have mercy."

Evolution of Words

DIANNE NELSON OBERHANSLY

From *A Brief History of Male Nudes in America* (1993)

I tried to see the city as he must have seen it—a miracle of light, the rain-wet streets opening from Battery to Sansome and finally down to Grant. Judd hadn't slept in four nights, and so, when he left his parents' house on the fifth night and walked downtown, the city must have spun with music for him. He was seventeen and sleepless and that close to what his mother would later call "release."

We cried at that. Release. The idea of Judd walking in Chinatown the fifth night, change in his pockets, the on-and-off rain a passage into something we had no knowledge of. He liked it there—Chinatown—the piles of foreign newspapers, the boys with braids, with needletracks dancing up their thin arms. San Francisco was a waking dream that my cousin Judd walked through tirelessly. He didn't want a car. *Leslie Prada and Her Topless Love Act* was something he had to see on foot, next door to The Condor, across from Dutch Boy Paints, and only a half block down from El Cid's *He and She Revue.* "Get a job and you can have a car," Judd's parents told him, but he continued to walk from Nob Hill to Lands' End in tennis shoes and T-shirt, with the long dark hair that would be cut before he was buried. No one knew where my cousin's spending money came from.

For months afterward I looked for answers by trying to re-create the scene of that shadowy fifth night, the world in rags. Even fish sleep, their bodies like silvery, shot arrows lining the Embarcadero and Baker's Beach and spreading outward on waves to Sausalito. Fridays were open buffet at Song Hay, and Judd could have been there that last night, but the restaurant was so busy that the cashier couldn't remember just one boy. An attendant at the Ginn Wall parking lot may have seen Judd, but there was nothing distinctive about my cousin's face, and in the darkness at the corner of the lot a slouching boy in a denim jacket was the least of things to notice. With a Chamber of Commerce city map, I tried to reinvent his path, tracing the cold hard steps he might have taken past the Greyhound Bus Depot and maybe on to the Flower Terminal where the chrysanthemums must have glowed, to him, like an eerie experiment set in white rain. North or south from there, perhaps unable to hitch a ride to Sonoma, cold and breathless and stinging with enough life to ground three people, my cousin turned, wherever he was, and finally headed for the nailhead lights of the Golden Gate Bridge.

That's where I stopped reimagining the scene—the place where Judd put on his Walkman and stepped into air. No one knew how he got past the attendants at the tollbooths. Magic, determination—my cousin wanted to fly, the music pounding in his ears, the rough wind making its momentary promises.

In the gloomy days before the funeral, no one thought about Judd's hair, about the way he had wanted to be. By the time we gave instructions, we were too late. Hyberland's Mortuary had already used army clippers on him.

Judd's mother, entranced, made endless pots of coffee, and it was not until months later that she said it: "release." Sitting at the kitchen table, our hearts turned liquid and we finally caved in.

Now, years later, there are other words we can't get past: "winter," "midnight." Even "water" hits us like a clap of thunder.

Ralph Goes to Mexico

ED ALLEN

From *Ate It Anyway* (2003)

Even at highway speed, the Ryder van's automatic transmission seems never to shift, just winds out faster and more frantic, like a washing machine on the spin cycle, revs up from ramp to interstate, to a high whinny at sixty-five. If Lydia tries to go any faster, some kind of governor comes on and literally pushes the gas pedal back up.

In his carrying case on the passenger seat, Ralph cries with what little strength he has left—a dry, lifeless yowl that after listening to it all day yesterday, Lydia hardly hears anymore. Sometimes she pokes a finger through a wide space in the wire door, but Ralph doesn't come toward it.

Interstate 40 seems to concentrate the August light into a sort of hazy tunnel cut into the thick of Arkansas, walls of pine forest on either side of the road broken up now and then by mobile home dealerships, all under a ceiling of blank sky the same color as the white pavement of the road. As she pulls off the interstate into another truck stop, Lydia can feel the allergy shots she got from her doctor in Cincinnati wearing off. In the truck parking area of the Union 76 Truck Plaza, she swallows three Excedrin Sinus with water from her old green wafer-shaped Girl

Scout canteen and hides her red eyes behind sunglasses before walking toward the restaurant.

She has left the van running, with the air-conditioning on, to keep Ralph alive a few weeks longer. It idles, dwarfed among the 18-wheelers lined up in a diagonal file from which they can pull out without backing up. Lydia's Mazda clings to the rear of the yellow van, its front wheels mounted up on the towing dolly, its windows piled with the washed whites and maroons of her clothes, most of which are probably too bulky for the heat that awaits her in Tucson.

"So," Dr. Tepper says over the phone, his little voice crisp in Lydia's ear. "Are we eating any better?"

"Not much," she says. "I'm still giving him water and that Nutri-stuff with the dropper."

She sits at a section of the counter where each seat has an individual telephone. The section is marked Professional Drivers Only, but Lydia, who is very good at asking for things, has been given permission to sit here.

She probably didn't need to ask; with her barrel-shaped body and her jeans, which she wears without those fashionable frayed rips in them, she could easily pass for one of the beefy women truckers who are always drinking coffee in these places. The freakish fact that she does not smoke would probably be interpreted here as meaning only that she is in one of those moments between the stubbing out of one cigarette and the lighting up of the next.

Lydia has often wondered if Dr. Tepper was originally a medical student who flunked out. He's the only veterinarian she's ever known who talks about dogs and cats using the iatric "we."

"I assume we're not going into Mexico anymore," he says.

Lydia says no, but she's really not sure. This had been her plan before Ralph got sick, and Dr. Tepper knows about it because she had to ask him for the vaccination records and health certificate so that Ralph could be readmitted to the United States. What she wants to do is to stop in El Paso and take Ralph briefly across the Mexican border. Somehow this is important to her: anything to do with airplanes and international borders and the way faces look when they have been somewhere you haven't. When Lydia was nine years old, before she had ever been in a plane herself, her next door neighbors had a pair of Scotties, and as she stood against the fence listening to the peppery staccato of their barking, she was fascinated to think that little Angus and Kyle had been up in a plane, coming from California. She would look at those dogs for long moments, trying to see if any residue of that flight was still visible in their stern little faces.

Ralph has already been in a plane, and if Lydia manages to get him into Mexico, he will be a truly international cat—the first one she's even known, if you don't count Canada. She can imagine that if he lives long enough it will be fun to show him off to her new acquaintances, the first time she has people over for dinner at her new apartment.

"You know," she will say as he pads from guest to guest beneath the red and brown concentric Navajo yarn constructions that by that time she will have put up on the walls, "he's been to Mexico."

She has another plan too, now that he is so sick, and this one she hasn't told anybody about. As soon as he dies, she has decided, she is going to take him to a furrier and have him made into a hat. Sort of a Davy Crockett style is what she is thinking—that might work well with his light gray stripes—but without the tail; the tail hanging down would be a little gross. If he can't be her cat, she has been telling herself since the day Tepper first announced that "we" had tested positive for Feline Leukemia Virus, then he will have to be her hat.

Texas thins out the next day into nubbled ridges and faraway gray tablelands. Ralph moans from time to time and stares through the bars of his carrier, moving something around inside his mouth, like an old man gumming the sores on his tongue. It is strange how little she feels for him now. Maybe that's the one merciful thing about FeLV: the personality is the first thing to go. By the time they are about to die, there's nobody to say good-bye to anymore.

She feels clearer in the sinuses already. Unfortunately, the main thing she notices at this point is how bad everything smells: the sweetish vinyl polish inside the truck cab, Ralph's deep yellow urine, a truckload of hogs up ahead, their thick outhouse odor trailing for miles behind them in the traffic.

Strange to think, in a country with MRI systems and CAT scans and little synthetic molecules that can fit into the puzzle pieces of the brain's wiring as cleanly as a digital key fits into the door of a Ramada Inn, that she had to spend five years feeling lousy, in the middle of a city of hospitals, and that after all the shots and pills and vaporizers, the most sophisticated advice her doctor could finally give her was to get out of town.

Everybody at work was wonderful about it. The director of customer relations at Procter and Gamble went out of her way to help Lydia find a good job at the Tucson office of IBM. The whole office held a party for her, gave her a card: "We're all sad you're leaving. Even the computer's down."

One of her friends drew her a cartoon showing the Four Horsemen of the Apocalypse (he labeled them Manny, Moe, Jack, and Shemp) breaking down the door to a deserted office marked 666. Inside the door, Lydia's computer, her phone console, and her desk, with its array of pill bottles and inhalers and nasal sprays, were strung with cobwebs.

The joke in this drawing had to do with Lydia's main function in the customer relations department. She had become the person who had to deal with customer inquiries about the number

666, which some religious groups believed was concealed within the company's trademark.

Lydia's job, as the 666 specialist, was to talk to those callers and explain that it was a hoax, to offer to send them a booklet that included the story of how the venerable trademark actually came to be, and, lately, to explain that P&G was suing two franchisees of a well-known pyramid-scheme cleaning products marketer, who were being charged with maliciously distributing a photocopied handout that accused P&G of being in league with Satan. She was also supposed to put a tracer on anyone who was blatantly threatening, though the tracers led almost always to public telephones.

She was good at it. It was the best feeling of the whole job, even on days when the bones around her nose felt as if she were twenty feet underwater, when she could actually calm down some born-again housewife and get her to admit that she missed being able to use Ivory soap. Sometimes a warm tingle would run up Lydia's neck, almost getting to the place where it would let the pressure out of her sinuses, on those occasions when she heard the voice on the other end soften and say good-bye without anger.

But most of the time it didn't work that way. Somehow 800 numbers always bring out the worst in people. Monday mornings were especially bad, in the lingering flush of Pentecostal gatherings from the day before. Women would ask a question about the Devil and then never stop talking long enough for her to answer.

The problem with talking to that kind of people all day was that later, when she went out into the real world and waited in line at the supermarket, she could never stop wondering who the angry ones were. Everybody always looks so normal and relaxed waiting in traffic; only after they're pulling away do you see the Assembly of God bumper sticker, furious in its red-white-and-blue block lettering. Every time Lydia and the man she had been seeing went to a Reds game together, she found herself paying less attention to the players than to the faces of strangers passing in the stands, wondering which ones God was talking to and which fathers were there not because they liked baseball but because they couldn't think of any other approved family things to do with the children. Some of those fathers had to be up there somewhere, on the other side of the field, hidden in the tweedish, red-sprinkled texture of crowd—sitting, staring, all that anger about the sixes compressed, hidden in their little family hearts like a handgun under a gang member's jacket.

In the El Paso Comfort Inn East, Ralph lies on his back on Lydia's lap, being force-fed. He seems to be calmly swallowing the molasses-brown amalgam of protein and vitamins and fat that she slowly pushes into his mouth from the graduated cylinder of the oral syringe. Then suddenly the muscles of his mouth and neck move forward in a spasm, and everything pours down the gray fur on the sides of his face, like a clownish extension of his mouth. He didn't swallow any of it. It would ordinarily be funny, but Ralph doesn't have a personality anymore. This is no funnier than paint dripping down a wall.

She wipes off what she can, looks into Ralph's blank eyes, and sees at once that he's not going to make it to Arizona. She does not cry because there is no longer anybody there to cry over, just a sick animal with a big cartoon Mexican mustache of Nutri-Vite running down the sides of his face.

So Ralph almost certainly won't be there when she has her first dinner party, which means that it won't matter by that time if he has ever made it to Mexico or not. But for some reason it seems even more important now than before, in the little time he has left. Plus, she has the papers from Dr. Tepper, and it seems pathetic to get the papers for something and then not do it.

"Mexico." That's what she says. She paces barefoot on the soft pinkish carpet, stepping around where she has set Ralph down and he has returned to his crouch without taking a step, bundled up in more or less the same shape he will be when be becomes a hat, if she can find somebody to do the job.

Ralph's whole life passes before her eyes as she walks around the motel room—all his travels, all the states he's been to; even cats are cosmopolitan these days. Born in Indiana, moved to Ohio, driven to Pennsylvania, New Jersey, Delaware, New York, other states she can't remember, yowling in the same carrier. And once by plane, unescorted, from Boston to Cincinnati, coming in shit-smeared and stinking on the U.S. Airways baggage wagon.

Now she does feel like crying but not enough to really do it. She paces, sniffing the motel's heavy carpet perfume with every inhalation. You would think that in these nonsmoking rooms they would need to use less fragrance instead of more.

And Tucson, everybody talks about how great Tucson is supposed to be: its sunlit avenues lined with cactusy gift shops, its good standing on the musical theater circuit, and its new Hispanic-American-Apache desert cuisine, which has been written up in *Gourmet* magazine, emphasizing green peppers grilled over mesquite.

But Lydia is prepared to face what she really expects to find there—the land of the allergic, the home of the geriatric: widowers in those supposedly glaucoma-preventive praying mantis goggles pushing their grocery wagons, called "buggies" out there, through the aisles of a store where for some reason Hellmann's has been renamed Best Foods mayonnaise.

Outside it will be so bright that if you forget your sunglasses, you will hardly be able to squint long enough to see the saguaros at the edge of the parking lot, poking up through the skin of the earth like something for which the doctor would recommend an immediate biopsy. She knows it's beautiful, but there's something horrible about it too, the unforgiving, Old Testament glare of light. She could see it everywhere last month on her apartment-hunting trip: the sun slamming down all day over all that cataclysmic beauty—if you can call it beauty—where the hills don't seem quite finished, and the valleys look like abandoned bauxite mines.

The manager of her apartment complex has warned her that her car's dashboard will crack in a week if she doesn't get one of those cardboard protectors that everybody puts under their windshields. She has already promised herself that when she gets one, she will never leave it up, the way most people seem to, with the "HELP! CALL POLICE!" side facing out. Decision taken: Ralph is going to Mexico.

When you get close to the border you can feel it, in the low clutter of cement-block houses, in the sunblasted look of storefronts. She drives the van, with the car following on the towing dolly, down streets full of signs for *Cambianos* posted above bulletproof money-changing windows, each with a concavity under the glass to pass the currency through. She has found a Mexican station on AM. The announcer's voice seems to be charged by some rapid and outlandish voltage, his syllables swooping up to a high note, then swinging down through an electronic reverberation of excitement. She took two years of that language in college and now she can barely make out a word.

Everyone on the pedestrian section of the Stanton Street Bridge walks in the same direction; you get back into the United States on a different bridge. Below, visible through the crosshatched security bars that run along the side of the walkway, the

By the time she has waited through the first long traffic light
ween the veterinary clinic and the ramp back on to the inter-
e, she has already decided that there will be no funeral. To
e a funeral you have to pray, and Lydia's standard joke with
friends is that she cannot pray because she is not a Repub-
n. She is thinking, now that Ralph can't be her Chicago hat,
the proper western burial would be to leave him out some-
re in the desert, as dinner for the coyotes. She is pretty sure
feline leukemia cannot be transferred over into latran leu-
nia. She has always loved coyotes, those beautiful dogs with
ir sidelong, haunted faces, and their bleached eyes, and the
able scruff of their coats that Price-Is-Right Bob cannot tol-
te seeing on a woman's back.

a parking area whose sign announces No Facilities, she parks
truck and walks away from the roadway, along a path that
ves behind a low rocky hill. The blue package swings at her
e. Tufts of toilet paper, white as chicken feathers and half
mpressed into a sort of poisoned papier-máché, mark the
ces around the trail where motorists couldn't wait for the real
t areas. She examines the ground closely as she walks, know-
g that only the lucky ones had paper.

She crosses a chain-link fence at the low point where others
ve tramped over it, walks a hundred yards further, until the
otpath has dwindled away and she seems to be out of toilet pa-
r territory. She can't see the interstate. It's rangeland out here:
t rocks and hardened mud with some kind of leathery-leaved
shes stirring around in the wind. It's hot, in that western way
u feel mostly on the bare parts of your skin. Some bloom, or
cay, in the desert has filled the air with something Lydia's
lf-recovered nasal passages have never smelled before: a deep,

Rio Grande flows along the bottom of a narrow sluiceway sunk
in the center of a white expanse of concrete. She is over the water now, the cat carrier swinging gently at her side, with Ralph's
veterinary papers tucked into a compartment, certifying that he
is not dying of any disease—and now beyond it, walking downhill
toward the barred full-height steel turnstile that lets people into
Ciudad Juárez. He is in Mexico.

Lydia stops nowhere, walking beside the traffic of Avenida
16 de Septiembre with her half-alive luggage, toward the other
bridge that goes back to the U.S., through the charcoal-sweet
restaurant smoke, the oily, distinctively Mexican exhaust, and
the soft bubble-gum smell that hangs over every corner. She
buys nothing from the wagons of ceramic dogs and fringed miniature sombreros, smiles blankly at the black-haired children
who beg for coins and stare into the cat case.

The next day Ralph can't walk. Lydia props him up and he falls
down, breathing hard. Outside the room, kids are shrieking and
doing cannonballs. It's one of those motels set up around a sort
of atrium, where all three stories of rooms face inward onto the
trapped noise of the pool.

She should have planned ahead about the hat. Whether it can
be done now on such short notice is problematic; maybe if she
just had him skinned she could send the pelt to a hat stylist when
she has time—which is a gross thought, but really when you
think about it no grosser than putting him in a hole and letting
fly larvae eat him. She holds him on her lap and pets him, feeling
every bone through the diminished flesh; his head hangs down
as if to stare at the floor. On television, Bob Barker announces,
with a nectar of love in his voice, that his next contestant on *The
Price Is Right* is eighty-five years young.

Lydia wonders what the fur-hating Bob would say if he could

see her this morning, with a live animal on her lap, and the motel phone book on the table opened to "Taxi" and "Taxidermy." She can see that there is something cruel about that old man's face, even as he fawns over his contestants, something sharp-toothed, hard, like the faces she used to imagine on the other end of the 666 line, face muscles clenched around the bones of their jaws like a fist.

Actually, Ralph might make a very good hat, now that he is just about finished with being a cat. His dignified gray stripes will go well with the winter gray of the air in a city, perhaps Chicago, sometime when she flies up there in non-allergy season.

"No ma'am," the first taxidermist says, in the gentle Texas drawl of a man not tough enough to have been a cowboy. "We just do fish 'n game here."

"Sorry," another tells her, "I don't do *pets*," coming down hard on that last word, as if there is perhaps in this region a whole underground dead pet business that decent family people hate. One more time, in her most diplomatic office voice, putting some warmth into it, the way she did with those toll-free callers who actually sounded as if they could be persuaded away from believing in the Sixes:

"Good morning. I'm on my way through El Paso, and I have a rather unusual request."

"Tell you the truth, ma'am, I don't know anybody in this state who could do that."

In the pamphlets Lydia used to read when she was waiting with Ralph in Dr. Tepper's waiting room, it always says that the vet-

erinarian will let you stay in the treatme
be there to witness the putting-to-sleep p
imagined that it must be a very healthy b
families. But they don't permit that in this
him into a hat, and now it turns out she
die.

It takes a long time. The waiting room
Hartz Mountain pet care pamphlets, noth
cept one of those very poorly organized w
the breeds of dogs in the world, in which
which description refers to which drawin
these hard-surfaced waiting rooms, with
smell, now stronger than ever in her clea
floors and their vulcanized vinyl couches
school bus.

Outside, she walks in the sunshine, in a
that makes her face and hands tingle but le
less under the dry warmth of her clothes,
Kmart, where she would like to find a mor
sunglasses. But the spaces out here can pla
turns back when she notices that she isn't g

Ralph has come back double-wrapped, one
side another. The doctor was required by Te
disinfect the body. Lydia can feel that the
cleaning fluid. She doesn't say much. The
think she's some kind of cold fish, to be able
ican Express card across the desk as casual
for a business lunch, and then to walk out b
even having to put her sunglasses on, holdin
ing case in one hand, in the other a bag of R
by the deadness she has just paid fifty dollars

spicy, scorched odor—something myrraceous and dehydrated, almost electrical, as if ragweed pollen had been sprinkled on overheated car batteries.

She opens the outer bag, then the inner bag, and pulls him out. He's clean and wet, all the force-feeding mess on his face gone, the gray fur draggled into little tufts, like a newborn animal, still warm, still loose in the joints. A strong peppermint smell, from the doctor's disinfectant, overpowers the sagey breeze of the desert.

She sets him on his side on a flat rock. She does not say good-bye. It occurs to her that maybe she *is* a cold fish. But then, you get that way, like a geriatric nurse overseeing the last weeks of what the obituaries always refer to as a "long illness."

What she hopes mostly is that the coyotes will get to him before the vultures and that they will not be put off by Ralph's peppermint smell. Coyotes are not known for being fastidious, but Lydia is too much of an outsider here to make predictions about the behavior of wild animals.

She pulls back out onto the interstate, the motor winding out to its familiar howl. The van, as usual, is almost out of gas. When a cat dies it leaves nothing behind. It is hard to remember anything but the color of its fur. Lydia has noticed that home videos taken of her friends' animals, even if they are played back just a few weeks after death, give a peculiarly unconvincing, cartoonish quality to things like the jerky motion of a cat's tail as it runs up the front steps of a house.

Perhaps it's an illusion, or exhaustion, or the thin air, or some neurological side effect of the pressure in her sinuses letting off, but when she opens the window, to air out the residual peppermint, she seems to catch a whiff, even through the heat, of Labor Day weekend in the high desert, the coolish breeze of work and school starting up again, the days counting down to the beginning of September with the same regularity as the green mileposts that count down through the single digits toward the "Welcome to Arizona" billboard that Lydia can make out, still a few miles in the distance.

Whether this move is a mistake or not she doesn't know (already having a thought entirely removed from Ralph, she notices), whether the men in the offices next to hers will be there by choice or by allergist's orders remains to be seen. She counts it as a good sign, though, as the van-and-car combination clumps over the seam in the pavement between states, that the governor of Arizona watches over the incoming traffic with the kind of confident smile that shows him to be the kind of person who would never have to move away from home because of something going wrong with his nose.

Snippet and the Rainbow Bridge

MONICA MCFAWN

From *Bright Shards of Someplace Else* (2014)

I

A pony hangs from a sling in the middle of a barn aisle in Indiana. His front right cannon bone is broken and in a thick white cast with a slight curve for the knee. He is a silver dun with patches of white on his head and belly and streaking his mane. His name is Snippet, and he is eleven years old and thirteen hands high. His past is unknown, though for a time he was likely owned by the Amish and used as an errand-running horse for the children. At some point he was neglected, and he ended up skeletal and shaking in an auction ring in Shipshewana, Indiana. There he was purchased, for sixty dollars, by Heart's Journey, an equine rescue nonprofit. After he was rehabbed, he became known as the Painting Pony, one of the few horses trained to lift a brush in his mouth, dip it into a bucket of paint, and press it to a large sheet of paper, again and again. Then he broke his leg.

His sling hangs from the rafters at four points, suspending him inches from the aisle floor. He is hooked to an IV that enters the arched muscle of his neck. Beneath him, white sawdust covers the concrete, and a Rubbermaid box filled with antibiotics, Vetrap, bandages, Betadine, bute, etc., is stored off to his right. His water bucket, grain pan, and hay net are propped up in front of him on a wooden cart. The stall doors, off to his right and left, are decorated with get-well cards. Most of these contain his crude likeness, drawn under rainbows or among a funnel cloud of hearts and stars. A few depict him painting, leaning back and dangling the brush from a dexterous hoof. A tinfoil helium balloon that says "Get Well Soon" is tied around the stall bars, and a small herd of stuffed animals is tucked between them. One of Snippet's own paintings—irregular puffs of green, blue, and pink floating over a linear red scrawl—stands on an easel in the pony's view.

It had been Marti's idea to put the painting there. Her thought was that the painting might inspire the pony's healing, remind him of what he needed to get back to. Marti is one-half of Heart's Journey, the founder and CEO. She's the emotive one, the one whose mascara is forever running down her face (why does she even wear it?) as she weeps in empathy over an equine's pain. She's forty-seven, with the rough look of someone with a *past*—drugs, spousal abuse, jail time—all this seems inherent in the cut of her Carharts, the crispy taper of her long hair, the tremulous wrinkles that seem to rotate around her mouth as she speaks in that confidential half-whisper, as if she were in hiding with whoever is listening. She seems threadbare, fragile, ready to break down or apart, yet she is so at home at the edge of ruin that she seems interred there, no closer to destruction than she is from health. She is sitting on a grain sack in the feed room.

Her partner, Judy, is picking up all the medical flotsam that has washed up by the pony, as if he were the shore of a toxic sea. She kicks the dog away from a bloody wad of gauze; she rolls up the Vetrap, combines two nearly empty bottles of iodine. She picks up several syringes and fans them in her hand, as if their needles must be kept apart, then drops them all in the coffee can for sharps. Judy is forty-two; like a twelve-year-old girl left in the elements for thirty years, she is faded, with faint cracks for smile lines, but her childhood form is essentially unchanged, right down to the sloppy long hair and perky joint-floppiness that marks her movement. Unlike Marti, she seems fresh and healthful; she speaks with an insistent but soft voice, as if she knew her good common sense is disruptive enough and aims to dampen its inherent blows. Often she is the one pulling friends and family back from excess or irrationality; she is that steadying hand on your shoulder before you do something rash. She cleans up around the pony and whistles in a strained and breathy way, like someone who has never really learned how. The barn is very quiet, apart from the padding of the dogs, the sighs and shifts of the pony, and the occasional plop of loose stool from him, which hits the aisle with a wet hiss.

II

Two vets are heading toward Heart's Journey. One is Dr. Jim, from Coldwater, a sixty-year-old large-animal vet who graduated from the land-grant college way back. He is extremely tall, with a concave thinness, like a sail full of wind. His hair is mostly white and his face has a grim, angular look whenever he is serious, which he rarely is. Most often, he's making smooth, small jokes to put people—taciturn farmers, waitresses, strangers waiting in a long line at the bank—at ease. He climbs into his truck adorned with the faded decal of a longhorn (though there are none in the area), turns the key, and smiles when an old George Jones song comes on. In the back of the truck, a canister of bull semen bounces like an antsy child as he eases over the dirt roads. He had to leave his dinner for this call, push his chair away from the peach cobbler and pull on his boots. As he laced up all the eyelets, his wife wrapped his pie slice in tinfoil and asked where he was going. "To see to the crazy ladies' horses," he said, and she nodded. She was never in the habit of asking further questions.

Dr. Jim drives by several farms he does business with—the Skitema dairy, the Yoder's pig operation, and a smattering of small farms and 4-HERS he seasonally visits. It is a cool day for early September, and the clumped beef cattle in the field resemble a large dark hand softly gripping the hilltop, like a father steering a toddler by the head. He needs to drop the semen off there on his way back from Heart's Journey. Out of the rabbit hole and onto solid ground. Heart's Journey—with its silly hand-painted sign, water troughs full of organic herbs and flowers, horses limping around the fields, and pair of unmarried hippie owners—was about as far from John Lidden's beef operation as you could get. Two women staggering around in rose-colored glasses, believing every beat-to-hell old horse farted rainbows. Still, there was something he liked about the place in spite of himself.

III

Dr. Merrill is also on his way to Heart's Journey. He is forty-nine years old and the lead veterinarian at EquiPerformance LLC. He rarely makes farm calls these days, and his assistant, Susan, seems startled when he says where he's heading. Horse owners usually come to the clinic, driving up in diamond-chromed gooseneck rigs with matching trucks. On most days, a fancy horse—a dressage warmblood, a jumper, a quarter horse reiner so muscled and slick it looks like rumpled silk—would trot on the pavement strip while he squinted to see any syncopation in the gait. Even when the irregularity was imperceptible, the owners would want a full workup. Dr. Merrill would snap the films up onto the lighted wall, gesturing at the blurred margin of a tendon, the slightly abnormal angle of a coffin bone, the compressed space in a joint capsule. Many of his cases involve vague complaints that sap a performance horse's brilliance: a short stride, a stiff jump, a sticky turn, all well short of an actual limp.

He instills hope in horse owners by hunkering down a bit, like a chummy waiter, and offering up a menu of edgy treatments: shock-wave, stem-cell, Aquatred, etc. He reminds his clients that there are options—there are almost always options, things to try—and his looks seem to second him. His eyes are wide set and show a lot of very bright white, so his hazel irises appear to be sinking in milk. This babyish feature is undercut by a bunched brow, as if his eyes were pulling toward each other, like drops of water on a tabletop laboring to flow together. His hair is youthfully tousled, his neck is loose, his ears are tight and thinly veined as buds. His form is hard and thin, giving the sense of having been whittled away from something larger.

Heart's Journey is few towns away, and Dr. Merrill merges onto the highway. The landscape is so bleary and overcast that the road seems hyperreal. It reminds him of bad cartoons, where the main characters and scenes are crisp and bright, while everything beyond is summed up in a few gesturing lines. Still, he is glad to push off the day's appointments. And the idea of the scruffy barn dogs and tame chickens swarming about his legs sounds nice, right about now. He'll show them, today, that he remembers their names. The bantam, for instance, is Oscar . . .

IV

It says something about you, the vet you choose. Early on, the two women chose vets like spouses choose sides of beds. They needed a vet almost monthly—for routine shots and for the problems rescue horses usually brought with them. Marti preferred Dr. Merrill—a vet who seemed a connoisseur of equine pain, able to treat it, she thought, because he knew all its guises. When he recommended a course of treatment, he spoke in a low, emphatic voice, full of caution and caveats, as if he were revealing some difficult private knowledge. It was that sense of painful confession, married with his intense bedside manner, that made Marti feel at home.

For Judy, it was Dr. Jim, the cutup country vet with the habit of slapping the horses' hindquarters like a car hood when he was done with them. He blurted out his diagnoses and waved his hands whenever the women asked for more specifics, as if details were an indulgence he was withholding for their own good. The particularly sorry cases—the really broken down horses—he had little patience for. "Best to let them move along," he said, his euphemism for euthanasia, as if they were already passing by on a conveyer. There was something honest, Judy thought, in his refusal to get caught up in anything murky.

Inevitably, both women see a character flaw made manifest in the other woman's vet preference. Marti can see that, despite her practical airs, Judy is afraid to delve into real troubles, to live with unknown outcomes. Judy, watching Marti and Dr. Merrill speak nearly cheek to cheek over some sketchy diagnostic, sees a woman who needs coddling, who relishes the minutiae of sickness under the guise of trying to heal it.

v

Over the barn, there is a bridge, a large bright-banded arch, as noxious as corporate branding bandied about in a boardroom. The bridge is self-contained; it is like a piece of garden décor that can be repositioned wherever it looks best; it performs no function other than to imitate a bridge, to give a sense of crossing. This is the Rainbow Bridge, and it is referenced often by Marti and Judy as if it were as solid as the feed store down the road. The Rainbow Bridge is animal rescuer parlance for the interfaith zone where dead animals go, the sphere where old, unsteady horses are restored to an eternal youth. Pet dogs who lived in different decades and never crossed paths on earth snort each other's buttocks in the sky. Cats cash in their unused lives for cloud perches near the sun. Or some such thing.

The Bridge comes up between the women with some regularity. They've kept horses from it and sent horses to it. They've pulled horses off slaughter trucks, they've outbid the kill-buyers at Shipshewana, they've carefully rehabbed starvation cases and neglect cases, calling the farrier in to trim the long, curled hoofs, like elfin slippers, on some of the worst. They've also had to put a fair number of horses down—Raven, with the ulcerated, cancerous eye; Henry, with the inoperable colic; the deformed colt Jet, who walked on his pasterns; the old mare Olena, whose ringbone and navicular kept her down so long she developed bedsores. Then there was Yankee, the off-track Thoroughbred who twice flipped over under tack, nearly killing Marti. A particularly troubling case, as he was young and beautiful and completely deadly—

VI

Before he left the office for Heart's Journey, Dr. Merrill had asked Susan to cancel his appointment with his client Deborah and her mare, Luna. Luna is lame again, this time in the hind end. Before, it was the left fetlock. Before that, a string of abscesses kept her out of commission for the better part of six months. Before that, she bowed a tendon. Before that, she popped a splint. There is another before that, but Dr. Merrill likes to pretend the mare has just appeared to him, in the hopes that he can view her present problem, whatever it is, with fresh eyes. The mare is tall and chestnut, with an excessive femininity to her face—long lashes, big, quivery eyes, fine ears, and a buttery muzzle. Deborah has the same kind of look, with jutting plump lips that seem to tussle, as if playfully trying to mount one another. She listens to Dr. Merrill and nods her head. Sometimes she voices a doubt—would Luna ever be right?—and blushes. *Of course*, Dr. Merrill answers, and Deborah goes brighter and looks down, as if her question were evidence of a small-minded faithlessness and not a reasonable question, considering. Then they move on to the next treatment. This has gone on for almost six years. Nothing in Luna's radiographs, X-rays, bone scans, ultrasounds, or blood panels has ever indicated anything beyond minor problems and good prognoses, so he never tells Deborah bad news. Nothing that has been wrong with the mare is unfixable, so he fixes each thing. But the mare will not stay sound. After two months of being ridden, she's dragging a toe around turns. Deborah too ages over these six years. He watches her ripen, then go oversweet on the vine. The lips get dewier, the eyes mistier, the clothing brighter, the figure fuller, so that during a certain appointment—perhaps when they injected the mare's hocks—Deborah is glaringly lovely, a nearly painful concentration of beauty. Seeing her makes his teeth hurt, as if biting into something too rich. He concentrates on her shoes—soft leather ankle boots, ill-suited to a barn—and sends her on her way with a breezy, encouraging comment: he hopes to see neither of them again soon. The next time he sees them, or the time after that, Deborah's skin is heavier. The red waves of her hair are dry and compressed into a clip on top of her head, like leaves flattened in a compost bag. The large, wet mouth on the slackened face looks pathological, seductiveness flaring like a growth. The horse still stands at the end of its rope and blinks its fawn eyes, then limps its little limp as Deborah leads her into a jog. She stops the horse and looks at Dr. Merrill with the shamed-hopeful look of a kid pulling back panty elastic to give a glimpse to a playground pal—*I dare you to say it's okay*. He pats her back. They bend over readouts and share breath. Assistants shuffle in the hall; he sees the shadowy blips of their shoes under the door, like flickering ellipses. Even as he murmurs assurances he stares at the image, feeling, not for the first time, that it is secretly enchanted, like those joke portraits whose eyes move as you walk by. The image is pristine, textbook; the lesions and edemas blink into view the minute he looks away. The horse is healthy. The horse is not well. Deborah smells gamy; he finds himself rubbing her hair absently, like he would a horse. Just a small problem, here, that's all.

Yes, good to get away.

VII

Judy wants to be blue. Everything in her midst seems blue. There's blue print on the bottle of bute. There's a blue plush goat in the stall bars, and the Vetrap securing the fraying bottom of Snippet's cast is blue. The sky outside the open barn doors, though it had been overcast for a week, is now a shocking shade of azure, bright even where the sun is not. Even the gray tomcat, who caterwauls high in the hayloft, looks bluish as he flicks his tail over a bar of light reaching through the eaves.

Judy had taken the True Colors personality assessment earlier that week; it had been free for the heads of local businesses (*I run a nonprofit*, she'd said). She was sure she'd be a blue (caring, creative, intuitive), but instead the results of the test had pegged her a green (analytical, logical, emotionally detached), and although the facilitators made clear there were "no bad colors," Judy knew all she needed to know from the other greens she'd been grouped with.

To her left, a Realtor woman with a drippy spray tan complained about the buzz of the fluorescent lights. To her right, the owner of a cheese shop droned on about her warring skin diseases, how one rash actually healed the other, oblivious to the discomfort of her listeners. Judy looked at the blue group across the room. They clustered around their table like bright birds at a birdbath, tittering with excitement, stretching up to flutter their colors—one woman bounced in her chair, her red hair in a chignon like a curled feather. They laughed, they spoke earnestly and quickly; to Judy they looked like artists transported from an earlier age, writers in a jazz club. I used to be that way, she thought. What happened?

Snippet is dozing, jerking in his sleep. The tips of his suspended hooves scrape the pavement, throwing off sparks. Judy puts her hand under his thick striped mane. She lays her face against his neck, feeling his long guard hairs, the vestiges of his winter coat that would have been fully shed if he were able to roll in the sand or if he were up to being curried. But he is a horse that hates being brushed, hates typical gestures of affection, and normally Judy's proximity would have caused him to dance sidewise, to perhaps nip at her coat, to roll his large black eye so the white sclera showed, so that he looked skeptical and affronted, although Judy always got the sense it was a put-on and that Snippet merely liked to play with expectations.

Which was why, when your back was to him, he would sometimes put his muzzle on your shoulder and nibble very lightly. But when you turned around, he'd gallop off with a squeal, so you were left wondering at his intent: was the closeness the point, and the wheeling away just a way to maintain his toughness, a kind of embarrassed back-pedaling? Or was the wheeling away the point, and the moment of closeness just a joke, just a commentary on how willing you were to believe in his affection, how vulnerable and dense you were?

VIII

Dr. Jim is a few miles from Heart's Journey. He's turned the radio off. He's thinking of the pony's radiographs and following what he considers to be a foolish train of thought. He doesn't look at many X-rays in his practice, and he felt bizarrely charmed when he slid them out of the mailer the other day. The pony's cannon bone—split white against the gray fuzz of the surrounding tissue—looked to him like a thin woman in a white shift, turning away from the camera. A high, small bone chip appeared to be the barest suggestion of a fine upturned nose, lost in the angling of her cheek. An oddly romantic image, like a frame of film from an old silent picture.

Of course he would recommend euthanasia—nothing else made sense. The pony was just a pet, but his advice would be the same even if it were a pricey herd bull. He has his kit with him and is prepared to put the pony down on the spot.

He drives slower and slower. The dirt roads, at dinnertime, are nearly empty, and his truck crawls. The films are in a sleeve on his passenger side. He reaches over and taps them out, idly, as if by accident. The image slides out. The woman, again. The crack in the bone is like a sash at her waist. What if he tried to fix the pony? His friends, the cattlemen, would rib him at the diner. They'd laugh and say he'd gone soft in the head, give him shit about retiring. His wife would shake her head in amusement or dismissal, he wouldn't know. His young son would bark a laugh, bits of sausage and milk spritzing the table cloth.

The break is open, but the bony column was aligned. The pony is small—five hundred pounds—that is key. What about a weight-bearing cast with longitudinal support? A sort of standing splint? He stops the truck and feels behind his seat. He lays the tire iron on the radiograph.

91

IX

Marti is in the feed room. The bag she sits on bulges and kernels work their way out of the plastic weave. Mumu, the obese calico, is curled on another bag, kneading and purring, rolling her head around, wishing to be touched. Marti wants a cigarette, but she quit. She wants a drink, but she quit that, too. She wants to leave the barn and go to Rosco's, dance with Jim, argue with the bartender, drive by the street she used to live on, write a letter to her first foster family, smoke a joint, shout at someone, try on a dress for someone, sleep on a floor, wake up someplace else, but she quit all that, too.

She's always had a lot of wants. It used to be she felt all of them, the way you feel each staggered drop when it begins to rain. Then they became a weather, nothing to blink at.

With a piece of hay she digs at the crescents of dirt under her fingernails. She hears Snippet struggle in the sling and Judy's voice quieting him. She should go out there and help her, discuss what should be done with the pony, but she doesn't feel up to it.

She squeezes her eyes shut and watches the pops of yellow and red, the light show playing in the dark. Those flashes of light—ghosts of light she'd seen, no doubt, the shapes of lamplight and bare bulbs like a visual echo—she bore down on them as if they were concealing something. They were bright shards of someplace else, she always thought as a kid, evidence of another world peeping through. Her stepfather once pushed her down and she hit her head on a planter. Her ears hummed and the light she saw was varied and streaky, as if she were being drawn through a nighttime cityscape on the back of a speeding motorcycle. It wasn't heavenly or spiritual—it lacked the solemnity—but wildly festive. It seemed more real than her stepfather or the push; both the man and the act struck her as chintzy in comparison, no longer substantial enough to fear. Even as he bent over her and begged her to be okay, rocking and holding her hand, she wondered if he knew he was barely there.

A chicken wanders into the feed room, moving to the beat of its clucks, turning its head and giving her a deeply skeptical look, its ruff of red-gold feathers fissuring as it drops its head to peck at the floor. Marti reaches down and brushes her fingers over his comb; it feels to her like the hand of a limp doll.

X

The thing he had to do, he knew, was to cut Deborah off. Tell her that, given Luna's long history of problems, she was probably just prone to unsoundness, and the best thing would be to make her a brood mare or a pasture pet. Just cut it off. The whole thing kept shaking him up. Sometimes he came home so distracted that his wife and son seemed to be just so much subclinical white noise, a side project he'd unwisely taken on. Laura would ask him what was wrong, looping her arms around his neck. All he could manage to say was that his mind was on a "hard case."

He couldn't tell her about Luna—he was loath to admit his obsession with the case, the lack of progress. There were far more dramatic cases that he could have on his mind, cases he did tell Laura about—a dicey colic surgery on a big-time jumper, a degloved pastern freed from barbed wire, barely salvaged, a breech birth unable to be righted. And of course he told her about Snippet, the minuscule pony with the catastrophically shattered leg.

"Is that the one who paints?" she'd said, and he'd looked at her blankly before remembering that yes, the two women had taught the pony to slop paint around. He and Laura had been watching the news when a local interest story on Snippet and Heart's Journey came on. In the clip, Judy and Marti handed a brush to the pony, who took it in his teeth then flung his head up and down, like an athlete making theater out of working a kink out of his neck. Paint spritzed on the women and the news-caster, an effusive woman with a smile so high and wide it showed all her gums, as if her upper lip were the corner of a yo-gurt lid, there for ease of peeling.

"That pony's hilarious," Laura remarked. She was in fact eat-ing a yogurt on the couch next to him—she was always watching her weight and working out—and her trimness had a parched, vacuum-packed quality, like a foodstuff that would need re-constituting with water to be palatable. His attraction to her had dribbled away as his practice became more consuming, but it struck him not as a loss but as a practical shift, the way you might rehab a horse with sore front heels by developing the car-rying power of his hocks and hind end.

On the TV, Snippet was creating a swirl of blotchy colors, his tail a counterweight to the brush, swishing left when he made a right stroke, flagging when he dropped his head and stabbed at the bottom of the canvas. The camera flicked to Marti and Judy, who looked especially eccentric in the studio lights; even with the camera makeup and hair they looked like drifters, gaping at some rare vision unfolding down by the overpass.

The donkey farm on his right tells him he's a mile or so out from Heart's Journey. Snippet hadn't been responding well to the soft cast and the sling, so the next step, if there was a next step, would be a table surgery and then a long, long rehab—at least a year, with much of that time tranquillized to prevent him from thrashing around and blowing out the pins from his bones. A twenty percent chance of recovery, if that. Normally he'd go for it if they would—which they would, at least if the same woman—was it Martina?—was at the helm. He recalled a hushed conver-sation with her in the tack room; her swimmy eyes searching his, translating all his nuance into two words: hope or hopeless.

He cringes at the thought of it—another vortex. He ought to just recommend euthanasia and be done with it. The afternoon sun moves through the cab of his truck like a hand feeling for something lost. It sets on the chrome details of his bag, where two files are tucked away—one for Snippet and one for Luna. If he puts Snippet down today—or just gives his recommendation and leaves—he can get back to the office and perhaps Deborah can come to a later appointment. There, he will let her know . . .

Dr. Merrill looks at his bag, the tongue of light on the left handle. Luna's latest radiograph flicks across his mind unbidden, like it often does. The black and grey fuzz of the image seems to crackle and squirm in his thoughts, as if he were in the process of tuning it in, moving rabbit ears to catch a signal that floats enticingly near. Something in the angle of the pedal bone? . . . not that it matters. No harm, though, in looking at the radiograph one more time, just to confirm.

XI

The problem is Marti. Being around that woman had changed her, made her harder, turned her green. Marti is so delicate, so emotional, that Judy has had to be strong and coldly logical just to keep some semblance of order around the farm. Marti's whole personality is like a sculpture Judy once saw of small, very thin reeds fed into each other to make a latticework so fragile it had to be protected from even the breath of the gallery-goers. It was in a glass case, in shadow, since light would degrade the organic material. Judy spent a long time staring at it, trying to figure out what, exactly, was holding it up. It was half-collapsed, so how . . . ? She'd looked at her program. *The integrity of the piece depends on the forces of gravity bearing down; it gathers strength as it falls into itself . . .*

Judy always has to do the dirty work: to turn away a horse from the rescue (otherwise they'd become hoarders—something Marti certainly was before Judy came on board), to cease treatment of a too-far-gone horse, to make the call to send a horse to the Rainbow Bridge, to hold the horse's lead rope while the vet administered the shot. How many lead ropes had she held in this way? How many times did she gently tug down on the rope, encouraging the horse, even as he blinked out of existence, to fold his front legs so he would settle down gracefully, rather than simply fall onto his side, convulsing and struggling, far from the peaceful send-off everyone wanted? And in these cases—when the horse left violently, messily, sometimes banging himself in the head, spraying blood through a smashed nasal cavity—how many times had she wanted someone there to comfort her? She wants to tell Marti about these times—Marti should at least hear it—but she doesn't.

There is something about Marti that forces a person to tread carefully. She seems flayed, like some sort of raw nerve flailing around in the world, and her pain seems elevated, deeper, more keenly and destructively felt. It is actually less painful, for Judy, to keep a sad image to herself than to risk Marti becoming upset. It is a kind of power, Judy thinks, to be so vulnerable. Sometimes she wonders if it's a kind of manipulation, too.

For once, Judy thinks, I want to be the irrational one. I'll be the one who can't let go. I'll call that wack-job Dr. Merrill for once. I'll keep Snippet going; I'll throw the rescue's money at him. We'll do surgery. Surgeries. Why not? He's a great pony. Why can't I lose my shit for once?

She wants to return to the illogic at the base of the enterprise, when they stood among all kill buyers, the slaughter-truck drivers, the farmers with the Skoal-can circles on their back pockets, the married Amish men with their heavy beards, gravely nodding, as if speech itself were too newfangled. The auctioneer, all chin and bald head, compresses and fans out his syllables in a showboating blurt, like a shuffler making an arc of his cards. And then, without even looking at Judy, Marti raises her hand. The auctioneer eyes her and nods. The men turn their heads and take her in: her stained Carharts, her long blond hair, the hard-ship-scored face with the stunned child-eyes. Some laugh, some grumble. The two women pull their pony—hip #467—from the pen. He is so thin and his coat so poor that he looks like a rug remnant tossed over a wrought-iron fence. His forelock is stiff with cockleburs and stands straight up like a plume; despite his condition he wears it that way, like he knows he is something to see. The two women lead him out, whooping and laughing, giddy with the absurdity of what they've taken on.

XII

The last time he'd fashioned a medical device he used a bamboo flute and a ripped shirt. The solider was in so much pain he'd bit a hole in his lip. He pressed the flute to the boy's shin, tore up his undershirt, wrapped it around and held the excess in his teeth to keep the tension, then tied it off. "Don't run off or your leg will whistle." Dr. Jim never joked crudely, nor swore, nor made coarse comments about women, nor employed gallows humor. He was an oddity in the barracks, and while the other men made fun of him often (his nickname was Norman Rockwell), they saw the resilience and subversion in his simple sunny jokes. "God-damn you, Rockwell," the boy had said, grimacing as Dr. Jim pulled him to his feet.

When he makes a comment to cut the tension, he likes to watch how it falls on the atmosphere, much like a golfer shades his eyes and traces the trajectory of his shot. The tense, silent people at the bank, for instance, ripple and shift, rolling their eyes, chuckling or smiling tightly. These slight movements break up the scene suddenly and dramatically; it is like a shat-tered pane of glass finally buckling into millions of shards. They can no longer be a line of silent strangers.

He is joking with himself, these thoughts of trying to fix the pony. He'd have to make this drive over and over to work on the patient. Probably he would work in a haze of incense, Marti or Judy (he never remembered who was who) would talk to him about the pony's feelings and thoughts, he would be made to contemplate the pony's paintings, and the pony itself would wobble around, comically debased in the walking cast he'd cook up in his basement shop. He looks at the film again. He thinks of the simplicity of the splint, how easy it would be to try. The look of the cattlemen when they found out.

XIII

The aisle is quiet and Marti ventures out. Judy is out riding the Gator, tossing flakes of hay over the pasture fences while the horses gallop around. Snippet dozes, the white Medicine Hat marking over his ears bright in the afternoon light, like a fresh doily on a worn couch. She pats him, studies one of his paintings, his last before the accident. Most of his paintings were sloppy, flung over the whole canvas and beyond, but this one is comprised of just a few frilly disks of paint, pressed over each other, as symmetrical as if it had been made with a spirograph. It looks familiar, somehow, and then she remembers where she'd seen something like it before.

Marti's foster mother, Gwen, used to wear a silk flower like that, every day, pinned to her headband, her scarves, or the hem of her shorts if it was hot out. It was blue and green and cheaply made with a fake pearl in the center, but Gwen never went without it. Once, Marti had gotten lost in an outdoor market, a swirling place chockful with wares of all kinds: herbs, blown glass, collectible pins, handmade clothes. She'd wandered away from Gwen to look at a table covered with tumbled stones. The man

98

explained the powers of each one: the bright flecks in the pyrite refreshed one's courage, while rosy quartz, held to one's temple, could catch the thoughts of others and refract them into your head. He leaned over the table, took her by her wrist, and tried to place a magnetic bracelet on her. His grip was wet, his eyes pink rimmed, and a winter hat with a leaping deer was pulled low on his gray head even though it was June. She jerked back and realized Gwen was nowhere in sight.

In the haze and heat she walked, looking for her foster mother, trying not to walk in circles, though she kept seeing the same blond women and their clumps of reed baskets swaying in the sun. She looked for Gwen's feet in their simple Greek sandals, or her streaming scarves, but there were many scarves and feet. Panic hit her. She had the awful feeling that this market was the whole of her existence and she'd be walking by these glass unicorns and bowls of beads forever. But then she saw, through the indeterminate mix of bare legs and colors, Gwen's perpetual flower. She saw it long before she saw Gwen, as if the flower were a prick of light that opened to reveal her, its petals an aperture.

She hasn't thought about Gwen in a long time. The flower's appearance on the canvas again suggested a keyhole to another place, and she remembers that Gwen used to say that she was an indigo child, possessed of a heightened vision and aura. No one else said that about her, so when Gwen got sick and Marti was moved to a new home, she tried to forget it. Auras and visions would not have played well in her second home, that was for sure.

She puts a hand on the painting and a hand on Snippet's sleeping forehead. She shuts her eyes. A tingle runs through her like a thread; it felt irritatingly minute, like a hair in your mouth. Gwen always talked about the inner eye, how it opened, blinked, and fluttered in response to the vibrations of emotions. Hers had snapped open. Snippet wants to go, she thinks. He wants to slip into the opening he made and enter the new place. She would call Dr. Jim, make herself hold the rope for once, and see.

XIV

To live in a horse's body is to experience a perpetual loop of sensation, as if each nerve ending were being plucked in a pattern. Sometimes the patterns change or stutter: this is thought. Normally you feel the hair at the base of your tail twice, then the inside of your esophagus; now the order is switched, and that has meaning. Then, of course, there are the eyes, set on the side of the head. It is like being at a themed ride at an amusement park: everything to the side is thrilling and bright, but the area right in front of the car is black. Your world is peripheral. The blind spot in the center of your vision is your center, dark and certain, a void you can retreat to whenever you want. Sometimes the people and buildings and grass and pasture fold over you and push you into that center, like a stone held secret in a fist. At these times, your sovereignty becomes a question, a source of suspicion, a mystery. People holler at you and peer in your eyes with a bright light, trying to see if you are still there.

What Happened

ANNE PANNING

From *Super America* (2007)

This morning at 10:30, Angela Mayer's husband died on his bicycle; he was wearing a helmet, in case any of you are wondering, though it hardly mattered. And Angela is doing all right, too,
despite so many things beyond the obvious, despite the fact she
lives so far away from both sets of relatives it will take them a
day and a half just to get there. What comes next is how it went,
what came before and what came after an event so circumstan-
tial yet conclusive. What comes next is an account of how people steer themselves through tragedy and freak accidents, and
of who Angela and Michael are, or were, together. What comes
next is something similar to—though far more detailed than—an
article you might read in the newspaper and find yourself unable
to stop thinking about. It is exactly the kind of thing you hope
will never happen to you or anyone you love, yet it intrigues you,
propels you forward into a strange pursuit to know more. Why,
then, do we seek blood, tragedy, horror?

Earlier today, a Monday morning in June: Angela and Michael
putter around the apartment, and Michael finishes off the last

101

of a second pot of coffee, despite the heat. In Honolulu, the only apartment they can afford is a small cinderblock walk-up on Date Street that gets very humid and cloistered and dark by afternoon. Angela is off to teach an English as a second language course at the Vietnamese Community Center, and Michael, a marine biologist, must run to the university and do research in the library. They Velcro into sandals, Angela swoops her long blond hair up into a tight knot, Michael fills his water bottle, and they kiss in front of the stove. Angela runs her hands up and down his back, over his stiff, line-dried T-shirt.

"Maybe we can go to the beach later," Michael says, and straps on his bike helmet, which looks, to Angela, like a peculiar, blue, shiny beetle perched atop his head.

"Yeah, maybe," Angela says, "unless I'm too exhausted." She slowly maneuvers her backpack onto her shoulders, trying to keep perspiration to a minimum. She must do everything slowly on days like this—walk slowly, eat slowly, get dressed slowly, think slowly. Outside, on the busy street, the sun pounds down like an assault, and Angela lingers by the door, imagining its rays pounding into her scalp, fermenting her brain, sunburning the side part in her hair. "I hate to go. It's too hot. God, why does it always have to be so damn hot here?"

The question is of course rhetorical, but Michael bristles and jeers. This bone of contention is old: Michael, an East Coaster, spent most of a year begging and pleading and campaigning for Hawaii Pacific as the school where he'd do his postdoc. With so many foreigners there, Angela could teach English as a second language, but as a Montanan, she had shirked. She had coiled up like a snake and spit, "Hawaii? Me going to Hawaii is like putting a polar bear in the desert! It's like putting a herd of cattle in the jungle!" And it's true—her parents were cattle ranchers, and it did get fantastically cold in Montana so much of the time. But still Michael hoped and held on to dreams of the clear ocean blue and all that heady sea life: bright yellow angelfish practically jumping into your hand! Parrotfish, dolphins, whales! About all of this, and more, he had read. For the rest of winter, Angela sat poised on top of a decision which would alter everything, and she knew it, and she roosted there long-term.

But they were married. Within three tiny chaotic years, they had already learned, like soldiers, to advance and retreat, listen and fight, give and take, and finally, to think things over in the kind selflessness of private time, which, when one is much in love, is the giving-in time. At last, Angela gave in, or agreed to try it, because she loved Michael: it was that simple. Yet, although Angela agreed that he should at least *apply*, she had no intention of going there; at her insistence, he had also applied to Oregon, California, and North Carolina. But as everyone knows, life more often than not throws you where it wants to. So when the Hawaii forms came and the funding was so good, even Angela couldn't say no. She, too, had job prospects waiting for her there, too good to refuse.

At the time of their decision, they were both working loathsome temporary jobs in a city they did not so much hate as endure. Angela was a clerk at a life insurance agency, and near the end of her assignment, an older female coworker with deep, smoky breath and tinted glasses took her aside and gave her a quick little lesson on how to hold a pen better so as to fill out forms more efficiently. Angela, a college graduate, had nearly fainted in exasperation and horror. Michael had fared no better on the temporary job scene; he had ended up in the county's social-services phone pool, with twenty-eight telephone lines ringing in his ears in a basement office, sans windows.

But this morning in June, in Hawaii, it is hot, both are distracted and busy, and from the window, Angela watches Michael unlock his bike. He weaves through traffic and stops, poised, at the light before heading up the hill and out of sight into Manoa. She, too, mounts her bicycle and is off. As she rides, heading toward Diamond Head, something in the air feels entirely too heavy, as if it might rain, though there is not a single cloud in the sky. Still, the air is thick and hard to get through. She plans in her head: she will teach, come home, make a cold fresh-vegetable sandwich, then, yes, go to the beach with Michael. They simply do not go to the beach as often as you might think, living in Hawaii.

Pay careful attention to Angela's return home, for upon arriving at work, she finds her two classes canceled, due to reasons of which she is unaware. There is simply a single white sheet of paper taped to the outside door, which reads, "Classes canceled today. Report tomorrow as usual." This note both angers and relieves Angela. Of course she is happy for the sudden freedom, but irritated at the knowledge that she could have slept in, that she has ridden halfway across town in the blinding heat and is soaked with sweat, that she had spent two hours last night preparing an innovative lesson plan having to do with restaurant menus and job applications. But she steers back toward home, coasting mostly downhill, sensitive blue eyes shielded by sunglasses.

The first indication that something is wrong is their friend Nate standing right outside their door, up on the second-floor landing. He never comes over in the mornings, and he never looks as sickly in the face as he does now. Angela waves to him, locks her bike, then sees in the lot a police car and knows then, knows for certain, there has been an accident. Her first thought is her family in Montana. Perhaps her father has been crushed by a horse; it has happened to people she knows. Or her mother in a car accident. It has to be her family; Michael seems practically indestructible—so careful, so smart, so beautifully alert and on top of things. She wonders if he is still at the library and how she can reach him in the stacks quickly.

Here is how Angela approaches the scene, in a way you may not expect: cheerfully. "Hey, Nate," she says, taking the cement stairs by twos and gasping, out of breath. "What's up?" She looks him bravely in the face.

Nate shuffles his feet and looks, for the first time, actually pale, despite his dark coloring. "Why don't we go in," Nate says, and Angela, for some reason, resists. She notes the policeman advancing up the other staircase.

"No, here," she says, and dumps her backpack, purple and worn, at their feet. "Tell me here. What is it?" She reaches out and touches his arm, which is warm, hairless, and smooth. Nate is their best friend; he is in Michael's department and a Hawaii local. He has shown them everything, driven them around in his Honda, warned them about dangerous beaches and jellyfish.

"It's Michael," he says, and puts a hand on her shoulder. "I really think we should go inside. I don't know how to tell you."

"Tell me here," Angela says again, and feels the sharp prickle of salt crystals form as the sweat dries on her face and back. "What is it? Is he all right?"

The policeman approaches them, introduces himself, and looks down, waiting for Nate to say it. And finally, Nate is able. "Michael was in an accident. It all just happened so fast—on his bike."

Angela feels fear rising in her chest, and her ears ring high and spinning. "Is he all right?" The sun makes her head throb, makes all the blood in her fingers and toes and chest pound and pulse and beat loudly inside her ears.

"Angela, Michael died," Nate says at last, then immediately opens up his arms and pulls her close to him. He begins to sob dryly, despite his aim at control, but Angela stands immobilized by the news.

"He died?" she says, patting Nate on the back, soothing him until he pulls away. "He couldn't have died! I just saw him an hour ago. He was right here."

The policeman takes his lead and intervenes as the force of

authority and stability. "We wanted to contact you before we called his parents." He takes a small notebook out of his breast pocket. It has a hard silver cover, which Angela notes curiously. "I'm really very sorry," he says, pink in the face. "It was a fluke accident. There was really nothing anyone could do. Are you sure you don't want to go inside? It's so hot out here." He wipes his forehead with his hand, then wipes his hand on his pant leg.

Angela murmurs back at him incoherently and unlocks her apartment door in a blur. Was she in shock? Yes. Was she about the throw up? Yes, to this question, and to all the rest, but she was merely functioning mechanically, as our bodies are somehow able to do in times of crisis. Later she will throw herself on the couch and sob and scream and grab her gut; later she will become nauseous at the mere thought of eating; later she will gather in her arms their stale pile of dirty laundry in the closet and suck in the smell with a terrifying thirst and stay there, stay in the closet, afraid to come out for hours; but for now, she is sedate with miscomprehension, glazed by the confusion of it all.

Oddly, once inside the apartment, she feels safe and immune, and seeing Michael's navy blue coffee mug sitting on the kitchen counter settles her somehow. She perches uncertainly on the edge of the couch and puts her hands on top of her head, trying to control the thoughts which are swimming like fish in her brain. "So tell me, I guess, what happened. I need to know this, right? I mean, I need to know." A slight breeze passes through the open doorway, and she jerks her head up, expecting Michael's lanky frame to walk in, his familiar, grainy face to lean against the door frame, his deep, kind voice which will laugh and tease and help her get through this.

The policeman sits on their one good chair, a rose-colored recliner, purchased at the Salvation Army; Nate hovers over the sink, cleaning up some unknown mess. The policeman explains the details of the accident in a calm, respectful manner.

This is what happened, what was told to Angela and later to

Michael's parents in Boston, and later to everyone who watched the local news: Michael was biking up the tiny road between the library and the medical school, which was also the road to the construction site for the new cafeteria. Large trucks and general campus traffic streamed through periodically. A line of parked cars was on Michael's right, and a large truck was chugging uphill on his left, going slowly, carrying construction supplies to the building site. Michael, probably in a hurry, decided to pass the big, slow-moving truck; he looked left, to see if any cars were coming, but in doing so lost his balance, ran into a parked car, tipped over into the street, and fell directly under the double wheels of the truck. He was crushed to death instantly.

More could be said, more fruitless attempts at "But why?" or "I just don't see how," but there are no answers, and even if there were, it wouldn't matter. Whether it's classified a fluke or a freak accident or bad biking depends on how you, as secondhand listeners, choose to interpret it.

Angela listens, hearing, head down. The policeman says Michael was wearing thongs, and that might've been part of the problem—he lost his footing. Angela snorts at this information; she doesn't know why. Michael loved his Surfah thongs with the bumpy, black massage soles, and to think of these innocuous $3.99 drugstore slippers causing his death is more than Angela can accept. Then suddenly, it hits her with a striking wet clarity: What is she going to do? What will she possibly do in the next ten minutes, or tonight, or tomorrow, or in a week, or for the rest of her life? Will she leave Hawaii? She thinks she will leave Hawaii, and sits with her own private thoughts, trying to plan and figure it out.

Nate must see fear mounting in her eyes and comes to sit beside her, to touch her and make her feel real. But another wave of disbelief comes over her, and she knows she will have to go see. It could've been her; it could've been Nate; it could've been her friend Patrice, who bikes Honolulu fast and furious, like a madwoman—they all bike cramped roads all the time, and so does everyone, but nobody gets killed. What could have gone through Michael's head as he made the short flight off his bike and out of his life? Angela tries to think of it, of what he would feel, but decides there was likely no more than three or four seconds of pure panic to think of anything.

Angela makes a motion now to go see the street, the exact sight, if she is ever to believe it. She agrees to let the police and the university handle the initial phone calls, since she cannot yet imagine talking to Michael's kind and loving parents, who were due to visit them in August. His father, Larry, will cry immediately and have to hand the phone to Michael's mother, Babs, who will stay on the line, pen in hand, notepad to her right, exacting facts and details. But then she, too, will hang up and stand in the kitchen, quaking with shock and grief. She will pray to her lord for strength, and they will slowly begin calling the siblings. Angela will talk to Larry and Babs later, after she has gathered herself, *if* she ever gathers herself.

She will also let Nate call her own parents in Montana, which momentarily seems an acutely remote and foreign place, as if, were she there, this death, this horrifying news would not be true. It could be a story told from the outside that they would all gasp and remark over but not have to endure firsthand. She will talk to them later when she actually understands more of what's happened. Everything, details, will be handled later, as if then it will all be okay, as if then the death will be old hat and yesterday's news, as if then Michael will be back and she'll be able to sit on the couch with her feet in his lap and tell him how awful it all was.

But on she moves through the confusion of the day, the hottest day she can remember since moving to Hawaii: ninety-nine degrees. Grabbing only her purse, though she feels as if she's forgetting something, she takes a ride in the police car. Nate sits in front; she sits in back. She is happy with it that way, so she can watch quietly out the window, try to discover what is happening to her life. All over Angela sees bike riders cruising slick and speedy between cars, helmets or no helmets, all of them sure footed and positive they will stay afloat. Be careful! she wants to shout. She wants to pound on the bulletproof glass window and warn them. Be careful! It could happen to you! But the big, bloated police car motors forward in air-conditioned silence.

They reach the accident site. This part may sound like television to you now, for you are used to seeing tragedy up close and immediately. *Cops. Hard Copy. Rescue 911.* But here, in real life, yellow Do Not Cross the Line tape is wrapped and knotted around trees. Police personnel stand around the sidewalk, taking notes and interviewing people. A fire truck is even on the scene, with one man in street clothes uncoiling lengths of canvas rope. He turns the water on, and—you may not have seen this part on TV—he washes away the pool of blood on the street. It rolls down the curb, watery red on dull concrete, and finds its way into the sewer drainage grate. The huge truck is still in the middle of the street, and a man, apparently the driver, paces the road, explaining, bending down over and over again to look underneath the wheels. He is wearing dirty working clothes—a tan T-shirt, jeans worn out at the thighs, dust-coated boots. You can imagine his guilt, the way that, even though it was no one's fault, it will always seem like his fault. To him it will. TV news reporters gather around him with microphones, and he speaks, though no one inside the police car can hear what he says.

"You okay?" Nate asks Angela. "You don't want to get out, do you?" But as he's asking, Angela does get out. She wanders, knowing no one will recognize her, feeling as if somehow she will forever share a relationship with this man, this truck driver. He is done with his interview, and she approaches him slowly.

"How are you doing?" she asks, and tries to meet his gaze, but he is busily looking again from the truck to the curb to the Honda Civic that has a small white paint scrape on its driver's door. This is the car Michael ran into.

"Not good," he mutters, hands on hips, as if, should he continue his investigation of the accident site, he will figure out why this happened. "Did you see it?" he asks, wiping at his nose. She can't place the gesture as from habit or tears. "I just didn't know what he was doing. He came from out of nowhere. You know, I got kids. I'm never gonna live this one down. I'm just never gonna get over this. Nope. Makes me not even want to get in that truck again. No, I don't think I can do it. Ah, Jesus. The poor kid. And his parents." He flips off his cap and scratches through his hair.

Angela glances back at the police car, which still houses the officer and Nate, who look back at her warily, as if she might commit murder. "I'm his wife," Angela says with neither conviction nor blame. "That was my husband."

The man reels. "Oh, God. No. I'm so sorry. I'm telling you—I just . . . I don't know what happened! I don't know what to say—he just . . . I saw him, you know, out of my right mirror, but—I guess he just tipped over or something and—and I was going real slow, too. I'm sorry—I'm just—so sorry." The man starts to cry, but Angela doesn't. She reaches out to him, sets a hand on his arm, and just then a newspaper photographer captures the moment on film. A woman comes running over with her clunky camera bag and begins snapping, which sets off a chain reaction of other reporters rushing over to get in on the beat.

"You better go," the man says. "They'll be all over you." He takes her hand away and leads Angela over towards the police car. Nate gets out and tries to shield her from any more people. As she's getting into the back seat again, the truck driver leans down and says to her, "I'm sorry. I just want you to know I'll be sorry for the rest of my life." He grimaces at her as the door is closed.

As they drive away, Angela looks back out the window. It's Michael's Surfah thong lying in the street. Or does she imagine it? The one lost thong—seeing it lying there haphazardly and overlooked finally opens up a well of agony for Angela. It starts in the pit of her stomach, rising, and she can feel it surrounding her heart: a new uncharted pain. Nothing will ever be right again, she thinks, as they deposit her back at the apartment, where friends are waiting. This, so many peoples' love and concern, must mean Michael is truly gone, and Angela sits for a moment with the thought.

"I can't believe it," she says, to no one. But, for lack of choice, she looks out the window, and starts to believe it. She makes an effort that will have to endure. For you, this is where the story ends. You can go back to your own lives—read and dream, eat and sleep—but Angela starts over, alone. She gets out of the car, squints up at the sun, and feels the heat pressing down like a punishment.

Taking Hold of Renee

MELISSA PRITCHARD

From *Spirit Seizures* (1987)

Twelve wives poke about the island cemetery, reading aloud the more tragic inscriptions.

Things must decay like mad in this heat and humidity! This from the young woman nearest Renee, the one closest in age to herself. Oooh, here's a saddy, Susanna Wicklow, two small sons and a husband aged twenty-nine, "all bleffedly removed from earth's mortal gloom," May 1789. Those poor British must have sailed over and dropped like flies.

With a trained decorum reminiscent of the schoolgirls they had all once been, the wives file into the stone church.

No one can locate Renee until a search finds her sitting on the ground within one of the churchyard's numerous hedged enclosures, her head like a flower, tipped heavily on her folded arms. It is an unkempt space, a place where dead leaves and broken branches are thrown, a sort of compost heap, is what the wives think, until they notice the little limestone hump beside Renee. The size marker used for a child.

A tactful retreat, so that the women, many of them grandmothers, can reconfirm the story of Renee's little girl, kidnapped less than two years ago, found dead in a forest preserve near the parents' home. Brisk cheerfulness is agreed upon, to behave as if unintimidated by such leviathan tragedy.

Renee dear, we thought we'd lost you! Some of the others have gone on to the shops before we meet husbands for lunch; the rest are heading to the little post office for stamps. Come with us, won't you?

Her skin glints, mother of pearl. Renee puts on her new red bathing suit, her limbs poking out from it like white eels. Her stomach never really flattened after Emily's birth. Her body's whiteness is an embarrassment. Like someone whose one over-prominent feature upstages the rest, Renee feels singled out by her skin. She looks freakish against the fiery green tropical backdrop, a specter beside the natives. She had watched, along with the other wives, when a black man in a red nylon bikini, his shoulder-length hair braided into dozens of wiry snakes, sprinted along the beach before diving elegantly into the sea. Now that's a jungle bunny, isn't it? one of the women said. I think he looks wonderful, Renee said distinctly, and the women looked at her with curiosity.

The librarian had suggested *Wide Sargasso Sea* for a trip to the West Indies, but Renee finds the novel risky, about a nineteenth century Creole heiress going piecemeal mad amid the oozy decay and red bloom of the tropics. It reads too much like a more lyric version of her own concealed voice:

"I never looked at any strange negro. They hated us. They called us white cockroaches. Let sleeping dogs lie. One day a little girl followed me singing, 'Go away white cockroach, go away,

go away.' I walked fast, but she walked faster. 'White cockroach, go away, go away. Nobody wants you. Go away.'"

Renee reexamines this passage. Is this what they think of us? She looks at the other women in the chaise longues, piled around her like reddening seals on rocks. The bolder few of their group are out snorkeling, their rented black tubes finning across the slightly peaky water. She shifts uncomfortably in her own chair, her limbs exposed and pale.

On her way back to the room to change for cocktails and dinner, Renee stops at one of the outdoor showers near the beach. Black birds with lemony eyes and doves the color of washed blood group in the coarse, choppy grass, waiting to bathe in her water.

Renee picks her way, guiltily, past uniformed employees on the curving paths bordered with yellow hibiscus and purple bougainvillea. Their taxi driver had said that over one quarter of the island men were without work except during sugar cane harvests. Security guards patrol their resort. Waiters are college graduates who move, dispirited, from table to table. The island, dependent on tourism and foreign investment, has, like most dependent entities, repressed hostility until it emerges as unctuous inefficiency. The majority of people live, poorly clothed, in cramped wooden shacks with no running water.

Nights, after rum punch and candlelit dinners by the sea, after sotted, jolly sing-a-longs ("Yellow Bird," "Down the Way Where the Nights Are Gay"), nights are the worst for them. Since Emily's murder, Renee rejects pleasure. Her mourning is vigilant, extended; she hates the weakness in Bill's character which argues for intimacy. Sex would be a selfish abandonment of Emily. Renee's ascetic grief, the sterility it imposes on them, ill suits the seductive tropics.

They have quarreled over this, Bill painfully asking that Renee seek counseling when they return home, Renee countering that he betrays their daughter, doesn't he, by so quickly expecting that she resume some normal life.

On their last day the group rides in open jeeps to a restaurant for breakfast. Tables have been lined up along a flowered terrace overlooking the Caribbean. Some of the wives deftly focus cameras, pressing about an ornate black cage recessed into a grotto near a fountain sloppy with brackish water. The frilly cage holds a green monkey. After the others go to their seats, Renee stays, sitting on the cool rock ledge beside the cage. The monkey, hyper-alert, is fuzzed much like a coconut, its fur greenish yellow like woodland moss. Tree ferns submerge its cage in watery emerald light. On the bottom of the cage is a life-sized baby, face down, in a torn pink shift spattered with watermelon seeds. One of the doll's arms is missing, its hair is in dirty blond screwcurls. The monkey thrusts its sinewy arm through the cage bars, touches Renee on the shoulder. Renee lets it hold her hand, its finger pads black, slick ovals . . . it seizes at her head, feathering through her long red hair with eerily intelligent fingers. Renee wants to sit forever near the monkey, never leave the broken baby at bottom, near the lip of muddy rainwater.

Later she tucks most of her breakfast into a napkin, hides it in the swallow of her purse, and feeds the fuzzed, parted mouth of the green monkey. Bill comes back from the parking lot, his face anxious, resentful. Please, Renee, everyone's waiting for you. Let's try, shall we? Today's our last day . . .

Renee has been gulping wine, eating a little bread, trapped at the dinner table again. Bill is asking the other young wife in their group what, in her opinion, gives a man sex appeal. He is a little drunk, she sees, and veering out of context. Next he stands, offers a gregarious, inclusive toast. A college education is mostly bunk, he begins, if you want to get into business and succeed, which—he gestures broadly—I seem to have done.

God, she thinks, he is that simple, content with himself, he suffers, recovers, goes on. Perhaps that is his gift, a certain over-looking of messy, unresolving grief. No slowing the machinery, no affecting the process. And he can still trust life; Renee almost envies him that.

After dinner Bill dances with the wife who had answered without a hitch that what makes a man sexy are two things—good eyes and great buns. Renee wonders if it is gratitude she should feel toward this woman dancing quite close to Bill, then feels as if she is suffocating.

Running from the party, the dancing, Renee drops her sandals at the edge of the manicured, torchlit lawn. Runs along the flat beach toward the fishing village, above which the moon lists, an apricot bulge. She nearly trips over a man squatting beneath a manchineel tree, cooking fish over a low fire. Runs by a man bathing himself in one of the resort's outdoor showers, rubbing soap over himself with furtive, quick slides of his hand. The sea is tearing up around her feet, sand crabs labor sideways, their eyes moist, human, trapped looking. The beach ends abruptly, and she takes a path leading to the narrow road with its nickings of stone and glass, the pain a joy against her feet.

Walking now past lightless wooden shacks on tottering brick foundations, past the Gospel Hall Church, a block of yellow stucco with windows shaped like rowboats. The fish market a gutted darkness with fish-taint, heavy as tarp, persistent.

By daylight she has seen village men dragging sacks bloated and bumpy with fish up the beach from their boats, upending them, slips of mercury raveling over spread-out newspapers, flies moving in, sparkling. Squat, mesolithic-busted women in tight, mismatched outfits and baseball caps, yelling prices for yellow dolphin, flying fish, women with string bags and cardboard boxes on their heads, buying fish rolled in newspaper. Now the market is black, echoing, pungent.

So I tell you, man, this grieving white woman in a fancy white dress, she's going like some damn starve cat, prowling dirt paths, she trip over the garbage between shacks, this resort white stops then to hear this one baby cry, she listen, alert as anything, hungry like she want to take that baby between her fingers like some meat ... us sitting on curbs like we do, outside the bars, she asks that we make obscenities to eat at her, she is that anyhow, she is telling us, salt eaten up. She has a dead child, she is telling us. Inside the bar she is asking you know, for rum. Then she thinks we climb like market flies on her. Get away. She flings her speech you know, packs her talk into what she calls our open monkey-faces. I have a baby child, a girl dead, she keeps forever telling.

So two of us, one at either elbow, we decide better to walk this poor damn white lady out of our town, so we take her back, cross her over to the whites' resort like she is some dangerous thing, some bomb ...

In their hotel room, Renee stands on the straw mat. Only the bathroom light is on.

Bill? I heard a baby inside one of those terrible shacks the people live in. It kept crying and crying. The sound went right through me.

Grayish fluorescent light halos her body. Renee steps out of its glare, closer to the bed.

I was going up and down their streets, running, yelling, I think I was yelling, like a crazy person. God. Anyone could have done anything, hurt me, killed me. They must certainly, in some way, hate us. But those people, Bill? Those two men? They didn't listen, didn't do anything to me like I might have wanted.

What they did, those men, was take hold. Just take hold, as if I were some lost, precious child, and bring me back.

Grace's Reply

NANCY ZAFRIS

From *The People I Know* (1990)

Grace's son joined the Navy at nineteen with vague but grandiose thoughts of espionage scuba diving. He drowned a year later. John's death was reported to her by men in uniform who knocked on the door. Their waists were tight and slim. It was a sailing accident, they told her; her son had been drinking. But Grace was sure he had been poisoned because he knew too much.

She remembered the day he left. She stood on the porch and cried. John pretended not to notice; he and his friend lifted their heads and yodeled some sort of war cry until Grace was forced to laugh. She held a finger under her eye to stem the tears. Then John shook his father's hand and as a last gesture of youth and frivolity jumped as high as he could over the door of his friend's convertible. He landed like a drunken sailor in the passenger seat. His leg had hit the door's partially opened window during his leap, but for Grace the flawed hurdle now resided in a memory that had perfected its arc.

Her son's sudden leap pierced her with feelings she had not seen coming. Her heart stopped as he drove away. It paralyzed her to remember it. Her nineteen-year-old son, struck down, would always be her nineteen-year-old son. He would always be jumping into a convertible like a TV detective. Forever young. Though a common enough theme, she embraced it like poetry.

She had always had this way about her. It was one of the things about Grace that set you wondering. She claimed to be an art lover, for example, but the only evidence of her taste was an oil portrait of herself. She liked to mention that the excellence of the painting lay in the fact that the oils would take decades to dry. It's worth it, she'd say, because of the vivid colors you get. To wit, the color of my eyes.

She managed to stand under this portrait of herself, with the frame-attached light aimed at the blue eyes, while a student from a community college interviewed her about her son's death. Grace had called the news stations about John, volunteered for radio shows, sent a telegram to Oprah. All for naught. Her husband steered her to the local cable station, but they told her they liked upbeat news for their community access hour. What about her other son? Maybe they could focus on him.

Finally a student from the community college came out to interview her for his final project. When Grace saw him, she couldn't help but gasp: he was so young, as young as John. He had brought his girlfriend with him. That was something John would have done, too. The student steadied his camcorder with one hand and held a microphone with the other. His girlfriend tried to move Grace away from the oil portrait to a neutral background. Grace refused to budge. She stiffened and became as motionless as the picture. Only her mouth moved, quivering slightly as she claimed that the autopsy which the Navy refused to perform would have revealed death from poisoning. Her eyes glazed to match the illuminated painted pair.

There was something obscene about two pairs of the same eyes staring into the camera. The student let the metaphor speak for itself. "Are you sure this isn't a pigment of your imagination?" he asked. He began stepping backward to bring more and more of Grace's living room into view. He panned the furniture and bookshelves. The books, selected for their height and binding, were like the slight mispronunciations of the self-taught.

And Grace was self-taught, if it came down to that. She was business path in high school, but it put her in too many typing classes. She didn't want to type. She wanted to own something, run a business. Her boyfriend had a car that she confiscated; mornings she drove it to school with the best of intentions, dropped off her girlfriends, and then flowed on by the school parking lot and onto the highway, her body drumming to a beat, her posture perked for a change of plans. Eventually she dropped out of high school, but she found herself missing those morning commutes gone astray. The peculiar air of a school-year morning had taken her initial good intentions and subsequent truancy and mixed them into an alchemy of happiness that somehow faded once her days stretched freely before her. She married and had her first child at nineteen. At twenty-three she had her teeth capped for no good reason except added white-ness and rectangularity.

She was a pretty woman and yet she had always seemed older than she was. Her teased beehive in the high school year-book made her look thirty. Even in her twenties you could sense middle age in her: she ordered albums advertised on TV and purchased a stereo/TV console at Sears. She steered un-steadily through youth like an old person on a bicycle. Even from a distance something gave her away. She was out of her element.

But now that she was thirty-nine, she had grown into her age. She looked the best she had ever looked. The platinum-colored hair she had worn for so many years no longer looked out of place on her. She sprayed and brushed it into a sensuous silver comma, up and around the ear and back to her chin. It was the perfect style to highlight her eyes—the hair seemed to draw back in respect for these two blue suns with their rays of tanned wrinkles—but until now it was hair that, like tattoos on a man, imposed certain expectations.

Even in high school she had dated older men whose hair was parted far to the side and cautiously sprayed in place. Shortly after high school she married a man who was regional manager of a large potato chip firm and who drove a company car. He had gone to college. His name was Jack and he was thirty-five. He was quiet and too grateful for her presence to issue orders or counterdemands or otherwise bother her. They had two sons. John, the older, dropped out of high school in his senior year and joined the Navy a year later. The other son, Gerald, went to college and worried about his grades.

When John was twelve, he left every day to hit tennis balls against the wall of a nearby school. Some days he scraped a pebble against the bricks and drew a strike zone so he could practice his pitches. Either way he was always at the school throwing strikes or serving aces. Grace often went up to watch. John was a pale, slightly freckle-faced boy with black hair. He had Grace's startling light blue eyes, but unlike Grace his black lashes made them look scored by heavy eyeliner. Two vivid circles of red appeared on his cheeks when he played. His body was scrawny and all-boy, but his face was disconcerting. He seemed to be wearing makeup on his lips, his cheeks, and his eyes.

One day Grace walked up to the school and saw an adult hitting tennis balls against the wall. The man wasn't very good: he held his backhand like a flyswatter. One ball sailed to the roof, and he dug into his pocket for another. When he saw Grace out of the corner of his eye, he kept to his forehand. He backpedaled and backpedaled to maintain a forehand. Finally he came to the end of the wall and caught the ball. He looked up at Grace as if surprised to see her.

"Johnny's mom, right?" he asked. He looked to be in his late forties. His stomach was huge but solid. It had muscled out a round sweat stain on his T-shirt. "He's over on the other side playing baseball."

Grace called John's name. She heard, like an echo, someone yelling "What?"

The man pointed his tennis racquet across the street. "I live over there," he said. "I see him here every day." He bounced the racquet strings off his stomach. "Got inspired. Thought I'd give it a try. So far I've lost five pounds." He wiped his forehead. "Probably a couple more tonight." He pointed to an expensive car in the parking lot. "By the way, that's not my Rolls-Royce."

Grace laughed.

"Mine's in the shop." He waited for a reaction. "Somebody dinged my Flying Lady."

Grace laughed even harder. She had a husky laugh that the man liked.

He walked toward her and extended his hand. "Name's Slim, by the way."

Grace looked at his belly. It was as big as a medicine ball. "Hi," she said. She felt her hand go limp in his.

"You have a nice son," he said.

"I have two sons." She sat herself on the parking bumper and her hand slipped free.

"Busy lady. And their daddy?"

Grace hesitated. "On a business trip."

Slim nodded at this and raised his eyebrows. "Let me guess. Real estate."

"No."

"Insurance."

"No."

"Something to do with a bank."

"No." Grace got up from the parking bumper and brushed her backside.

"Is it animal or vegetable?"

"You don't give up, do you?"

"I see you laughing," Slim said. "Is it something that takes place indoors or outdoors?"

"Both."

"This sounds fascinating. What is it?"

"Potato chips," she said. "It's not as stupid as it sounds."

"Potato chips? Of course! It's not stupid at all! Rippled? Barbecue? Green onion? Lightly salted?" He had her now. Each word sent Grace rocking with laughter until she was back down on the bumper and holding her sides. "Honest, Officer, I didn't touch her," Slim was saying.

John showed up as they spoke. "We've got to go," Grace said. "Summer camp."

"Summer camp. Both of them?"

Grace gave an embarrassed smile and nodded. "Tomorrow."

"Summer camp." Slim considered this. "Summer camp, potato chips. Potato chips, summer camp. Tomorrow." His mouth moved in sucks and slices. He looked up. "Perhaps I should see you to your door."

On the way home he told them that his real name was Charlie. Charlie Pascal Samarov. But Grace continued to call him Slim.

Slim stayed for dinner. Then he left but came back in time for dessert. Afterwards he escorted everyone to his car and lifted up the trunk. Inside were Army-green duffel bags and backpacks. The boys were delighted to dump their suitcases. He gave Gerald a compass and John a small hunting knife with a leather sheath. Grace hesitated at the knife. Slim shrugged his shoulders and held out his hands. "So the kid murders his tentmates."

Grace leaned against the car to hide her amusement from the boys.

"Yeah, I'm gonna murder my tentmates!" John's body bounced with an impatience to get started.

"A clear case of self-defense," Slim said.

"Don't," Grace pleaded.

When the kids had gone to bed, she fixed some drinks. Slim told her about his job. He was a Navy recruiter. There were all kinds of problems you ran into, he told her. "You wouldn't believe some of the stuff the Navy pulls. Ho ho ho. You wanna buck the Navy? Uh-uh, don't try it."

"What would they do?"

"What would they do? What wouldn't they do?"

"Like what?"

"Like I am not at liberty to divulge what. Let's just say they stop at nothing. Nothing. They called me up about a year ago, right? and tell me I don't have enough—uh—colored boys. Not black ones, browns. Spanyolies. Like I'm gonna find some around here. I've got a friend in New Jersey, okay? New Jersey. Surprise surprise, turns out he's got the same problem. Only reverse."

Slim thought this was the funniest thing he'd ever heard of. So did Grace.

"So I offered to trade some of my good clean wholesome all-American white boys for—you know, and it all worked out. We fiddled some papers, we diddled our quotas . . ."

Grace wiped her eyes and sighed. "I don't know why you make me laugh. You've got the knack."

"But, boy, I'll tell you," he said, "we've got some crazies up there giving us orders. Okay? Okay. Now one admiral—this is a few months ago—decides that—uh—you know, the Female Recruits, as it were, have a low comely percentage. The WAVES are not making waves, if you know what I mean."

Grace happily agreed. Not making waves was not one of her problems.

"They're dogs."

"My stomach hurts," Grace said. "Please stop. I'm telling you to stop but I don't really mean it."

"Now you, if they saw you . . . but that's another story. What we are talking about here are dogs."

Grace blew her nose into a tissue. "Oh dear," she said.

"So you can guess what happens. Orders—*requests*, I guess I should say, let's be official here—come down from the admiral that he'd certainly appreciate seeing a—uh—Different Breed of Animal. I.e., get rid of the dogs. Get some bazookas. Get some weaponry. It gets so bad that they start offering bonuses for this." He began tapping his head with his forefinger. "Bonuses. So Slim starts to get an idea. The light bulb . . ." He gestured as if twisting bulb into socket. "Goes on. All systems go. Slim's circuits . . ." He gave her a wink. ". . . are erect."

Grace punched Slim on the arm with a pert little jab.

"Okay? Okay. Let's think this over. There's a beauty school right down the street. Obviously they need business, right? It's just a bunch of students. So I work out a deal with them. I invest in a better camera, you know, so I can get depth and angles, and I do some pretty serious shopping at Goodwill. Long slinky gowns. Girdles. So I take my new recruits down to the beauty school. I get them all done up, hairstyle, makeup, makeup three inches thick—this thick, thicker than lasagna—red lips, false eyelashes. Then, if they're buxom . . ." He cupped his chest to show what he meant. "I load 'em up. I haul in the low-cut gown, which I have to slit down the back, throw over a feather boa to hide their fat arms and stomachs, and take a picture aimed right at their grenades, if you know what I mean. If they're short and squat, I photograph them from the floor up. They come out looking tall and lanky."

Grace nodded cheerfully. Being short and squat with fat arms and no grenades was not one of her problems either.

Slim patted her on the back. "I tell you, I really had to pull some tricks. Now you, I wouldn't have to pull any tricks with you. I'd love to photograph you in one of those gowns."

"Just a minute," Grace said. "Pour yourself another drink." She left the room. In a few minutes she reappeared in an evening gown.

"Now that's what I mean!"

"But you don't have your camera."

Slim looked thoughtful. "Hey!" he said. "I guess I'll just have to come over here tomorrow!"

"When the kids are at camp."

"I guess so. I don't see any other way, do you?"

"Just a minute," Grace said.

She was gone for several minutes this time. Slim took his drink and lay down on the couch. He closed his eyes. He felt someone taking off his shoes. He opened his eyes and saw Grace in a negligee. It was blue like her eyes. "Do you want to come in the bedroom with me?" she asked.

Slim looked at her. "That's a direct question if I ever heard one," he said. He unbuttoned his belt, jerking the leather flap from its hook as though ramming in a carbine. He rubbed his stomach, dyspeptic and hard, a solitary yearning bicep. For a moment his hand glided lower than his stomach and he winked. "I'll tell you," he said. "This is just about the most comfortable couch in the world. Right now I must be the most comfortable person in the world." He gave her a salute. "I love this couch. I'm telling you, I love this couch. Where'd you get it, Goodwill?"

Grace retreated alone to her bedroom.

The couch was empty in the morning but Slim came over in the afternoon. Grace had already returned from the summer camp where she dropped off the kids. She took a picture of them in front of their cabin. In a week, when she picked them up, she would take their picture again in the same spot. She liked these before-and-after shots.

At the camp one of the women in charge of the counselors had looked at John and then at her. "He's got pretty blue eyes," she said. "Like his mother." Grace was seldom complimented by other women. Usually they were either taken aback or jealous. This was a momentous occasion. She was thrilled. She wanted to tell someone. When Slim showed up, she told him. "I'm happy," she said, "and I don't mind saying so."

"You should be, baby, because you know, that is the God's truth," he said. "You do have beautiful eyes. We've got to do something. We've got to do something special."

Slim had brought his Polaroid. He showed her how he posed his female recruits. He took a shot of Grace from the ground up, one from standing on a chair, one in the shadows—"This is when they're really ugly"—and a few close-ups of her face.

Grace looked at the pictures. All the angles made her look out of proportion. "I guess it really works," she said.

"Don't you think it's time we got a little racier?"

"Sure." Grace laughed.

"So do I, but dammit all, we're out of film."

She shrugged.

Slim chucked her under the chin. "Aw, poor kid's already missing her little boys. Come on, let's just hop in the car and get some more film."

The Quik-Mart they drove to sat beside St. Rita's church, which was holding its summer festival. Slim parked his car and went after a couple of hot dogs. He ate one hot dog while checking over the other one. He appeared more anxious about the second dog, which he jiggled absently in the direction of Grace's breasts and crotch. They both noticed this at the same time. "Knew I'd get you perked up sooner or later," Slim said. Then he ate the other hot dog.

Several local artists lined the church's parking lot and hung their pictures on the clothesline that cordoned off the lanes of art from the lanes of food from the lanes of games. Most of the artists specialized in charcoal portraits, sketched on the spot. Their samples were hung up behind them like T-shirts drying in the sun. Grace strolled over to look. Fat women had lost their double chins; men had recovered their hairlines.

One woman sat apart with oil portraits lined up behind her

and a Polaroid camera tied to her leg. She caught them looking at her. "I make a preliminary sketch!" she yelled. She waved a pencil in the air to illustrate. She lifted up her leg. The camera dangled from a strap around her ankle and Grace saw white underwear under her flowery skirt. "Then I take some pictures. And then I go back to my studio. It's ready in a week!"

Grace and Slim edged closer.

"Take a good look," the woman continued. "This is an *oil* painting. This is not a charcoal fifteen-second caricature. This is art. Charcoal is okay for some. Watercolor, I'm not knocking watercolor, it suits many others fine. But oil takes years to completely dry. Years. There are not many things I'd be willing to spend years on, would you? To be honest—may I?—most of the faces I see I'd just as soon tell them: Forget it, it's not worth your time, you don't have the face for it."

"Look at this, Grace," Slim said. He pulled her over to one of the portraits that had a light attached to the top of the frame. "This is something. This is it, Grace. This is what I was talking about. With this thing shining down on your eyes."

"You have gorgeous eyes," the woman said. "I want to capture them. Beautiful and expressive."

"And with a light shining down on them . . ." Slim held out his palms. "Grace."

"You'd be an angel."

"Does the light come with it?"

"Everything. Frame, everything."

"Hey," Slim said. "How about knocking off five dollars since we brought our own pictures?" He showed her the pictures he had just taken of Grace.

"I can't use these," the woman said. "They're too dark and out of proportion. I need something taken in the natural sunlight."

Slim raised up his hands in surrender. "Far be it from me to stand in the way of great art. Sit down and pose, Grace."

Grace sat down. "I don't know . . ." she said.

"You have beautiful eyes," the woman said.

Grace smiled. "You're the second person who's told me that today. And I'm not kidding and I'm not bragging on myself—I'm just repeating what happened."

The woman flicked her wrists like a magician. "Voilà! There you have it! Do you need any better reason?"

Grace looked at the woman's hands. Tight rings garroted each finger, and metal bracelets dangled from her wrists. "Are those rings going to interfere with the brushwork?" she asked.

"These are only for show, my dear. I paint completely denuded of jewelry or other affectation."

"Denuded," Slim said. He let out a whistle.

"My son has the same eyes I do," Grace said.

"Again! There you have it. Immortality. Progenation of the race. Can you think of a better reason?"

Grace looked at her. Her eyes flickered toward the woman's hands.

"Can you think of a better reason?" the woman repeated.

Grace hesitated.

"There's only one answer, dear."

"No," Grace said.

"That's the answer."

"How about like this?" Grace asked. She struck a pose.

"No no no!" the woman shouted. "Wipe that smile off your face. This is art. I want you pensive."

It took a while, but Grace finally managed to look pensive.

When they returned from the festival, it was late and they still didn't have any film. "No problem," Slim said. "We'll just pick some up tomorrow. When does Big Daddy come home?"

Grace laughed. "Day after."

"Perfect. I just hope this doesn't get too serious because I'm starting to fall head over."

"Me too," Grace said. She sat down beside him on the couch.

"If you're so crazy about me, don't I even get a little drinkie?"

Grace jumped up. "Excuse my manners!" She ran to the kitchen and came back with two drinks and a photo album. "That's me," she said, pointing to some pictures of herself as a teenager. Her hair was teased a mile high.

"Jesus, Grace," Slim said, "you look like that little girl who married Elvis."

"That's me too," Grace said, pointing to another picture. She was older and there was a little boy by each knee.

"Your hair got a flat tire," he said.

"Here's another one." She directed him to a picture of her in a bikini.

"Damn! Don't do this to me, Grace. I'm burning up. I'm afraid to turn the next page."

"And that's my husband there."

"What's his name?"

"Jack."

"Jack's an old fella, ain't he? Gives me some hope. You must like 'em old."

"It's true, I do," Grace said. She moved her hand to Slim's stomach and began to massage it. It was hard and explosive. She wondered if it would start to sweat during sex. These were the kinds of thoughts she often expressed aloud to alarmed friends.

"You've got a cannonball waiting for me," she whispered in his ear.

"This ain't no cannonball," he said very loudly, as if to an audience. "This here's a bowling ball." He patted his stomach. "And this bowling ball wants you."

Grace began to sit on top of him.

"Why don't you slip into something more comfortable first," Slim said, holding her at bay. "And would you hunt me down some Di-Gel or something?" he called as she turned the corner.

When she returned, Slim had the television on. "Am I psychic or something, Grace? Answer me that one. Do you believe this? I say I'm a bowling ball and what's on the tube? A bowling tournament live from Canton, Ohio."

Grace was naked.

Slim turned up the volume.

"It's high," the announcer said. "The three-six pin. Thumb went down early on that one."

Grace moved over and stood next to the TV. Slim kept his eyes glued to the screen. He adjusted the contrast.

"You're throwing the ball sixty foot this many times," the TV announcer commented. "The fatigue factor has got to take over."

Grace paraded in front of the screen. Slim looked down for his drink. Finally she sat down next to him. "Here's your Di-Gel," she said. She left the room and came back with her clothes on. She threw him a pillow and sheet and walked back toward her bedroom.

"What, no lovey?"

"If you want!" She turned around.

"Oh Jesus, he missed the bucket!" Slim screamed. He jumped up and flung an imaginary bowling ball. "The Bucket Crumbler missed the bucket!" He sank back on the couch exhausted.

"Goodnight," Grace said.

She continued to see Slim every now and then, although that was the last night he stayed over. But every time she passed the incandescent eyes of her new oil portrait she thought of him.

During John's eighteenth year, Grace ran into Slim in the grocery store and nothing was ever the same again. She looked down in disgust at the mountain of hamburger meat in his cart. "Boy Scout troop," he explained.

"Boy Scouts?" she said. "Well, speaking of Boy Scouts..." She cleared her throat. "Speaking of Boy Scouts, my little Cub is a Boy Scout no longer." She paused to admire her opening line. "Ever since you gave him that hunting knife and told him to murder his tentmates," she added for good measure. She went on to tell him that John had dropped out of high school. He was hanging out with the wrong kids. He was starting to get into trouble. "So what am I going to do about him?" she asked.

"A nice kid," he said. "Eyes like a girl. A good backhand. Not as good as mine . . . "

"This is no time for your jokes." Grace picked up a few pounds of his hamburger and flung it angrily into her cart.

"I need that meat, Grace." Slim's fingers inched cautiously into her cart.

"This isn't funny. This is my son. I would like a suggestion." Slim shrugged.

So Grace gave him her suggestion. Boot camp. John needed discipline. A makeover.

"Boot camp . . . " he said. "It's not a bad idea. Those were good times, Grace."

"Oh shut up," she said. "And just do me a favor. God knows you owe me one."

She pointed a finger so dramatically that Slim drew back in fear. He searched his mind for the debt he owed. "Anything," he promised.

"Convince John to join the Navy."

Now she could kill herself for saying it.

At times she would stop dead in her tracks. She saw John hurdling over the convertible. A cocky, immortal leap.

She should have listened to Slim's Navy stories—the things the Navy did, the way they got rid of you if you knew too much. She should have listened.

She began to write letters. She persisted in the belief that John had died under suspicious circumstances. She wrote to the president, congressmen and senators, Billy Graham (ear to the president), Jack Anderson, the Pensacola Police Department, the Game and Fisheries Commission, Burt Reynolds (influential in Florida), *60 Minutes*, the American Civil Liberties Union, Bruce Berube (a friend John had mentioned in letters), and the Navy itself.

The Navy wrote to the senator who wrote to her. John had drowned while on unauthorized leave from the base. He had been drinking.

Of the others she wrote, only Bruce Berube, the Navy friend, replied:

> Thank you for the check, it will come in handy. Maybe he was poisoned like you say, I can't say for sure. Because John knew a lot of things but he wasn't saying. He kept his cool. He kept his mouth shut and his fists open. Everyone loved him. He was just like a brother to me, he's got a girlfriend he was going to marry before he drowned. She's about to have a baby who's your grandson, she's got no money and she refuses to marry anyone else she loved John too much. She has a lot of pride but write to me if you can do anything for her.

Within a few weeks a regular correspondence had been arranged with Bruce as the liaison between Grace and John's pregnant girlfriend. "She don't speak English," Bruce explained in one of his letters.

"Neither does he," said Grace's husband Jack. He did not support her in this venture. He wanted to bury John. He had already suffered enough heartbreak. A stroke had left him with a useless left arm. He tucked it under his belt to keep it from straying.

"No English. That means her eyes are brown," Grace said. It was very important that the baby have John's blue eyes, which John in turn had inherited from her.

In the time spent before any photographs of her grandchild arrived, she read about heredity. She learned how to draw genetic tic-tac-toe charts to predict eye color. There was not much hope. The browns always outnumbered the blues. Only a 25 percent chance if the mother had a recessive gene for blue eyes. No chance otherwise. And if she didn't speak English, Grace thought, chances were she was brown through and through.

But she kept drawing her gene maps. Maybe the results would change and blue would come out ahead. She wrote to Bruce and asked him to find out the color of the mother's eyes. Bruce wrote back that the baby, a boy, had been born the week before. He had blue eyes and his name was John. Grace asked for a photograph. She enclosed a check to cover Pampers.

Her husband kept away from it. He consoled himself with thoughts of his other son, who had just made the dean's list in college. He stayed outside in the yard. Grace watched him hit fungoes with a plastic ball and bat. Forced to do everything with one arm, he had purchased something advertised on TV called a pop-up batting practice kit. It allowed you to throw up balls with your foot by stomping on a pneumatic tube. If you jammed your foot down hard, a fast ball came surging out of the tube. If you torqued your foot, a curve ball came out.

From the window Grace watched Jack try to master this machine. The plastic, corrugated pump that shot out these balls looked like a caterpillar spitting eggs. The balls came out crazy. With each swing his useless left arm flew out like a boomerang and bounced back against his side. She wondered if the neighbors were watching too. If she hadn't been grief-stricken she would have been embarrassed. Because he looked ridiculous. But he kept at it every day. Every day he asked Grace to shag the fungoes he hit, but she refused. Usually she didn't even answer him.

One afternoon he caught her watching him from the window. He came back upstairs and forced her out, practically pushed her outside into the spring air. "It's spring! Grace, it's spring!" he called. Grace shuffled lifelessly down the stairs, hoping to irritate him—*anyone*—with her dead weight, her dead grief, her sadness heavier than a body. Jack pulled her into the garage where he sat her on a bicycle. "Just do it for my sake," he said. "I've been practicing."

Grace sat on the bicycle like an Indian chief and remained mute. She watched vacantly as Jack attached his left hand to the handlebars with Velcro strips. "I've been practicing," he said. "Watch this." Then he pushed off, pedaled once with his right leg, and fell off. She sat there and listened to the sounds of his failure. She heard the rip of Velcro. He tried again. Fall. Velcro ripping. Velcro being reattached. A pedal clicking. Velcro ripping. She heard it all but she looked studiously in the opposite direction. It had been weeks and no photograph of the baby. When Jack got to the end of the driveway, he turned around. "This is great!" he yelled. "Come on!"

She pedaled reluctantly to the end of the driveway. Then she took a break. She decided to walk up the slight incline that took her to the stop sign. Without a word or sidelong glance of acknowledgment, she walked her bike past Jack, who was frantically pedaling once or twice, catching himself, and then pedaling again. He was not making much progress. At the stop sign she turned right. When she could no longer hear the crunch of Velcro, she stopped. She supposed she should wait for him.

Then she decided not to wait. Why should she? What had he done for her lately? How many letters had he contributed? She pedaled two more blocks until she came to the school where John used to hit tennis balls. Across from the parking lot of the school was the dead end where Slim lived. She rode down the street and stopped in front of his house. The door was open but she could see nothing through the screen. At the bathroom window, whose frosted glass was pushed up, Slim's face appeared behind the screen. His features widened into a brief look of panic and then disappeared. She jumped off her bike and ran toward the house. She slammed against the door just as he arrived to push it shut.

She grunted and threw her hip into the door. "Let me in!" she screamed. The door was shutting. She shoved her hand into the crack that remained. "Okay, break my hand!" she yelled. "Go ahead, break it!"

He opened the door. His face was red and steam rose from his scalp and stomach. The towel that he held was too small to go around him. He held it in front of him like a matador's cape. "Just give me a minute," he said.

"I have a bone to pick with you, Mister."

Slim slowly backed up toward the bathroom.

"You didn't come to my son's funeral. You didn't send a card. You got him into this mess and you didn't even send a card."

Slim ran into the bathroom and slammed the door.

Grace pounded on the door. "Come out of there!"

Slim reappeared in his boxer shorts and T-shirt. "I'm sorry," he said. "I really am. I thought I sent a card. I remember mailing it." He shrugged helplessly. "I'm sorry."

Grace was at a loss. She couldn't find the proper words. She had no words. There were things seething inside her.

"What about that oil painting?" she finally said. "I thought you were going to pay for the oil painting."

"Jesus, Grace, I forgot all about that. It's been years. Has it dried yet? I thought I told the lady to send me the bill. I remember mailing her something."

"You remember mailing just about everything, don't you? I'm the one who got the bill. What about those other things you told me? You know the Navy did something and you're not helping me find out."

"Honey, I never told you that."

"You're the one who told me what they did."

"Honey, now wait a minute, you've just got to calm down. What are you doing out here riding your bike in this hot weather?"

"I'm riding with Jack," she said.

"Where is he?"

"He's slow. For God's sake, Slim, the poor man's had a stroke! Don't you have any mercy!"

"Grace, now calm down, baby. I want to tell you something. Honey, I've been thinking about you. Grace, would you believe something?" Slim moved toward his monaural record player. It was turquoise with a white plastic turntable. "I've thought about you so often I bought this record. Reminds me of you, Grace. I want to play it for you." He leaned down and fiddled through his records. "Do you know Dan Fogelberg?"

"No I do not know Dan Fogelberg, not to change the subject or anything, Mr. Slim Slime. You think I'm not on to you?"

"You must have heard this. Listen to this. Grace baby, listen to this."

A guitar and voice began. She knew immediately that this would be a sad song. *"Met my old lover in the grocery store."*

"Remind you of anyone?" Slim came up behind her and slipped his arms around her waist.

"Snow was falling and . . . "

"Well, not that part. This is really an all-seasons lullaby."

The song continued. The tinny voice of the singer matched the plaintiveness of the song. It was about a man who met his old girlfriend by accident on Christmas Eve. They sat in the man's car and drank a six-pack and talked. The woman was married to an architect who kept her warm and safe and dry; she would have liked to say she loved her safe architect husband, but she didn't like to lie.

"Said she married her an archi . . . "

"A Potato Chip Man," Slim sang into her ear.

Grace smiled and leaned back. She sank into his body and felt his stomach at the small of her back.

"Now here's your line coming up," Slim said. "Here it comes."

"I said her eyes were still as blue oo hoo."

"That's your line if I ever heard it," he whispered in her ear. "That is your line."

Grace felt the breath in her ear. She turned around and found Slim's earlobe. She moved her lips to his mouth and began kissing him. They were deep kisses that pushed him backward. Her kisses became more desperate. Slim's legs buckled and Grace landed on the couch. He undressed her. His hand attacked her breast like a rubber plunger; he sucked it hard into his palm. He pulled off her pants and got down on his knees to remove her shoes. He stood up with the shoes in his hands. "Let me get these damn things out of the way," he said. He walked into the bedroom and rattled around. She heard a theatrical commotion. There were muffled thumps and bangs as he threw things in and out of his closet. "I know I had a shoebox around here somewhere," he called to her in a loud shout.

Grace lay on the sofa, studying the ceiling, the walls, listening to the excavation in the other room and his earnest shouts of minor progress. Eventually she sat up and sighed. She leaned down and snapped up her bra. She buttoned her shirt and looked: her son's leap into the convertible sprang into her mind's full view like the jump itself. The hurdle was so perfect it stopped her breath. John could beat even the rules of gravity. Those who remained behind were all victims of gravitational pull. All but one. She would write to him someday. Congratulations on your blue ribbon, she'd say. I'm not surprised you won it in the high jump. Your father was quite a leaper too. One time he jumped over a whole car. I'll never forget it.

Death and the Maid

ROBERT ANDERSON

From *Ice Age* (2000)

She and Clayton and Our Boy Bubba had eaten dinner, the dishes were done, and it was just after eight when Sophia left the house. When she stepped down off of the pine porch, there was only the red earth and its spitefulness nettled the bottoms of her bare feet; the screen door, its six-inch tear advantageous to all but the barn bats, screeched on its hinges three times over. The footpath to the field had the worn sheen of an old saddle and the sky was sunless, but still pale. She guessed that she had perhaps fifteen minutes of what would serve her better than actual daylight to say her piece in.

She was rehearsing the opening words in her head: "Well, Mrs. Buxton . . . So, Mrs. Buxton . . . How do you do, Mrs. Buxton?" She reached the field before she had made up her mind. The redness of the freshly turned earth threw her. She said simply, "God," and her forearms ceased walking the air like rudimentary batons.

Mrs. Buxton," she said, "you're not in Brownsville no more. You're in McAllen. My name is Sophia and this here's my field. I'm gonna . . . well, I'm gonna . . . "

She couldn't decide between "keep you" or "look after you" and soon she found that the choice itself dried away on her tongue. She had to lick the roof of her mouth and she tasted railing as she began to speak again. She apologized for taking up the better part of the day in getting Mrs. Buxton "settled in" and particularly for the three-hour wait in the tractor shed—her pastor was undergoing therapy for his pedophilia and she was foolish enough to put her faith in Owlington County's Reverend Heisler. When he hadn't presented himself at noon, as arranged days ago, she phoned his parsonage and spoke to a talcum-voiced female who insisted that she was his housekeeper. The housekeeper explained, with regrets, that the Reverend had sudden business in Tijuana that morning.

Sophia thought that "sudden business in Tijuana" meant he was selling his last rite writs door-to-door, or under a rock to under another rock—that is, if the city remained anything like it was on her distant and dismal honeymoon. The writs contained a Latin excerpt on the front and an adhesive patch on the back and they were commonly glued to a dying person's chest like a candy store tattoo. Sophia said that they were considered a great convenience all across the vast backyard of Texas because they saved the bereaved the trouble of summoning a clergyman at the hour of death. She wasn't even sure that the Reverend's faith—Protestant something—sanctioned extreme unction. Mrs. Buxton didn't seem to know either.

The powder-voiced housekeeper asked Sophia if she were speaking on a cell phone. Sophia told her she wasn't. The housekeeper thought that that was a pity, since she had half a mind to dial up the Reverend's hotel in Tijuana and ask that he bequeath Mrs. Buxton's "otherworldly remains" unto the Lord Almighty from the other side of the border, while Sophia held the cell phone, the one she did not happen to have, over the grave. She heard the very beginning of a hum coming from far down the gravel road that fronted the absentee-owned portion of the acreage; a speck appeared on the horizon, soon revealing itself to be a neutral-colored sedan with its headlights already on. Even with the day holding, she could not ascertain the make of the car and this unsettled her because the traffic on that road was usually limited to her neighbors. She did know that if a stranger had strayed onto her road from the interstate, then that stranger was either pitifully nearsighted or someone who had gotten lost on purpose. She held up her hand in commiseration. Across the field, the car came abreast and Sophia had to drop her hand for fear of being mistaken for a scarecrow.

"So how you like the country?" she asked, knowing that Mrs. Buxton had spent most of her life in New Jersey. She joked that Texas had much to see and most of it was hardly worth looking at—it was the size of the state and the relative paucity of human beings that pleased Sophia: "Good for keepin' things in the family, if you follow me." She talked of the free fall of crop prices over the years and how at present the average South Texas farm could not feed a family of gerbils. She told the grave how the land developers had appeared "thick as bonebirds" in the early 1980s and how much of what was once their land had been auctioned off and bonded to tract housing.

"Mexicans," she said, "dew-eyed and damp-back Mexicans and they're comin' this way. Hang around the streets of town ten minutes and you find out that they don't know the difference between a marble birdbath and public pisser. You know what I think, Mrs. Buxton? I think we're about to end up just like the Alamo."

The burial field was now all that was left of the land her husband had inherited from his father and his father from his. She and Clayton and Our Boy Bubba planted without a harvest; they sowed and they did not reap. The county gave them three hundred dollars a grave, less the occasional kickback. Weekday afternoons, she earned extra cash by delivering foil-wrapped meals from the parsonage to the elderly in the trailer towns that ringed the city limits while Bubba sometimes landscaped by day and outlawed most every night, running the interstate with a band of boys who could strip a hobbled vehicle down to its skeletal essence in a matter of minutes, and Clayton chased the roseate genie through endless jugs of border wine, and Sophia claimed to be grateful to the liquor for the tranquility it brought her husband. She sipped a glass now and then, but it tasted like "hot and sour Hi C."

"We actually manage quite well," she said.

She heard the screen door, loose on its hinges, and she looked back toward the house. It was only the wind. She peered as best she could from the distance, and she caught the blue phosphorescence of the television set beaming through the front window.

"'Scuze me, Mrs. Buxton," she said, "I thought that might be Clayton or Bubba come to fetch me in. Truth to tell—and I am one straight-shooter from the old school—neither one of them thought that it was necessary for me to come out and speak with you this evening. Truth is, if you'll pardon me for sayin' so, they didn't want to take you in altogether. They said you'd bring bad luck. Can you imagine? Like blamin' the rain on the sky."

She paused and waited as she would with the living. Mrs. Buxton's silence emboldened her to continue.

"Pardon me again for sayin' so, but they were rightfully suspicious, I reckon. 'Least from their standpoint. We never had a case like yours. County's sent us their vagrants and their mole peoples enough to stack like lumber. We've even had convicts. But you, ma'am, are our very first Texas State executed."

The paleness of the sky hadn't altered—the enfeebled day was squatting and listening and Sophia wished for twilight. For one thing, the burial mound seemed so obscenely red, and this reminded her of the ghastly Halloween pranks she had seen perpetrated upon defenseless graves, which were, in the end, anything but defenseless, since these acts of malice shamed only the living. Death, in all of its belligerent inevitability, was never mocked.

"But finally," she said, "I lined 'em by eye, Clayton and Bubba, and I told 'em, 'Bad luck, hell. Ain't Our Girl Aubrey a Carmelite nun-trainee with the sisters in the city of San Antonio? Why, that's just like havin' a little lobbyist up at the gates of heaven.'"

Her daughter Aubrey had seen a fanning angel in the very same field they were now conversing in. Sophia told Mrs. Buxton how the child could not be dissuaded with talk of sundown shadows and how she would neither sleep nor eat until her mother phoned the Archdiocese to report the news of the Catholic miracle. The good sisters of San Antonio had sent their van for Aubrey within the week.

"I don't miss her much on account of I know she's with God," Sophia said.

She apologized for going on about her family matters when it was really her task tonight to welcome Mrs. Buxton to the field. She explained that she felt a keen sense of duty to get to know her "interreds" as though they were relatives.

"Lost relatives, I guess you'd say," she said. "Long lost. Don't you go thinkin' I'm crazy, now. I am a Christian and a Christian believes, by book, that the dead retain an awareness of their earthly remains. It's like when I donate a blouse to Goodwill. A little while down the road I'm sure to see it in a Mex clothing stall, or maybe just some Mex kid raggin' shoes with it."

Her eyes roamed the field. "You know," she said, "maybe I better just watch what I say. This bein' the border, not everybody in this field is altogether Anglo-American."

"Well I ain't to judge. Likely you can't help it how you're born and I'm beginning to wonder if you can help it how you live. And although I am not to pass judgment, I am meant to try to understand within the confines of what God meant for me to learn. I said the same long before my only daughter was deemed holy and havin' one saint-child to my name has only strengthened my belief. Understanding is dearer than judgment and harder to come by, to boot. I tell you, most of the time what I understand for certain is a mystery to me. This life will knot your head like a nigger bonnet."

She paused and waited.

"Sorry."

She puffed her cheeks and let the air out, slowly. "Fact of the matter, Mrs. Buxton," she said, "the county, by law, has to inform me of the backgrounds of every body I inter. Therefore, the reason why you're lyin' here in my field has not escaped me. I asked right off about your daughter, little Muhibbi. Clerk said your mama, her grandma, had buried her up in New Jersey eight long years ago. I naturally asked why she wouldn't do the same for you, now that your debt is done and you ain't able to harm nobody else. The clerk told me he didn't know why she wouldn't have anything to do with disposing of you, but neither our county nor Texas State has any legal means with which to compel her. That's what he said and I said that's a shame. A damn sight of a shame you and your daughter ain't layin' together back where you belong. The two of you could have made it all up over eternity."

All at once the sun dimmed and Sophia saw that she was casting her shadow directly upon the grave. For fear of being thought rude, she moved slightly to her left and the shadow did not move with her. She switched back to her original position like someone trying to outwit a mirror.

"If only you hadn't done it in Texas, ma'am. I expect up in New Jersey this sorta thing happens all the time. I ain't never been there, but from what I get from the TV its pretty much one big rumpus room, ain't it? A New Jersey jury, even if they didn't believe your story, mighta stifled their shock long enough to see their way clear to send you off to an asylum. Be the most humane thing to do, if you ask me. For all goings on around here, we still don't get much daughter killin' per se. We don't have the first notion of what to do about such a thing 'cept to kill the one who done it."

She moved again and her shadow did not move; she raised her hand and the shadow refused to wave back at her. She bit at the web of her palm and it hurt—she was alive, but dreaming; it was important for her to listen closely to what she herself had to say.

"I just got to hand it to you for sheer gumption."

She moved a step closer.

"You plain old went to bat baldface in that courtroom. Tellin' 'em all about those Nazi skinheads runnin' your car off the road. How they molested you and your daughter for three straight days and then knocked you out with a shot of dope. You woke up short a child and you drove clean across the state, huntin' for her. You never bothered to contact the police 'cuz with their big bellies and their fat, red necks, they didn't look all that much removed from the skinheads. And, right hand to God, you had no idea that your daughter was in your back trunk all the while. Neither did those eight thousand witnesses within five city blocks when you pulled into that Phillips station. They just figured maybe you had a rotted hog in the car with you.

She turned her back to the grave; she hunched forward and the long nozzle of her spinal column showed clearly through the fabric of her sweater, her fists balled into the base of her stomach, and her elbows in the air. Viewed from Mrs. Buxton's perspective, it would have looked as though Sophia were straining to take flight.

"I'm sorry, Mrs. Buxton," she said, turning back. "I forgot my manners. I tend to do that with my dead."

She was standing now on the roof of the grave and the earth was warmer and kinder to her toes than the outlying dirt had been. When she turned away to laugh, she had felt a breeze upon the back of her neck, and she wondered if the occupant of the grave wasn't laughing with her. Just to be certain that there was no ill will in the air, she reached down to give the earth a reassuring and apologetic pat.

"Wasn't anything personal, I hope you know," she said.

A bracelet of ice seized her wrist and her right arm wrenched forward—she found herself offering the grave the emptiness of her right hand. Again, she apologized, saying that her rudeness might have to do with something she ate and she tried, with difficulty, to recall her dinner of roughly forty-five minutes ago. The numbness of her fingertips promised an end to the needlepoint that had salvaged so many evenings for her. She gauged the tensile strength of the grip, tug of warring for an instant. Her shoulder socket began to give ground and she had to ease off.

"Mrs. Buxton, I know mothers and daughters," she said, evenly. "I've been on both sides of the issue. It's a beautiful thing, sure. Sometimes too beautiful. Havin' somebody so close to you wearin your eyes and your former mind. Every moment and every memory comes shootin' right back at you. It's like havin' a person in your skin with ya."

She paused and waited, as she would with the living.

"I can truly say I almost understand, and understanding, honey, is a duty to me, whereas judgment abides by God. What with you bein' chased out of New Jersey by that gun-totin', cuckolded boyfriend. You wheelin' all across the country, lookin' for what work you could find on a sixth-grade certificate. Just what was you supposed to say when the child asked you, "Where we goin' to, Mommy?""

She felt the grip loosen a notch and she considered trying to snatch her hand free, but decided that it would be foolhardy to try to outquick the dead; the ghost would have to be lulled into letting go.

"Between you and me, we can call this thing you did self-abuse. You killed this precious little part of yourself and then you tried to keep on drivin."

The ghost released her hand. She wanted to stand up, but, given the situation, she distrusted sudden movement. She looked back at the house; it seemed impossibly distant and remote, as though the household already slept and the house now existed only in the compression of sleep and dreams. She lived in that house for over half her lifetime. She had sex and babies and fits all within its walls. The idea that it had been a drowsy mirage all along delighted her. She looked at the grave and her smile dried up.

She said to the dirt, "You tried to keep on drivin', but now you're lookin' at a red light you know damn well you can't never run."

She felt the front of her sweater separate from her skin. She murmured, "I just meant . . ." before the burning of the fabric into the back of her neck caused her jaw to clench. She was on her knees and the weight of her body upset the burial mound. The earth under her knees became larval.

"Is it that you want me to pray with you, Mrs. Buxton?" she asked, her voice going high and small. "You could have tried askin' kindly, you know? I never been one to shrink from prayer. I do have to have both hands, however."

The ghost did not respond and Sophia made an attempt to sound stern and severe. "Look here, do you want the good Lord to hear us or don't ya? I expect we've both given Him enough reason not to listen as it is."

Four bone-cold digits latticed into the spaces between each of the fingers of her right hand. She felt the chill down to her toes and she was afraid that she might commit the sacrilege of voiding her bladder right where she knelt. She joined her left hand to the prayer pyramid, and though her mind was blank with terror, her appeal to heaven came out as assured as a sermon.

"Dear Lord, I ask upon the soul of my daughter Aubrey, now a Carmelite nun-trainee, and upon the soul of the lost lamb Muhibbi, only daughter of Mrs. Yasmina Buxton, that You bestow Your grace and tender mercies upon the wayward spirit of the newly departed here with me. She is, as I am and as I have mentioned, a mother. A chosen vessel of Your life-givin' power. You did see fit to entrust a life to her. Lord, she nurtured that child just as long as she possibly could. When she could no longer nurture and when she knew that she had no life worth givin' life to . . . well, Lord, she slaughtered."

Sophia could scarcely believe that she had said that, nor could she believe that she was presently being pulled face-first into the burial dirt with her arm contorting higher and higher up her back. She opened her mouth to protest and she tasted earth. She felt her fingers bending back toward the joints and she saw a succession of blue-steel match heads, flaring into tiny zips of lightning.

"She slaughtered in the spirit of sacrifice," she got out between clenched teeth. "In accord with Abraham and Isaac and all that. Believin' that it was to Your will and Your greater glory and that she was only givin' You back what was Yours all along."

Her arm fell freely down her back, as limp as a sleeper's. She had bitten into her tongue and when she spat the issue was darker for the combination of blood and earth. She remembered that it was a grave she was lying upon and she said, "Sorry, ma'am." She wiped the spot with her fingertips and patted at the earth.

"That's all right," she said, nursing her bitten tongue. "I ain't about to get into a fight with someone on their first full day of bein' dead. I would like you to know that your quarrel is not with me. I mean, I've lost just like you. It wasn't that awful long ago I had fifteen hundred whole acres of land and a daughter closer to me than my own heartbeat."

She pushed herself up by her elbows; she stood there, shaking the dirt from her hair. She smiled down at the grave through the cloud of fine gravel she had just filled the air with, her own blood now bright at the corner of her lip.

"Do you know what my heart whispers to me, Mrs. Buxton? It whispers, 'Good for you.' Night and day, that's all I hear from my heart. 'Good for you, good for you, good for you.' Well, all right, good for me. 'Cuz I let my lamb bleed, lady, and you best believe you never did. You just hung on to your girl's windpipe for three minutes and she had heaven on a plate. Aubrey, hell, she ain't in no convent. That's just somethin' I tell in town when they ask me where my youngest is at. One too many times I had to chase her off from over yonder, our sold-off fields. I says to her, 'Girl, you mean to tell me I sent you to school for five-and-a-half whole grades and you can't so much as read "no trespassing?" It ain't like you ever worked this land or lost any sleep worryin' about an early frost, or the grasshoppers, or the blood mortgages on it? This here's my field, or least it was. Maybe it's time for you to find your own land. Get somethin' of your own and then lose it, so you'll know what I know. County workers are always sayin' how thin and peaked you look; I got me a mind to let them take you off my hands.'"

She waited as she would with the living.

"Then the county came, Mrs. Buxton. Aubrey didn't wanna get in the car with them. My eyes stayed dry. I just said, 'Go on, Lamb. Go on up the road. Go on and bleed like I bleed.'"

The north wind struck her full in the face; it electrified her clothes and she felt bits of Mrs. Buxton's soil spraying her ankles. She looked around and saw that night had fallen.

"There ain't hardly a man, woman, child in the county doesn't know what I did," she said. "But I'll be goddamned if I'll ever admit it to a livin' soul. So, much obliged, Mrs. Buxton. I'm gonna have to get back to the house now; it's past time I be on about my business. Might be I'll be back to check on you, I don't know. Depends on how heavy Clayton and Bubba sleep tonight. Mind you don't move around too much and disturb the other residents. You try to get some rest now, y'hear?"

She turned up the path. She halted, digging in her heels. She said, "Oh, the rock," and she hurried back to the grave.

"Mrs. Buxton, I usually take a small rock from the grave of a new arrival. I like to wear it in my apron for a day or two and then I put it in the breakfront in the dining room with the others. It's a memento of the bond between me and my interreds. May I?"

She reached down and the icy bracelet again closed around her wrist—she did not struggle.

"Mrs. Buxton," she said, "would you like to come in the house?"

Rough Translations

MOLLY GILES

From *Rough Translations* (1985)

There was so much to do that Ramona felt dizzy, and when Ramona felt dizzy, Ramona lay down; once down she stayed for
the count and then some. Shadow and sun took their turns on
her ceiling, the phone rang unanswered, a Mozart sonata spun
silently on the turntable by the window. Ramona dozed, and
dreamed she was dancing. When she awoke she found her own
hands clinging to her own ribs as if for dear life. It's the funeral,
she decided. It's the funeral that's killing me.

She must have spoken out loud because her son Potter stared
from the doorway. He was balancing a bag of groceries in one
arm and his pet cat and violin case in the other. In his slipped-
down glasses and long brown pony tail he looked as careworn as
any young housewife, and Ramona felt the familiar urge to apol-
ogize, an urge she stifled with a shamed little laugh and a wave
from the pillows. If my timing had been better, she thought, Potter could be touring Europe right now, playing music with his
friends, having some fun . . . can Potter have fun? Potter frowned
and said, "What is it? You okay?"

"Alive," Ramona cried gaily, "and kicking." She lifted one moc-
casined foot to demonstrate and knocked the phone book off the
bedspread. Potter's frown deepened. He had never smiled at Ra-

mona's jokes, nor had his sister Nora; finding their mother un-
amusing was the one trait they shared. Sometimes Ramona
thought: It's because they can't forgive me. Other times she
thought: It's because they have no sense of humor. She watched
as Potter, frowning, put down his burdens and moved into her
room. He snapped the record player off, drew the curtains
closed, turned the lamp on, plumped her pillows, and pressed his
lips gingerly to her forehead to feel her temperature. Ramona,
tucked under his chin like a violin being tuned, tried to sound
the right note. "I had the funniest dream," she said, but even as
she began to tell the dream she saw Potter didn't think it was
funny; his face was so pained she started to lie. One lie, as always, led to another, and down she went, deeper and deeper.
"So there I was," she finished, breathless, "tap-dancing among
the gravestones like Ginger Rogers in a horror film. Isn't that a
scream?"

"It might make a good drawing for *The Beacon*," Potter
said. Ramona bowed her head, contrite. She knew what Potter
thought of her drawings. She had heard him describe the cartoons she did for the village weekly as "illustrated idioms, the
kind you find on cocktail napkins," which she supposed was a
fair description—not kind, but fair. A few days before, propped
up in bed, she had finished her last assignment: a pen and ink
sketch of a little ark floating on a sea of question marks with a
caption that read "Flooded by Doubts." Her very favorite submis-
sion, "Tour de Force," had showed a docent dragging a group of
tourists through the Louvre at gunpoint, and it was true she had
seen a cartoon much like it etched onto a highball glass at the
church rummage sale; she had bought the glass, of course, and
pitched it into a garbage bin at once. She tried now to imagine
how she would draw her dancing dream. She'd sketch herself as
she was: a small, wide-eyed old woman with bad posture and a
frizz of gray bangs. She'd dress herself in a straw hat and tux and
set herself among the headstones at Valley View . . . Valley View?

Was that right? Was that the cemetery she had finally decided on? Or was that the one where Hale had been buried? Should she be buried by Hale after all? Would he want her there? Would he let her stay? Her fingers started to clutch at her ribs again, and again she sighed and said, "So much to do. So many decisions. I hope you never have to go through this, Potter."

"Right," said Potter. He replaced the phone book on the bed, gave Ramona another of his shy hard stares, and left with the cat meowing at his heels to start cooking their dinner.

Ramona reached for her glasses, picked up the phone book, and turned again to the back. She had memorized the five listings for Funerals, but she had not yet found the nerve to dial. She stared at the ads again, narrowing in on the Manis Funeral Home, which said, "Call at Any Time," and The Evergreens, which advertised air-conditioned chapels. The air-conditioning tempted her, for the summer afternoons had been growing warm, but when she finally started to dial and her finger slipped, she took it as an omen. She did not think the Manis Home, despite its insistence, should receive calls at dinner time; she'd call them tomorrow too.

She fell into her old habit of reading the phone book, leafing through the classifieds for Mourners, then for Paid Professional Mourners, then finally for Mummers. She still wondered where Hale had found that little blonde who wept so competently at his graveside—a waitress Ramona had not been told about? an extra secretary? How delicious it would be, she thought, if I could hire the equivalent of that little blonde—some good-looking young boy, an acting student down on his luck . . . someone who would be willing to fling himself down on the coffin . . . She shivered happily, thinking how that would shock Nora, and then, penitent, she reached for the phone again and dialed Nora's number, the words "I hate to bother you" already forming on her lips. She knew Nora would be busy. Nora was always busy. Right now, Ramona feared, Nora would be kneading a loaf of whole wheat bran bread, knitting a sweater, cutting the baby's hair, balancing her husband's business accounts, checking the twins' homework, and drafting a proposal for a new gymnasium while her old mother, with nothing better to do, lay slumped in a filthy bathrobe on an unmade bed covered with overdue library books, wanting a chat. Oh Lord, Ramona thought, gazing around her cluttered room, but Potter and I live like two French whores, underwear everywhere, and jars full of dead roses. I can never have the funeral here. The best thing to do is go to Nora's at once and get buried in Nora's backyard like a pet hamster in a shoe box.

"I can't decide between the Manis or The Evergreens," she said, when Nora picked up the phone. "How can I find out which one is the best?"

"I'll find out for you," Nora said. "Next?"

Nora's knitting needles clicked like static on the other end of the line while Ramona tried to think of something else to ask for. "Medication?" Nora suggested. "Has Potter been giving you the right medication?"

"I think so." Ramona glanced at the bottle by the bed, rechecked it to be sure it was labeled for her and not the cat, and leaned back. "It's just planning this funeral."

"Do you know what I'd do about that funeral if I were you?" Nora said.

Ramona waited, grateful.

"I'd forget it," Nora said. "I'd file it away in my Not-to-Worry drawer."

"Not-to-Worry drawer?"

"That's right. I'd file it away and swallow the key. Do you understand?"

"I'm not a child," Ramona began, but Nora, her voice flat, sweet, and dangerous, said. "Have Potter cook you some real food for once. I'll come by and see you in the morning. I don't like the idea of you thinking about your funeral all day. It's not healthy."

Not healthy? thought Ramona. That's a good one. She said good-bye to Nora and lay back. Her heart began to race and her fingers raced too, drumming and tapping on top of the phone book. What should she do, what should she do? Perhaps there was still enough time to go crazy? She had always meant to spend her last days tiptoeing around in a flowered hat with a fingertip pressed to her lips, but no luck. These were her last days and she felt no crazier than usual. She felt as she always had when there were decisions to be made: harassed and dreamy, wildly anxious and unable to move. She reached up to twist one earring off, realizing, with dismay, that one was all she was wearing; in her haste to prove she could still dress herself she had forgotten to put on the other. Her bathrobe buttons—were they closed? They were. She wished she could push a button and make herself disappear, right now, before her body became a burden to them all, before they learned how complicated, dull, and expensive it was to dispose of even a small person's final remains.

"You know who I admire?" she said to Potter as she joined him in the kitchen for dinner. "Junie Poole. Junie sat down in the hall outside the coroner's office one night and tried to kill herself by drinking a thermos of gin mixed with pills. When they arrested her she was too drunk to talk, but they found this note pinned to her mink coat saying she hoped her children would appreciate the fact that she had at least taken herself to the morgue. Of course, no one's appreciated anything Junie's ever done, before or since, but that's not the point. The point is that she did try to make things easy for her family. I want to make things easy too." She picked up her fork and looked down at her plate. "Liver? Won't Nora be impressed." She tried to eat a little. But when she saw the cat, in the corner, licking from an identical plate, she put the fork down and regarded Potter, who had done this to her before, once with canned salmon and once with pickled herring. He was either trying to be very economical or his values were more confused than she suspected. "Potter," she said, watching the old gray cat huddled murmurously over its plate, "do you think I should just crawl off to the woods?"

"There aren't any woods within crawling distance," said Potter. Ramona smiled; Potter did not. "I think . . ." Potter began. He stopped. Ramona folded her hands and waited. Potter, born when she was over forty, had been a talkative child, full of ideas and advice and so original that even Hale had paid attention, but Potter had stopped talking years ago, at least to her. "I think," Potter repeated, one thin hand fluttering before his downcast face, "that you are using this funeral to mask your real feelings."

Ramona waited, her own head bent. "And what are my real feelings?" she asked at last.

"Rage," Potter said, his shy eyes severe behind his smudged glasses. "Terror. Awe. Grief. Self-pity."

"Heavens," said Ramona. She was impressed. Once again she wished she were the mother her children deserved, and once again she found herself having to tell them she was not. "I'm afraid, Potter," she said, "you give me credit. I don't feel any more of those 'real' feelings now than I ever have. What I feel now is a sort of social panic, the same old panic I used to feel when Hale wanted me to give a dinner party for his clients and the guests would arrive and I'd still be in my slip clutching a bucket of live lobsters. I'm sorry, dear, I can't eat this. I'm too nervous. I'm going to have to make a list."

She sat at her drawing desk, staring at a piece of paper, wondering where to start after printing "To File in the Worry Drawer" across the top of the page. In the next room Potter talked to Nora on the telephone, his voice reluctant and slow. If only my children liked each other, Ramona thought. She sighed and pressed her palm to a few of the places that hurt. Sometimes the pains were gone for hours altogether and sometimes they felt like ripping cloth; sometimes they widened and sometimes they narrowed and sometimes they overwhelmed her completely. Right now she was being treated to a new pain, a persistent jabbing in her chest that tapped back and forth like an admonishing finger. It feels like I'm being lectured by a bully, she thought. Lectured on my failures. If I had been lovable, Hale would have loved me, and if Hale had loved me, I would have loved myself, and if I'd loved myself, Nora would have loved me, and if Nora had loved me, Potter would have loved her, and then Potter wouldn't have had to grow up loving nothing but his music and his wretched cat. Hale and I, she thought, set a bad example for the children as far as loving went . . . the children! she thought. She pushed her chair back and stood up. "Tell Nora," she called out to Potter, "tell Nora I'm sorry but this is going to be an adults-only funeral, X-rated, no grandchildren allowed. Maybe the boys, but by no means the twins. By no means the baby. I've seen little children at funerals before," she added, when Potter finally returned from the phone, "and it's no picnic, believe me."

"Nora said to give you this." He handed Ramona a mug of warm milk and his eyes were so sad that she drank it all down even though there was a cat whisker floating on top.

That night Ramona dreamed her funeral was held outdoors on the slope of a mountain; it was a bright summer afternoon and everyone she'd ever cared about was there: her parents, her grandparents, Hale, all her friends from childhood on. She was there herself, hovering in the sky like a Chagall bride, her pretty shroud rippling around her crossed ankles. She had never felt so happy. Tables set up under flowering trees were laden with cakes and roasts and sparkling wines; music came from somewhere; there were rainbows, fountains. The conversations she overheard made her laugh with pleasure; people were saying kind, affectionate, funny things to each other, some of them so wonderful, so insightful, that Ramona could scarcely wait to wake up and write them down.

Half-asleep, she groped for pencil and pad and quickly, in the dark, jotted down every scrap of conversation she could remember. In the morning, unsurprised, she studied her notes. They were illegible, as frail and choppy as an EKG. Lost, she thought. Like everything else. Lost like all the words I've tried to string together throughout my life. For a brief, bitter second she thought of all the poems, stories, prayers, and revelations that had evaporated like breath in cold air when she tried to express them. I have never said anything right, she decided. Even my jokes, even the drawings I do for *The Beacon* are wrong—rough translations of a foreign language I hear but cannot master.

She took her pen and quickly tied all the choppy lines on the paper together, making a scrawl across the top, and then she drew herself at the bottom of the page, an anxious old lady staring straight up, and then she wrote "Over My Dead Body" and tore the paper up.

She shook the day's second dose of Percodan into her palm and thought again of Junie Poole passed out in front of the coroner's office. It was then she saw how her own funeral truly would be: a small gathering of silent relatives sitting in uncomfortable pews in a little Consolation Chapel somewhere. Pink and yellow light would fall through the stained-glass window over the casket where she lay. The air would smell unwholesomely floral. Muzak would be piped in. She would be wearing an evening gown that Nora, at the last minute, would have had to alter to fit, a terrible dress, mauve, with long sleeves and net at the neck. Her nails would be painted mauve to match, and her lips. Her five grandchildren would be wild with horror and boredom. The boys would be thinking about basketball and sex, basketball and sex. The twins would be cracking their knuckles, glancing cross-eyed at each other, giggling. The baby, whose damp quick hands were never still, would be digging a design into the plush seat with a thumbnail, a design no one but the baby would know was a skull and red flames. Nora would be shushing and clucking the children as she counted the heads in the chapel, trying to decide if she had made enough potato salad. A minister chosen by Nora's husband would give a speech. The minister would say that Ramona was in a far better place than she had been before. Potter, picking cat hair off his pressed blue jeans, would think about this. He would regret he had not gone to Europe with his friends when he had the chance; he could be in a better place, too, he would think, if it weren't for his mother. After the ceremony the mourners would bunch on the sidewalk in the sun, ill-at-ease and restless . . . and I'll still be lying beneath the pink and yellow lights, Ramona thought, reeking of hairspray and formaldehyde—and the garnet necklace I want Nora to save for the baby will still be around my neck, forgotten in that damn mauve net.

She eased herself out of bed, walked unsteadily toward her closet, opened the door, and peered in. The darkness surprised her. At first she could not see the mauve dress and she even had a wild hope she had thrown it out, years ago, but then she saw it, hanging in its plastic bag like a hideous orchid. As she reached up to strike it off the clothes rod, she lost her balance and fainted forward. It was so strange to fall face forward into soft dark clothes that when she came to she was not even frightened. She tried to tell Potter how strange it had been, how comfortable, how sexy really, like falling into outheld arms, like dancing. Oh but that time Hale twirled her at the Christmas party and she was feeling almost beautiful that night and so deeply in love and as she came out of the twirl Hale turned to another woman, neglecting to catch her, and she lost her balance and spun across the dance floor, all the colored lights a blur, and she was completely alone and she was laughing, even before she fell and cracked her coccyx she was laughing, prepared for the laughter of others, prepared to say, "It's all right, I'm not hurt a bit," even though it wasn't all right, even though she *was* hurt a bit. Quite a bit. Always after that she saw herself as Hale saw her: a clumsy woman with breasts that were too big and lips that were too wide and little awkward hands that couldn't hold a man. She saw herself as someone who could be dropped. "Oh Ramona bounces back," Hale drawled, and didn't she though, bouncing back like any old kickball. Well, the secret was not to take yourself too seriously. No matter where they kicked you it couldn't hurt if you didn't let it, if you got right down there with the dancing shoes and laughed—if you could do that, you could rise like a rose in the air when they toed you.

"I have something to say," she said to Potter. "I have a statement to make. Are you ready? You should write this down. It's very important. Listen, Potter. Words of wisdom: Lie low. Move fast. Bounce."

"Don't try to talk," Potter said. He knelt beside her, stroking her forehead with the same light scratchy touch he used on the cat. "Don't keep making jokes. You don't have to be funny any more. Just breathe slow. Relax."

Ramona flushed with temper and turned her head away. She could not relax. She was angry at Potter and at Hale and at Nora and at herself too, angry at everything that wasn't funny any more, angry at everyone who had let her down, down, so far down that when young Dr. Seton stood up from the chair by her bed it was as if he were stretching up toward the ceiling and she was sinking down through the floor, sinking faster and faster, and only the thought of her funeral made her stop: the last straw, she thought, and wouldn't you know it's the one straw I reach for. "Good girl," Dr. Seton said. "You're coming back to us."

Coming back? Of course she was coming back. How could she leave? There was so much to do. There was her life to understand and Hale to forgive and Nora to charm and Potter to cheer up. There was the novel. Where was the novel? Lying in a cardboard box somewhere, half-alive, unfinished, unformed. There were all the paintings, the little canvasses of pastel flower arrangements that Hale had called "stillborns" instead of "still lifes"—where were those? Facing the walls of the garage? She didn't want anyone seeing those paintings; she didn't want anyone reading the

journal she had kept in the first years after Hale's death, or playing the tapes she had made of her own voice, singing her own
songs to her own accompaniment on an old guitar. She was not
ready to be judged; her work wasn't done yet; it wasn't begun;
she didn't even know what her work was, for God's sake. "You
seem to have developed a faintly comedic point of view," her last
art teacher had told her. "Have you thought of doing cartoons?"
And he had dismissed her, turning his head, stifling his yawn;
he had dropped her, not bothering to watch the direction of his
kick, nor the way it hooked, nor the way she bounced, landing on
both flat, splayed, calloused feet before the editor of *The Beacon*
with a sheaf of drawings in one shaking hand. She had an occupation now. But was that her work?

"Those cartoons," she said, looking up into Nora's puzzled
face, "those cartoons were the hardest things I ever did and they
were never what I meant to do. I meant to do something quite
important and beautiful with my life, you see—something that
would astonish and delight and make you all proud."

"Still trying to talk," Nora said. "Half-alive and she's still trying
to talk. She's probably worried we're going to take her to the hospital. Well, don't worry, Mother. Dr. Seton said you might as well
stay here—although why you'd want to, I'm sure I don't know.
The house is a mess. It's filthy dirty and there's nothing in the
cupboards but cat food. I've sent the boys out to rake the yard
and the twins are making cocoa, and the baby, here's the baby,
the baby will keep you company while I discuss a few things with
Potter. And his cat."

After Nora left the room, the baby—a lanky, curt, fast-moving
four-year-old whose given name, Hope, was so unsuitable that
Ramona had never been able to use it—sidled close and peered
down into Ramona's face. "Ba?" said Ramona. It was all she
could say. "Ba? Ah wa pa."

"You. Want. Paper," the child repeated.

Ramona pointed toward her desk and Hope tugged at the

drawers until she found the drawing supplies. She gave Ramona one pad and one pencil and then, engrossed, she chose a thicker pad, a sharper pencil, for herself. Ramona struggled upright in her bed. For a long time she and Hope sat quietly, thinking. Then Hope ducked over her pad and started to draw a city. Ramona sat immobile. Even if I try, she thought, I won't succeed. I've never been able to organize my life; how dare I attempt to order my death? My funeral will be as disastrous a failure as my childhood, my marriage, my motherhood, my dotage. There will be the same dry coughs, the same scraping of chairs, the same artificial smiles I've seen all my life. I'll be put to rest like all the rest, and no one will ever know how much I had to give the world, or how I longed to give it. She glanced at her granddaughter's page. Hope had finished the city and was peopling it quickly with vampires and werewolves. It's enough to make the old blood stagger, Ramona thought. In the next room Potter and Nora were arguing. The smell of burnt cocoa drifted in from the kitchen. Ramona dozed. She dreamt Hale was in bed with her, asleep, his back turned to her, his weight warm, familiar, a great comfort, and she snuggled close, glad to have him there but afraid to wake him, afraid he might awaken saying some other woman's name.

When she opened her eyes it was dark in the house. She turned on her light, picked up the pad and pencil, and began to write. She had just had the one idea that would make her funeral the successful occasion she knew it could be. She knew the music, the foods, the psalm, the location. She wrote quickly, covering the page. She wrote until she had said everything she had to say, and then, content, she slipped the paper into the top drawer of her nightstand, lay back, and slept.

It was a restless, busy, broken sleep and it seemed to go on for a long long time. Dreams came and went, some of them nightmares, some so full of light she fought to stay in them. Nora nursed her with unsmiling vigilance, bathing and dressing her with swift cool hands. Nora's children took over the house, the boys mowing and trimming the lawn, the twins scrubbing the kitchen and bathrooms. Only the baby refused to pitch in. She sat at the desk beside Ramona's bed, covering page after page with intricate, disordered drawings. Potter too ignored Nora's orders; he locked himself in his room with the cat and tuned and retuned his violin. Ramona, listening to him play over the sound of the vacuum and the dishwasher, felt a robot was playing to her from the moon, so strange and cold and simple the music. Sometimes one of the children would drag a chair to the bureau and bring her the photos she asked for—portraits of Hale, his smile lean, gleaming, and enticing as ever, group pictures of old school friends standing arm in arm in sunny gardens, photos of her own children as children and herself as child, girl, and mother. When Ramona looked from these pictures to the face in the mirror Nora held up, she was pleased. She finally had a face she liked, sharp-boned, flushed, with enormous eyes—a stylish face, at last. She still could not speak clearly enough to be understood and when visitors told her she looked beautiful she could only tip her head, a queen accepting homage. There's a price tag to all this glamour, she wanted to tell them. Nothing big. A pay-later plan.

One afternoon Nora said, "Come on, Potter, help me for once. I want to carry Mother outside." The two of them linked hands and carried Ramona out into the garden, pausing to point out the bright banks of amaryllis and filling her bathrobe skirts with Japanese plums from the unpruned trees against the fence. Ramona looked into their pale distracted faces and said, "If you two would just like each other a little, I think I could go to heaven this second," and Nora said, "Still trying to talk? I wish she'd give up," and Potter said, "She can't give up; she's tough; she's not like us," and Nora said, "Speak for yourself; I don't slop around feeling sorry for myself all day," and Potter said, "That's because you don't know how to feel anything, period," and they carried

Ramona into the house and dropped her on the bed a little too roughly. That night Potter announced that since Nora had taken over so well, he was leaving. He was moving in with another unemployed musician who had a house by the sea. "I'd like to move to a house by the sea," Ramona said suddenly, and this first clear sentence after weeks of gibberish made Potter turn and Nora stop in mid-sentence. "I'd like to go there right now," Ramona said, "and never come back."

"Don't make me cry," Nora said sharply.

"She means she wants to die," Potter said.

"I know what she means," Nora said.

Potter picked up the cat and held it close to his heart, then laid it by Ramona's side like a bouquet of gray flowers. Nora came and stood beside them. "She's asleep again," Nora said. "No I'm not," Ramona said. "There's so much I've wanted to tell her," Nora said. "But I don't have her gift. I've never known how to put things."

"Well," Ramona answered, pleased, "I thank you and I think I finally have put things in place myself. I've taken care of everything at last." But nobody heard her. It was dark in her room and she was alone. Why look at me, she thought. I've gone and died with my big mouth wide open. She started to laugh and in that same second she started to spin, which made her laugh harder, for she knew that with this last breath she would fall, fall and break herself and bounce, bounce far beyond laughter forever.

The cat leapt off the bed and meowed for Potter, but Potter and Nora were sitting in the kitchen drinking coffee together and talking about a time when they had both thought their mother the gayest and most beautiful woman in the world, their father the richest and kindest man. The only one who heard the cat cry was the baby. The baby had slipped from her sleeping bag and was prowling through the house, searching for paper. She let herself into Ramona's room and went to the desk, but the drawers were depleted, all paper gone. In the top drawer of the nightstand by the bed she found some paper, one side ruined by her grandmother's writing, but the other side fresh and clean. She turned to the clean side and went to the window. Squatting in the moonlight with the cat winding around her, the baby drew the dream that had awakened her: a woman shooting off the edge of the planet, her lips like two red wings, flapping up toward the stars. She studied the drawing, shook her head, and tore it up.

Nora made the arrangements for the funeral. It didn't take long. She was pretty sure she knew what her mother wanted. She found a long purplish evening dress in the closet that looked brand new, and she gave it with instructions for matching nail polish to the cosmetician at The Evergreens. Her husband knew a minister who agreed to say a few words. After the service, which was mercifully short for such a warm afternoon, the mourners were asked to return to the house for refreshments. Most of the mourners seemed to be truly mourning; some of them were weeping. Ramona had been so brave, they said, so uncomplaining. She had kept her sense of humor to the end, they said, and they paused to study the display of drawings from *The Beacon*, their faces long and somber. The cat wandered companionably through the crowd. Potter sat in the garden with his violin, playing a song that everyone knew but no one could place. The notes seemed to come together in little rushes, rise, fade off, rush in again. "My Mother's Voice," Potter said, when the minister asked the name of the piece. The baby, swaying to the music, pushed open the door of Ramona's room, climbed the chair by the bureau, brought down all the photographs, and dropped them out the window, chanting "Bury Bury" as they fluttered down. She was about to throw a garnet necklace out too when her father caught her and gave her a spanking. Nora, handsome in black, was too busy to pay attention to her daughter's screams; she was telling everyone how childlike Ramona had seemed toward the end, how dependent and docile. "It was as if

I were the mother . . ." Nora began, but she was interrupted by a large lady name Junie Poole who hugged her impulsively, spilling gin down her dress. "This is the best funeral I've ever been to," Junie declared, and although the others turned away to hide their smiles, they all said later they agreed. It was a good funeral. The weather was fine and sunny, the house was welcoming. The only thing missing was Ramona herself.

The Brotherhood of Healing

BARBARA SUTTON

From *The Send-Away Girl* (2004)

"What they do is take a vein from your leg," Mrs. Rodgers had been told by the fat contractor always hanging around the counter of her sister's bakery. "They go in there and get the vein from your leg, stick it in your neck—the old switcheroo. Zip, zip, zip." With each "zip" the fat contractor used his index finger to make a zig, a zag, and then another zig motion, as if slashing his throat—as if slashing his throat would dispel any doubt as to his expertise on surgical repair of the carotid artery. "I seen it on that cable station," he told Mrs. Rodgers, "the whole thing—no commercials."

"Better check your own plumbing" is what Mrs. Rodgers thought at the time, but this was before her second minor stroke. "Three strokes and you're out," she figured after Stroke No. 2, sitting in the Catholic hospital's emergency room, subtracting numbers from one hundred so that the young guy pretending to be a doctor would believe she still had a brain. Intern, resident— what did it matter? The kid had acne; he needed a dermatologist or at least things in tubes from the drugstore. "You're a walking time bomb," he told her confidently when the nurse was out of earshot.

It was the primary care physician of Mrs. Rodgers's sister

who'd diagnosed the initial stroke of bad luck, prescribed another blood pressure medication, made a referral. Mrs. Rodgers let a month go by before acting on the referral. Her own doctor was dead, like most everyone she knew, so she had to rely on her sister. It wasn't just that Mrs. Rodgers did not like this man whom her sister had recently chosen as primary care physician from a long list of unpronounceable names the HMO sent out (the guy's first name was Lambert, followed by something else that read like a ransom note). It wasn't just that Mrs. Rodgers didn't like this Lambert character. It was much more philosophical. Some time ago she had decided that she wasn't afraid to die, and the disposition not only grew on her but began to feel like an accomplishment. Not being afraid to die, it seemed, was just about the only thing that Mrs. Rodgers had up on most people. Plus, there was something almost gluttonous about old people being afraid to die—a tenacity that seemed to tip the order of things, as if the more that old people clung so desperately to life the more that small children would run out in front of cars. Mrs. Rodgers didn't want to go back to the Lambert character. She didn't want to go back to the Catholic hospital named after some nun from Montreal. She especially didn't want to talk to residents with acne. But then not being afraid to die was not the same thing as wanting to die, so after the second stroke Mrs. Rodgers began to think seriously about a vein from her leg going into her neck—"zip, zip, zip," no commercials.

The vascular surgeon to whom Mrs. Rodgers was referred was called Dr. Jay. "He's the best," the Lambert character had said. "The best at what?" Mrs. Rodgers thought—"gin rummy, lawn darts?" His office was in a big to-do clinic attached to a hospital, and she dreaded taking the senior shuttle down there because the place had its own exit on the highway. That seemed to Mrs. Rodgers a bad sign. That seemed to indicate that this was "a place where they take you," which is how the oldsters were always phrasing it—to show, she imagined, that they now considered themselves cargo. Even though she herself had been described as real estate (i.e., "Christ, you're as big as a house!"), Mrs. Rodgers didn't want to think of herself as cargo.

The clinic's sections were color-coded, an orders-from-headquarters setup that made Mrs. Rodgers think of the lousy trip to Disney World she'd made with that Foster Grandparents outfit. In Disney World you checked your brain at the parking lot, where the sections are named after Disney characters, and for some reason Mrs. Rodgers expected the same logic to apply at the clinic. If the cardio unit is Goofy, neurology must be Donald Duck—Minnie Mouse for female problems (but then nowadays even men seemed to have female problems). Three-purple, four-yellow, two-blue. "That's my problem," thought Mrs. Rodgers. "I'm too blue. Send me to purple. Wheel me to yellow." All the people in the waiting room looked like they belonged there, as if waiting in a waiting room was why they were born. Most didn't seem to be reading anything, and some were in various stages of outpatient recuperation. All of them were big, so big that on those space-age white swivel chairs soldered to the floor they seemed to Mrs. Rodgers like livestock—livestock that were trained to be indoors, like the horses that wore party hats and braids on *The Ed Sullivan Show*. She wondered who those skimpy swivel chairs were made for anyway. Healthy Finnish people probably. Made in Finland for healthy Finns who never got sick.

The nurse doing the ultrasound rubbed the paddle on Mrs. Rodgers's neck like she was a barber giving a shave. "Leave the sideburns," Mrs. Rodgers said, although her comment was inaudible to the nurse squishing Mrs. Rodgers's mouth to the right side of her face. "OK there, hon?" the nurse asked. "Just a lil'bit more to go."

While her mouth was being squished to the right side of her face, Mrs. Rodgers saw a man walk past the doorway; then he came back and picked up and opened the folder in the trough on the hallway wall. "For the love of Mike" was all Mrs. Rodgers could think, because this is what her sister-in-law always said whenever she saw a person she didn't understand, a person who seemed out of his element. Dr. Jay was young; he had a shaved head and an expensive suit. "They must be trying to make this hospital something else," Mrs. Rodgers thought, "like the modern world with all those different types of coffee." On all the TV shows, the doctors were young and didn't have acne, but in real life most of the doctors she's seen have looked like the actor Karl Malden. Karl Malden up close—that's what a real doctor looked like to Mrs. Rodgers.

"Why do they shave off their hair these days?" Mrs. Rodgers thought. It's the ones going bald, so they figure no pretense. Maybe her poor husband should've done this, rather than grow his hair long at the sides and comb it over with Vitalis. Maybe her poor husband was born at the wrong time; he probably would've opted to shave his head if he were young today. Like he always said, "The only way out is through." But then he never said that. It must've been some other husband, some husband on TV, whom Mrs. Rodgers heard say that. If her husband had a hair motto, it was "The only way out is to comb it over with Vitalis." Before that it was Brill Cream—she could still hear the jingle as clear as day: "Brill Cream, a little dab'll do ya, for men who use their head and not their hair"—and after that it was Grecian Formula that came off on the pillowcase.

Here at the color-coded clinic was a man who obviously used his head and not his hair. "I'm Dr. Jay," he said in a soft, almost muffled voice, yet the tone suggested to Mrs. Rodgers "Hold your applause till halftime." Mrs. Rodgers sat in a chair; he sat on an examining gurney that was high, but he used a footstool so that he wouldn't look odd sitting on this too-high gurney. The way he moved the stool into place while he was listening to her describe her symptoms made Mrs. Rodgers think of a priest on an altar. When you watched most people do things with their hands, you thought of cooking shows, or of Martha Stewart making a patio lantern using a tin can, a hammer, and a really big nail. Or maybe you thought of Martha making Thanksgiving dinner for eighty-five people and sixteen dogs. But this guy made Mrs. Rodgers think of a priest. There was solemnity in his placement of the footstool, as if somebody were about to make a confession. To Mrs. Rodgers, the gesture said, "Pay no mind to this gesture (but only a fool would pay no mind to this gesture)." Dr. Jay positioned the footstool like he'd had some experience with swinging a canister of incense. He asked Mrs. Rodgers questions and nodded when she answered. She had the feeling he was being deceptively kind. She had the feeling there was a shtick—mainly on account of the ends not matching up, the incongruity of the modern world with all those different types of coffee and the footstool ritual that seemed older than the hills.

From the ultrasound, Dr. Jay estimated that Mrs. Rodgers's right carotid artery was 95 percent blocked with plaque, mucked up with the crud of life. All those doughnuts consumed around the age of thirteen, when she was skinny as a rail, her half-slip always slinking down ("A family without elastic," thought Mrs. Rodgers, "that was us"), and now everything that had ever been slinking down was catching up with her. The surgeon called the blockage "stenosis," which sounded to Mrs. Rodgers like a cramp you'd get by taking dictation. Also from the ultrasound, however, he saw that something was wrong with the blocked artery for a good four inches. He called the situation something that Mrs. Rodgers could not remember—she hoped it wasn't "diseased." Maybe he said it was "squirrelly." But then she doubted a man like him would ever use the word "squirrelly"; "squirrelly" was her word—really her dead brother's word. A car goes squirrelly on the racetrack if you don't accelerate before the curve.

Dr. Jay had told his secretary to make an appointment for Mrs. Rodgers to have an angiograph the next day. The secretary's name was LuEllen, but the way the surgeon said "LuEllen" gave Mrs. Rodgers the impression that he did not think of Lu-Ellen as a person but a job title. Mrs. Rodgers figured that if Lu-Ellen's husband got transferred to a ball-bearings plant in Georgia, Dr. Jay would have to advertise for another LuEllen. Because the doctor's LuEllen couldn't get the person on the phone to give Mrs. Rodgers an angiograph until next week, the surgeon grabbed the receiver and started negotiating. He wants it tomorrow, he wants it today, he wants it yesterday. "I'm admitting her," he kept saying. It seemed to Mrs. Rodgers to be some sort of game, hospital politics. From what she could tell, if she was admitted she could have the angiograph tomorrow. She half expected the surgeon to cover the mouthpiece and say, "Pretend you're sick—here, cough into the phone."

Two or so hours later she called her sister to say, "They've finally admitted me."

"I didn't even know you were waiting to be a member," her sister replied.

"Just get down here and bring me my denture cup."

Mrs. Rodgers, her sister, and her sister-in-law all lost their husbands at the same time—stomach cancer, heart attack, bridge freezing before road surface. "Bad things happen in threes" is what everyone said, as if this was the right answer that you said on TV and won a million bucks. But there they were, three medium-old sadsacks in black—"I'll weep at your wake if you weep at mine." At least Mrs. Rodgers's sister and sister-in-law had children—grown children with children of their own. And her sister had the bakery and her sister-in-law had something going on in Florida—a doughnut shop on a golf course, maybe some beachfront swampland with a gambling parlor—something anyway; they didn't talk much these days. Mrs. Rodgers had had none of these things—no commercial property and faulty fallopian tubes. She and her poor husband tried and tried to have babies until he called a time-out for good. Of course this was way before sticking test tubes in the freezer and way before there were ads for Viagra behind home plate at Yankee Stadium.

Even though it seemed to Mrs. Rodgers that she was only in the hospital because of hospital politics, the nurses kept calling her "sweetheart," like she was an old lady who needed to be spoon-fed sugar-free custard. Just a few months ago Mrs. Rodgers had visited just such an old lady at the Catholic hospital—someone who, on top of everything else wrong with her, needed her cataracts removed so that she'd be able to describe the color of her urine to one doctor after another. Mrs. Rodgers wanted to tell the nurses, "Call me that again and I'll sock ya in the kisser," but she decided instead to call them "sweetheart" right back, even though most of them didn't get the drift, didn't get that she was being a wiseguy. "How's thaaat, swee'heaaart," one screamed while rigging her up to a heart monitor that she probably didn't need, "aw-wright?" Mrs. Rodgers figured that the correct response was something like "Yes, dear, that's just fine." Instead she shouted, "Thaaat's aw-wright, swee'heaaart!"

"These nurses," Mrs. Rodgers thought, "how do they know what to wear?" It's like when they took away uniforms at the Catholic schools—total chaos. Now all the kids have their pants falling down. She made the mistake of calling one such kid to task on this issue in the drugstore parking lot. "Hey, kid, haven't you ever heard of a belt?" "Hey, grandma, haven't you ever heard of my fist?" At least Mrs. Rodgers could be relatively certain that the nurses weren't going to mention their fists to her. They all wore flowered blouses like they were a team of Japanese flag-twirling girls. Or was it the Chinese who were always twirling flags? "You can't lump together all slanty-eyed people anymore" Mrs. Rodgers had been told by some droopy-eyed Seventh-day Adventist who looked a lot like her dead brother-in-law. This was on a religion/shopping station way up there where she hardly ever went, way up where you had to pay or get the V-chip for the kids of the kids you never had.

The next day Mrs. Rodgers had the angiograph, a process in which they put dye in your veins and take X-rays. After the procedure she had to lie flat on her back for six hours—lie flat with weights on her stomach, like she was a fish drying in the sun. She was waiting for the six hours to be up, but she was also waiting word from the surgeon. She assumed that he wanted to operate, but she didn't know when. He needed to look at her big picture; he needed to "confer" with his "colleagues"; then he'd decide what to do about her squirrelly artery.

Mrs. Rodgers's sister and her sister's two grandsons kept her company some of the time she spent on her back. The boys kept running off, going down to the vending machines.

"You shouldn't keep giving them dollars," Mrs. Rodgers told her sister.

"That's what you have to do with kids these days—buy them off."

"I guess I'm lucky my days are numbered."

"No they're not," her sister said, not looking up from the brochure she was reading—*Carotid Endarterectomy and You*. "Listen to this: says you're supposed to 'refrain from sexual intercourse' for one week after you're discharged."

"So what do they expect me to do instead?"

"Have regular bowel movements."

"How do they do it?" Mrs. Rodgers asked her sister.

"Prune juice."

"I mean how do they keep cutting people open?" Mrs. Rodgers continued. "They must make mistakes. On some days they must make mistakes."

"Maybe nowadays they don't make mistakes."

"How can they never make mistakes?"

"They must get themselves all relaxed. Maybe they listen to classical music while they wash their hands."

"Classical music?"

"Look at it this way," Mrs. Rodgers's sister advised. "You've never listened to classical music, and you've made all kinds of mistakes."

Mrs. Rodgers's sister had intended to be there when the doctor showed up to talk turkey, but she and the bought-off grandsons got tired of waiting. "Just don't take anything with bad odds," she advised, "and find out what you're supposed to do while refraining from the intercourse."

At half-past ten Dr. Jay appeared in Mrs. Rodgers's room; he was followed by a little crew—boy-girl-boy-girl. More of the residents—people who lived at the hospital, too tired to read a thermometer let alone sew an arm back on or find themselves a tube of acne medication. She wasn't surprised at the residents, but she did have to blink a few times at what the surgeon was wearing with his surgical getup—a gold chain. The doctor wore a braided gold chain like he was an NBA player or a drug dealer. This is what Mrs. Rodgers heard Charles Grodin once say about men who wear gold chains, as a joke, to a couple of basketball players wearing gold chains. Or maybe the lily-white Dr. Jay was compensating for the hospital's having no black surgeons like they have on all the TV shows. That's what the protesters on TV would've called the Dr. Jay types in the sixties—"lily-white," because even though the sixties were gone and would never come back, he was that type. And this was the type of hospital where people—the livestock people sitting on the swivel chairs made for the thin and healthy Finns—would have conniptions about a black doctor. Still, in this day and age, with the hundred-kinds-of-coffee mentality going full throttle, Mrs. Rodgers figured that you could sneak in a doctor with a shaved head and a gold chain, but he sure as hell had to be as white as Dr. Jay's lab coat.

"We got some good pictures," Dr. Jay told Mrs. Rodgers, who was now fixated on the lab coat because he had his "Dr. Jay" embroidered in perfect cursive script. "How like him," she thought, "perfect cursive script." She wondered how she could think "how like him" without even knowing him, but when she looked at the blue embroidery again she swore she saw "Dr. J." Her poor husband used to talk about Dr. J. Her poor husband liked to watch the basketball games on television. Her poor husband would've had conniptions if they made him see a black doctor with a gold chain.

Dr. Jay told Mrs. Rodgers that she could either have the surgery to repair her carotid artery tomorrow or go home on a blood thinner. He gave her the odds—35 percent chance of a stroke on the blood thinner, with no surgery; pretty much smooth sailing with the surgery, but a 10 percent chance of a stroke during the operation. The hitch with the surgery was that Dr. Jay had to replace the squirrelly artery with an artificial artery or else graft a vein from Mrs. Rodgers's leg.

"So the fat guy was right," Mrs. Rodgers mumbled to herself.

"What?" Dr. Jay said.

"What the fat guy said," she repeated loudly.

"What guy?" he said, irritated, wiping his palm over his bald head. Then he sighed and told Mrs. Rodgers that she should think about it and decide in the morning.

"I don't want to think about it," Mrs. Rodgers said. "My sister told me not to take anything with bad odds. So I'm going with the surgery behind Door No. 2."

"Ya wanna watch your soaps, swee'heaaart?" a nurse asked Mrs. Rodgers two hours before her scheduled surgery. "They're not my soaps," Mrs. Rodgers thought. And what was this "soaps" business anyway? Mrs. Rodgers's sister called them her "programs." Her sister watched her programs on a thirteen-inch set in the kitchen at the bakery, two hours' worth. According to Mrs. Rodgers's sister, Procter and Gamble was nowadays keen on sponsoring murders, homosexual relations, and terrorists' bombs going off during what people used to call the ironing board hour. Mrs. Rodgers had watched only one such "program" in all her life, *The Doctors*, which the announcer would always describe as "dedicated to the brotherhood of healing." All of the doctors in that show were white, some even lily-white; all had good manners and wore long gowns for surgery, things that looked like the aprons that meat cutters wear, but there was never any blood. Everything these doctors wore in surgery looked spanking clean and just-starched, which, Mrs. Rodgers guessed, made you think of the ironing you were supposed to be doing. There was one "lady doctor," the beautiful wife of a surgeon who was graying at the temples, but you never saw her doing any doctoring. She just cried a lot about whatever candy striper her husband was running around with. In those days, the healing racket really was a brotherhood.

If there still was a brotherhood of healing, Mrs. Rodgers thought, it was probably still a racket—healing for dollars, sort of like bowling for dollars. Healing for dollars to golf with. Even with the HMO mess, Mrs. Rodgers knew that surgeons made a lot of money. *Ka-ching*—there's the addition to the kids' bedroom. *Ka-ching*—there's the six-car garage. "Who knows what they spend their money on nowadays?" Mrs. Rodgers thought. "Sex-change operations for their boyfriends in Singapore." She knew about these things; she watched Montel every day—a black man with a shaved head. One time at her sister's bakery she'd heard the fat contractor and another fat man discussing whether Montel was a homosexual on account of his shaved head. "Them bald faggots make my skin crawl," the contractor had said, to which the other fat guy replied, "Lots of 'em have big dough though." Someone else in the bakery had noted that Montel had a wife and multiple sclerosis, but the fat guys insisted that a bald faggot was a bald faggot.

Some gal who wasn't quite a nurse—a junior nurse—came in and said, "I'm going to have to shave your groin." Mrs. Rodgers thought it sounded like something a cop would say when he caught you speeding. "I'm going to have to ask you to step outside the car, ma'am, so that I can shave your groin." Soon after that, some guy who wasn't quite a doctor—a resident, or maybe a doctor who just wasn't Dr. Jay—came in and said that Dr. Jay would make the incision high on Mrs. Rodgers's leg so that the scar wouldn't show when she wore shorts. She hadn't worn shorts in thirty years. She can remember the last pair of shorts she bought, seersucker shorts at Sears. Mrs. Rodgers imagined that Dr. Jay would be appalled at this pair of size sixteen shorts— that was a good word, she thought, "appalled." He was probably appalled at a lot of things.

Mrs. Rodgers's sister and sister-in-law would certainly have been appalled at Dr. Jay's gold chain. He had it on again with his blue outfit when she was wheeled into the operating room. He told her things about the procedure that she didn't understand; he spoke slowly while nodding: "First, we're going to *blah-blah-blah*, 'kay? Then we're going to *blah-blah-blah*, 'kay? Then we're going to *blah-blah-blah*, 'kay?" Mrs. Rodgers felt like he was calling her Kay. "I'm not Kay," she wanted to say, "and I'm not 'kay." Then someone wheeled her back out into the hall because there was a delay with the anesthesiologist. "Delay-shlemay," she thought. He was probably stuck at the end of a long line of cars in the Dunkin Donuts drive-through.

It seemed to Mrs. Rodgers a long time that she and the gurney were abandoned in the hall. It was very quiet; all you could hear were the elevator bells. From her experience with her husband dying, she knew about "the elevator law," that people weren't allowed to ask doctors questions about patients when the doctors were held captive in the elevator. This is why doctors usually took the stairs. "It's good that you doctors take the stairs," she had said to her husband's doctor on the day her husband died. "That means you'll live longer." "Longer than what?" her husband's doctor replied. He was Pakistani; he liked riddles. Or so he said. "What part of India are you from?" Mrs. Rodgers had asked when she met him, to be friendly. "I'm not from India," he said. "I'm from Pakistan." Mrs. Rodgers's husband said with a laugh,

"What's the difference?" He was in a funny mood that day, probably because he'd just been told he was dying by the minute. The doctor looked at Mrs. Rodgers, not at her husband. He was sitting on a stool; he had leaned back. The nametag on his lab coat was upside down. "What's the difference?" he repeated. "I'll tell you the difference, Mrs. Rodgers. Indians like jokes; Pakistanis like riddles. That's the difference."

If the anesthesiologist is Indian, Mrs. Rodgers thought, maybe she should tell him a joke. She tried to think of a good joke to tell the Indian anesthesiologist who'd been detained at the Dunkin Donuts drive-through, but she also wanted to make sure that he didn't forget to give her the full dose of anesthesia. She knew a joke about a man who is rejected by the woman he is courting. He tells her, "It's just too much for me to bear that you don't love me, so I'm going away, far, far away, to forget—to forget you, to forget everything." And the woman replies, "Well, just don't forget to go away." Mrs. Rodgers wasn't sure if this was really a joke, but it might remind the anesthesiologist not to forget to give her the full dose of anesthesia.

Mrs. Rodgers tried to kill time by thinking up the top ten reasons why Dr. Jay would wear a gold chain with his surgical getup. Reason No. 10: He couldn't wear a wedding ring when he did surgery, so the gold chain was a proxy for the wedding band. Dr. Jay wore a gold chain because he was a devoted husband. Reason No. 9: The gold chain was given to Dr. Jay by a grateful patient whose life Dr. Jay had saved by grafting some veins onto some arteries. From that day forward, Dr. Jay always wore the chain during surgery to remind himself of his duty to save lives. Reason No. 8: Dr. Jay had left on the gold chain once by mistake when he was called in to perform a difficult emergency operation at ten o'clock on a Saturday night, and because this emergency operation was miraculously successful, Dr. Jay always wore the gold chain when he operated, as a lucky charm. Mrs. Rodgers didn't like this reason because it meant that Dr.

Jay was wearing the gold chain in real life, which somehow seemed worse than his wearing it with his surgical getup. What was he doing wearing the gold chain in real life? Did they have to go fetch him off the disco floor? Mrs. Rodgers skipped ahead to Reason No. 1: Dr. Jay had operated on an NBA player from Philadelphia who insisted on wearing his gold chain during the highly risky surgery because this chain had brought the man so much luck on the court. During the operation the man died; it was a national tragedy. The man's fiancée later threw the gold chain at Dr. Jay, shouting, "You killed him!" From that day forward, Dr. Jay always wore the chain during surgery to remind himself that he was not God, that he sometimes made mistakes, that a lot of people died all the time, that life is sad.

"You got any more jokes?" Dr. Jay was saying to Mrs. Rodgers. The surgery was past—it was a success, because she wasn't dead. "You were telling us jokes before the operation." Dr. Jay was leaning over Mrs. Rodgers. This time she did not focus on the gold chain; instead she was trying to get a look at his face. He really did look lily-white, like a blanched almond. If he was the blood man, she thought, where the heck was his own blood? He even looked a little sick himself, like he was having chemotherapy. He looked young, too—too young to have cut into her squirrelly blood vessel, even younger than the resident with the acne. He looked like a kid on a St. Jude's poster, a chemotherapy kid who had no hope. She couldn't see that well, but the skin around his mouth looked funny, like he'd broken out in a rash, a purple rash. It had a definite shape, this rash, and then she realized it was from wearing the surgical mask. His face, despite the rash, felt intensely familiar to her. "I know too much about him already," she thought, trying to resist the way that fear can make us resort to pretend affection, and for some reason she told him, "I'm not afraid to die."

"You're not going to die."

"I mean I'm not afraid of it, when it happens."

"You're doing just fine, 'kay?" he said, holding her hand. She knew he was holding her hand because she had a sensation of something soft but cold, very far away.

"It smells like iodine in here," Mrs. Rodgers's sister said in the ICU after Mrs. Rodgers was wheeled in from recovery. "You're lucky you're half-asleep, or you'd be sick to your stomach."

"It hurts in different parts," Mrs. Rodgers told her sister. "That must mean the parts are working."

"Or that they're not working."

"I just saw Kojak," her sister whispered conspiratorially. "He shook my hand."

"Maybe he's running for office."

"Him? What would he have to say to people?"

"I dunno," Mrs. Rodgers muttered. "'Who loves ya, baby?'" She thought for a moment, feeling too groggy to even swallow. "He told me I wasn't going to die."

"I guess that means he really does know everything."

"He's not God," Mrs. Rodgers said bluntly, even though her voice was hoarse. "He makes mistakes."

"What do you mean he's not God?" her sister replied with hushed alarm. "How can you rain on my parade like this?"

Mrs. Rodgers scrolled through all the stars and bit players she remembered from heaven; she thought of Dr. Jay reminding her of a priest in his suit; she thought of an Oprah show in which a woman with big frizzy hair, a woman who looked like she'd just come back from a few rounds of electroshock therapy, babbled on about angels.

"He's an emissary," Mrs. Rodgers told her sister, because this is what the frizzy-haired woman had told Oprah when Oprah asked what, exactly, is the point of an angel: "They are emissaries," the woman had said, making her eyes bug out toward Oprah. "Sometimes they arrive on the scene wearing suits; sometimes they wear overalls." Mrs. Rodgers could feel that now it was her sister who was holding her hand, and she felt obliged to clarify, "But not the kind in the overalls."

Because Mrs. Rodgers's blood pressure would not stabilize, she was kept in the ICU overnight. She could administer morphine to herself by squeezing the button on the cord taped to her left hand—cheap fun, she thought. Whenever she squeezed for the morphine, she was able to isolate one sound from the ICU's beeps, blips, and alarms. Sometimes it was a voice. She heard someone say that all the fish in the pond were dead. It was a child's voice, probably someone's bought-off grandson; she'd heard this as the child was being ushered out of the ICU; she heard a nurse say that no one under eighteen was allowed. "I was just tellin' him that all the fish'er dead," the boy argued. "The fish'er just floatin' there." He was just a boy, but already he had the voice of what he would become—a big guy who ran a business using his truck, probably a tree and stump removal service, or a fat contractor who'd sit for hours at the counter of a bakery eating apple fritters and French crullers. Probably this kid's name was Bob, the soon-to-be-famous Bob of Bob's Tree and Stump Removal Service.

She didn't even know that the hospital had a pond. Apparently the senior shuttle had strategically avoided the scenic route of dead fish just floatin' there. She kept thinking about her sister's grandsons running down to the vending machines with their dollars; she thought how nice it would be to be a kid, to run down to everything, even though you never wore a belt and your pants were falling down to your knees. She pictured Dr. Jay in his surgery duds and gold chain running down to some vending machine. He must've been someone's little boy once, even though now he was either a devoted husband and pillar of the community or else a bald faggot rolling in the dough. That thought struck Mrs. Rodgers with great heft: every vascular surgeon was once someone's little boy—or little girl. Someone's little fussbudget, someone's little widget, someone's little who's-it.

Mrs. Rodgers was sent to a room on the ninth floor so that she had a good view of the hospital's pond. Every morning when he made the rounds in his expensive suits, Dr. Jay called Mrs. Rodgers "Kay": "We're going to start you on one hundred milligrams of Atenolol, 'kay?" It seemed to Mrs. Rodgers like "Kay" was his secret name for her, and she found that she didn't even mind it. He also told her she was doing "fantastic." All of his terms of praise seemed to have at least three syllables. It struck Mrs. Rodgers that nowhere else in the world could she be praised three syllables at a time for just lying there as her cells grew back together like mold grew on cheese. And the more Dr. Jay praised her for just lying there like a moldy piece of cheese, the more ashamed Mrs. Rodgers became of her life in relation to his.

The nurses in their flowered blouses had lots to say about Dr. Jay—he was a "saint," a "wonderful saint" no less (as opposed, she imagined, to the un-wonderful kinds that nobody bothered to put on the Mass cards); he worked all the time, like a resident himself; he always talked to the families, always returned their calls; he was often in on the weekends in his jeans and sweatshirt. Mrs. Rodgers became ashamed of her life in relation to Dr. Jay's because she knew quite well that her life was a mistake, what doctors nowadays were not supposed to make. No, it wasn't really that. Not a mistake, because that would imply she at least attempted something else. Her life was more like a firecracker that didn't go off. That resident with the acne didn't know diddly-squat. She wasn't a walking time bomb; she was a dud firecracker. "Who is it that makes the firecrackers," Mrs. Rodgers asked herself, "the Chinese or the Japanese?" But then she remembered the warning that "You can't lump together all slanty-eyed people anymore." Nowadays firecrackers were probably made by Seventh-day Adventists in St. Louis. Wherever they were made, Mrs. Rodgers was sure that she was an old one that didn't go off, because if a firecracker never goes off, you can't tell what it was supposed to look like—its shape or its colors, whether it would fan out like a giant dandelion tuft or give off a boom like a speedway light hit by a shotgun bullet. A firecracker that doesn't go off was probably less than something, less than even a tree falling in the woods.

Every time Dr. Jay came near her, Mrs. Rodgers wanted her look to convey, "I am going to try to be a better, stronger person from now on. I'm really going to try to be Kay for you, Dr. Jay." She knew that if her poor husband had heard a spoken version of this thought, he would've waved his hand in front of his face and said, "That don't mean shit." Like a lot of people in these parts, Mrs. Rodgers's poor husband didn't worry about using the right verbs. She imagined Dr. Jay being appalled at the way her poor husband didn't match up his verbs. She also wondered why her husband always came out of her mouth as "poor." He wasn't financially poor. He wasn't much of a success in life, and he had the hair issue to contend with, but he wasn't any worse off than most men she knew. He would criticize people he saw on TV; he hated most Democrats. In what way was her husband poor—just because he was dead?

And what did Mrs. Rodgers really know about Dr. Jay? He was a slow talker, a fast thinker, a sharp dresser. He had no hair and sensitive skin. But like her poor dead husband or somebody else's poor dead husband always said, "Ya never do know." How could she have known that one day he'd stop at the doorway of her room, read from her chart, and then shout at her from across the room? Coldly, abruptly, he asked her, "How'd you like to go home today, right now?" He seemed to be dismissing her forever from his life, from any proximity to his profession of healing, by reciting the script of the three blood pressure medications she would take. Something happened—she was suddenly poison, a leper. She was suddenly no longer his Kay. "He wants me out of his hair," Mrs. Rodgers thought, almost bitterly, "even though he doesn't have any hair." She kept thinking of all the things he wasn't saying. *Who loves ya, baby? Who loves ya, sweetheart? Not me, Kay. Not me, 'kay? And by the way, Kay ... thank YOU for shopping at Sears.*

He was gone, gone for good it seemed, when Mrs. Rodgers felt imperiled, when she thought, "Don't leave me, Dr. Jay!" She had not thought about the time when he would not be around. No one's being around or not being around has mattered to her in years. She had not known there were things she wanted out of him. For instance, she wanted him to tell her husband's doctor that she wished her husband never said "What's the difference?" between an Indian and a Pakistani doctor. She had wanted Dr. Jay to find this doctor and tell this doctor that it was because her husband didn't have children; it was because he didn't have hair; it was because he didn't have good odds. She wanted Dr. Jay to tell the doctor that it wasn't her fault, that she wished her husband were another way. She had thought that Dr. Jay truly was an emissary; she was sure that if Dr. Jay had said this to the Pakistani doctor, the doctor would believe it was true, because both this doctor who liked riddles and this doctor with the shaved head were dedicated to the brotherhood of healing.

By coincidence, the Pakistani doctor was present when Mrs. Rodgers's husband died. Mrs. Rodgers thinks of it as a coincidence because everyone says that you can tell when a doctor's patient is going to die because the doctor is never around—off skiing in the Alps, tagging turtles in Costa Rica, murdering his mistress in Barbados. The doctor had stopped in between operations he was performing that day. He took Mrs. Rodgers's right hand and held it to his forehead, like he wanted her to feel for a temperature. He held her hand there for what seemed like a long time. When he released it, he said, "This is so I never forget sadness." "Did he still never forget people's sadness?" Mrs. Rodgers wondered. She also wondered what her hand had felt like when he held it to his forehead, because she wasn't at all sad in the several minutes after her husband died. She wondered if the doctor was looking for sadness but found something else. She remembered thinking, at this very dramatic moment, that the doctor must've kept his nametag upside down because he figured "Why bother?" Why even bother with people who don't care about the difference between an Indian and Pakistani doctor? She was sixty-two then but looked much older. Maybe everything about her said to him "sadness." This dead man was all that Mrs. Rodgers had in common with the Pakistani doctor, and now she would never see him again. This had seemed to her the saddest thing. "Do you really never forget?" she longed to ask him, again and again and again.

Mrs. Rodgers had to wait for her sister to come and claim her, and her sister wouldn't be there till well past five, till her sister had finished watching her programs. "What is it we're all chomping at the bit to get back to anyway?" Mrs. Rodgers asked herself. "Do we really want to be out there with the dead fish?" No, she thought. Most people would rather stay here; they'd rather be called "swee'heaaart" by nurses in flowered blouses. She walked over to the window because she realized she was lucky to have had such a pretty view for a full week. The thought of dead fish reminded her of her poor husband, of meeting her poor husband at a tavern, just like in the song that goes "there's a tavern in the town," only the song they were playing when she met her husband was "Little Brown Jug." When she met her poor husband at this tavern in the town, when he was still a stranger to her, she should have asked him, first off, "Why do you think it's ok to marry someone you won't care to ever know?" It struck her that perhaps her husband always came out of her mouth as "poor" because she knew the truth: he was not a man to be loved. She was too stupid at that tavern in the town to have said no to anything; there was nothing she could've done to change her life, to make it a working firecracker. She started to sing that song they were playing: *My wife and I live all alone in a little log hut we call our own.* If you live for forty-odd years all alone in a little log hut, why is it surprising that you're not afraid to die? Maybe living is what you were afraid of. Mrs. Rodgers looked down at the pond with its own little marsh, a special feature of this world unto itself, this world with its own exit on the highway. *Ha ha ha, you and me, little brown jug, don't I love thee! Ha ha ha, you and me.* "I love thee," thought Mrs. Rodgers. Now that was certainly a good joke to tell a doctor.

Passerby

JACQUELIN GORMAN

From *The Viewing Room* (2013)

Some people view life as a gift, and some people view life as an entitlement. But Ellie knew she was different. She viewed life as a short-term bridge loan, and she was always behind on the payments. She was aware that at any moment the collateral could be repossessed. When anything bad happened to her, she asked not *why me* but *why not me*. She wondered if this was the beginning of the end that she had expected even earlier. She knew firsthand that sight is an anticipatory sense, its greatest value resting in the warning of danger coming straight toward her. She knew this because she had lost her vision for an extended period of time, enough time to live the rest of her life, once recovered, with one foot in the blind world and one foot in the sighted world, teetering between, never sure where both feet would end up, like a person who can't swim must feel stepping down from a dock into a boat, unsteady, rocking back and forth, legs growing wider apart, until finally a choice must be made.

Ellie had fallen many times before, but she knew that this was the last time. It was dark ahead, but she walked toward it anyway, feeling certain that a light would emerge to guide her steps, motion-detector lights like the ones she had installed around her house. She took the stairway that she thought was leading

to a parking garage, pleased that she would get to her car before the other people leaving the theater, who were still waiting
for elevators. She took that first air-step and knew immediately.
There were no stairs, and there would be no soft landing. Here it
was, the abrupt ending, and she relaxed into the fall, grateful to
be reclaimed at last.

She was not afraid of death. She knew many people said that
they were not afraid of death, just of suffering beforehand, but
in her former days as a hospice nurse she had seen how people
clung to life, wracked with ferocious, unrelenting pain, confess-
ing in a whisper, *I am so afraid, so afraid.* But her worst suffering had already happened, when Mandy, her only child, died,
taking the poisonous sting out of her own death. The other
mothers in her bereavement group had said the nights would be
the hardest, but that was not true. She welcomed the setting of
the sun, making her feel as if it were practically normal to crawl
back into the waiting, unmade bed. No, it was the mornings that
were excruciating, waking up into one more day without her
daughter, needing every bit of emotional strength to move her
eyelids open.

"Eleanor, can you hear me. Can you tell me where you are?
Eleanor! Eleanor!"

A strong male voice of increasing urgency and brisk impatience. This man's voice was entirely different from the two voices
she had heard a few minutes before. After she fell, a husky older
voice, not asking questions, but talking to her, "Oh, my, you've
done it now. Poor thing, you can't get up from this," and then
later more questions, a young, breathless voice, "Where does it
hurt, squeeze my hand if you can hear me and show me where
it hurts. Blink if you understand me." And she had tried to blink
but her body, every piece of her body, was disconnected from her
mind. And now this voice, a doctor's voice, and she knew that
this man was highly educated and was irritated with her, or with
the nurses around her.

Now she wanted to open her eyes and answer the orientation questions, the who, what, where, and when of the moment, oriented to person, situation, place, and time, but she had nothing left. She had asked these questions of people herself, trying to gauge the flimsiness of their grasp upon the solid world. She wanted to answer him because she was not in any kind of pain or discomfort and she wanted to reassure the voice that everything was all right. And she wanted to tell him to call her Ellie, not the formal name on her driver's license.

"Unresponsive," he said, in a quieter, resigned voice, to someone who was taking notes. "Severe head trauma, probable skull fracture, massive bleeding from lacerations, need a head and neck CT stat if she makes it that long."

Well, none of that sounded very encouraging. But the good news was that she must be breathing or they would be forcing a tube down her throat. The brutality of the emergency room had always disturbed her, and she had left instructions about what procedures she would allow at the end to prolong her life. Damn few, actually. But the directive was locked in her glove compartment. Did she drive here? She could not remember a car or an ambulance. No, she flew here! And she was getting ready to fly again, up through the ceiling, up past the clouds, flying away, far away from the voice, drifting into a deep silence that swaddled her, arms and legs folding in, now certain that she never had to move by herself again. It would all happen without her trying. And she was too exhausted from all the trying to turn back, anyway.

Henrietta had been dreading this moment ever since she took the hospital chaplaincy position. She had hoped it would never happen. But now that moment was here. She was paged to the viewing room and the dead patient was not a stranger but someone she knew and loved.

She had reviewed the ER notes over and over, sobbing at her

computer in the Spiritual Care Office. She wished someone else could read it with her and help her understand how this had happened. But she was the only chaplain on call. Apparently, Ellie had fallen from a forty-foot height and landed crumpled against the partial concrete wall of the construction site, a new parking structure for the theater. Her head had been pierced— oh, God, pierced—by a rebar. And worst of all, she did not die right away. Poor Ellie, poor dear, sweet Ellie. Why would she be walking there, in the dark, so late and alone? Was her MS in relapse, and was she walking with a cane and lost her balance? But that would not explain why the paramedics had told the doctor that she must have torn down the thick yellow caution tape and then carefully squeezed herself through the opening between the locked fence gates to tumble to her death.

Unless this was what Ellie wanted.

They had talked about suicide, more than once, actually. Ellie had asked Henrietta if she had ever contemplated taking her own life. Henrietta had answered quickly, and now she realized probably too smugly, "I would never give back the gift," sounding as if she believed that suicide was an act of weakness, a fatal character flaw, an unforgivable failure to appreciate life. Ellie had not seemed offended by the remark, but it had effectively ended the conversation until later, until necessity demanded that they revisit the subject in the most painfully direct way.

It was Halloween night, almost a month ago, and Henrietta had attended a mothers' bereavement group, one that Ellie had been leading for years. A disturbed woman had pulled out a gun and threatened to kill herself. Henrietta, a practiced crisis interventionist, had managed to call for help just in time. She was concerned about what Ellie had said to her later.

But that was not what bothered Henrietta the most about that night, now that she looked back on it through the lens of this terrible possibility. It was not the things Ellie did not do or say that night but what she did say to Henrietta later, after Rachel had been put on psychiatric hold, after the rest of the group had been counseled and escorted home. She had said that if she had been alone in the room with Rachel, with no witnesses, she doubted she would have stopped her. And she might have asked her to kill her first.

How louder a cry for help could there be than that? Yet Henrietta had let that statement sit there between them without comment, mistakenly thinking that if she silently listened to her friend's true feelings, she would never act upon them once they were let out into the night air. That it would all disappear like a harmless ghost, as if there had ever been such a thing. Ghosts always haunt somebody for a reason, usually to tell them something important. Well, Henrietta had missed that message.

But so many people loved Ellie. Didn't she know that? All those mothers who had leaned on her strength, all those dying hospice patients who borrowed her deep faith, desperate people who counted on her to see them through the darkest time of their lives. And she had done that so well that one of them had called to ask for a viewing at two o'clock in the morning, only a few hours after Ellie's death. The nurses who prepared Ellie's body had also known her and had taken greater care with her, wrapping her in layers of freshly laundered and warmly dry hospital gowns, as if she could still catch a chill.

Henrietta stood by the gurney in the viewing room and hesitated for a moment before sliding her hands into the black vinyl bag that covered Ellie from the neck down and pressing a rosary into the folds of cloth, close to where she thought Ellie's hands would be. She was careful not to touch her skin even though she wanted to change the bandage on the left side of her head, which was no longer bleeding but still had yellow antiseptic stains weeping through. Ellie was a coroner's case since the accident was still under investigation, and nobody could touch the body directly until the Medical Examiner's officials came. Were they even thinking homicide now? Could it be true that somebody had pushed her, that anybody would want to kill her?

There was a knock at the door that made Henrietta jump. She looked up to see a tall, elderly man walk through the door. He was African American, quite thin, wearing a thick down coat that was caked with mud at the edges. He stood at the back of the room, and Henrietta went over to him.

"Do you want to come closer to say good-bye?"

He shook his head and backed away a few steps but did not turn around to leave. He was shaking as if he were scared she was going to rise up and go after him. He looked at the body from a safe distance. Then he reached up and took the black wool cap off of his head and held it to his chest, closing his eyes.

"Would you like to pray with me?" Henrietta asked.

He blinked at her and then narrowed his eyes to inspect her hospital ID badge.

"No, thanks. I just came to pay my respects is all."

He put his hat back on and turned to leave, but Henrietta called out to him.

"Did you know Ellie long?"

She avoided asking the more obvious and interesting question about how he knew Ellie. And then she remembered that Ellie volunteered at a homeless shelter several afternoons a week. This must be one of her—clients? No, she called them something else. Guests. As if they were guests in her own home and she were hostess for parties every day.

"No, I never met her," he said quietly. "Not until tonight."

"You saw her fall," Henrietta said.

She knew it. She could tell by his expression that he had seen Ellie die. She knew exactly how that kind of guilt wore on a face. She had seen it her first night as a chaplain, in this room, when a father came to see his infant son, whom he had shaken and thrown against a wall.

"Yes, and I'm so sorry," he said, looking at her with tears in his eyes, confirming her fears.

She knew he was about to confess, and she wanted to stop him, to make him wait until somebody else, anybody else but a minister, came into the room to hear him out. There were rules about this kind of conversation. The boundaries were set clearly in the case law. Confessions of a crime already committed are protected by priest-penitent privilege. Only a clear intention of causing harm in the future waived the privilege.

But what about God's law? Why wasn't she held to that law, the law she had promised to obey above all others? Why couldn't she hold this murderer accountable, at least here, at least now, when she could drag him over there and make him look closely at the damage? She would start by showing him the thick dried blood that streaked and flattened Ellie's silver hair against her cheeks, hideous dark-red earmuffs.

"What did you do?"

At least she could hear the details, hope that it was fast and he had not hurt Ellie before he pushed her.

"I took down the tape. Like I do every night. It's where I keep my roll. I slide down into there, and I get some sleep where nobody can bother me. I take the tape off, but then I always put it back up before the workers come back. I never thought anybody would come there at night. I never told nobody where I keep my roll."

"Roll?"

He sighed. "My sleep roll. I found that place two months ago, just as it started to get cold. It's warm down in that hole. And I was safe from the cops, from the security guards kicking me awake."

"You were sleeping there?"

"Yes, I was asleep but then I heard her cry out, and I looked up, and there she was coming down. She landed against the wall and there was this metal—"

"No, don't!" Henrietta interrupted him. "Enough! If you pushed her, if you did something to her, just tell the truth. To me. In here. In God's name, tell me the truth!"

He stared at her and then slapped his hands together, holding them up, mock prayer, in front of her face. She flinched and held her breath.

"You calling me a killer? I'm homeless, Lady Minister, but not brainless. I wouldn't kill a person and then show up here later."

He was right, of course. Why had she been so quick to accuse and judge? And now she throbbed with regret, endless, irreparable regret over words said or unsaid and things done or never done, the same regret that she used to try to assuage when a visitor expressed it. Always remembering the last scenes, the last words. If only I had said this or if only I had done that. And now it was her turn.

"I am so sorry. She was my friend. I am trying to understand why this happened."

"I am sorry for your loss then, Ma'am," he said.

"Why are you here to see her, if you never knew her?" Why would a stranger ever come into the viewing room to see a stranger?

"They dragged me in—the paramedics. It was her blood on me, not my own, but they wouldn't listen and made me get checked out."

Henrietta could now see that it was not mud on his jacket, and she had to look away.

"I tried to stop the bleeding, and I couldn't. And then I went up and got help. It was the last thing I wanted to do, let me tell you, to let them know where I was, but I thought I had to do it. Somebody had to do it. I thought about running, and I don't know why, but I didn't want to leave her there alone, so I pointed my flashlight up and swooped it back and forth. They saw it."

She looked at him closely now and saw that he had blood-stains on the arms of his jacket and across his chest. Had he held Ellie as she lay dying, at least, so she knew somebody was there, somebody cared?

"I don't know. I just wanted to see her one more time, in the light. I saw her fall, like you figured. Only witness. They called me a Passerby in that report. But I didn't."

"Didn't what?"

"Didn't pass her by."

He smiled at her then, and she saw him clearly. His upper front teeth were missing, so it was a child's smile in an old face.

"Is there a word for that? Stayingby? Should be a word for that, 'cause I seem to be stuck here staying by. I'll be honest. I don't think all of her has left us quite yet."

She looked at him, and his eyes were bright. He was afraid. But not of the body, and not of what he had done, but of something that would not let go, had not left this room, and she felt it too. How to release it?

She smiled back at him. "There is a word for it. For you. For what you did."

"What?" he asked.

"Angel," she answered.

He shook his head, scowling. "No, don't be saying that! Don't be thinking that I'm some kind of saint in dirty clothes or prophet just because I'm on the streets. Don't be thinking that by being nice to me, you will get your own halo polished up with a poor soul's gratefulness."

He must have given that speech before. It packed a hard punch. Henrietta had never had anybody speak to her this way. She had people in here mad at other people, mad at God, but this was the first time somebody was genuinely mad at her. It was a stupid thing to say. As if she decided who the angels were in the world.

"I'm sorry. I was trying to give you a compliment, to praise you for . . . "

"For doing the right thing? Save it. You don't have to believe in God or angels to know what's right."

Henrietta held out her hand. "Let me start over. My name is Henrietta, and that lady over there is Ellie."

He gave her a gummy grin, and touched her hand briefly. "Name's Leo, not Passerby."

"Well, Leo, we are all just passing through, aren't we?" Henrietta said.

"And some of us just can't ever stop moving, that's for sure."

"Ellie worked with the homeless. She went down to a shelter and volunteered every day since her daughter died."

"Well, at least she wasn't one of those do-gooders who show up only on Thanksgiving when the news cameras are out."

"No, she loved the work. She said that after Mandy died, she could not stop making her lunch every day, and so she put it in the car and handed it out to the first needy person she saw. And then she just wanted to help more and more people."

"Yep, plenty of them in this city, that's for sure."

"It's the warm weather," Henrietta said.

Leo smirked. "Damn, I'm tired of hearing that. It's not the warm weather, or Florida would have more of us. It's the cold-hearted people sealed in their cars, not seeing anything but the road ahead."

"Ellie was not one of those people, Leo. She had a tough life, a lot of losses. She always had a roof over her head, but she said she knew what it was like to lose your place in the world."

"Yeah, your kid dying on you will do that. My life turned to shit after my boy was killed. Drinking was the only way I could see fit to breathe. And even so, it was hard to breathe for the longest time. The air had knife blades in it."

"I'm sorry," Henrietta said.

"Don't be sorry for something you had nothing to do with, Preacher-Lady."

He was a prickly character. She did not know how to talk to him.

"Leo. Is there anything I can do for you?"

He seemed startled by the question. Then he walked over to Ellie again and stood by the gurney. Henrietta went over to stand beside him.

"I think it was part of God's plan to take her now. I really do," Henrietta said quietly.

Leo flinched. "You know what I think? I think we say death is only part of God's plan when we agree with the timing, that's what I think. So you must have thought this was a good time for her to die."

"No, I didn't mean that! I did not want her to die. I loved her."

"Well, then, tell me something. How come you know God's plan? What makes you so special you can speak for God? Explain why He does what He does. No disrespect, but I just wanna know."

Henrietta bowed her head, ashamed at the turn the conversation was taking. This man was asking an impossible question. She did not know God's plan any more than anybody else, but in her religion, ministers mediated for God, were expected to explain away the inconsistencies and attribute it to mystery. Yet, how could death always be part of a plan, when babies died of brain cancer or were burned alive by their parents? After almost a year in this hospital, the place she had come to renew her faith, she had come instead to the terrible conclusion that she did not believe in a loving New Testament God but the Old Testament punishing God. This changed the whole picture, not necessarily for the better. But Leo was waiting for her answer.

"Tell me about your son," she said, trying to distract him. "I know that losing a child is the worst thing that a parent has to bear."

He shook his head and sighed. "No, it is not the worst. The worst is having a child die and it's your fault."

Oh, God. This was a mistake. So this is how the guilt on his face came about. And her heart lurched because she knew her legal obligation. The rules again. Any criminal act regarding a child was an exception to the confidentiality privilege. But Henrietta did not want to hear another sad dead child story. She had only the capacity to grieve for Ellie, and not a drop more left. She closed her eyes, and only then did she feel it. A draft of cool air against her face, in a room with a closed door and no windows. She felt her hair gently smoothed back. Ellie. She always called her Cool Breeze. Ellie. She would have forgiven him.

She opened her eyes.

He sighed. "She's completely gone now," he said.

"Yes," Henrietta agreed. "She's gone."

And she took a long last look at her friend. A few seconds later, when she looked back to Leo, he was also gone.

Leo knew how to disappear from view in a matter of seconds. Those seconds between the shout of a cop and the pounding of his stick. Those seconds between a scared woman walking her dog and the spray of pepper in his face. He always had an exit strategy. He had to get out of there, that viewing room. He had to run, even before he could tell the woman in there something that might have eased her pain.

He would have told her about what he saw when he shined a flashlight in her friend's face. A look of beautiful peace, even with that metal sticking into her brain. She was still breathing, but she never opened her eyes. Yet there was not a bit of hurt in her face or in her body, no flailing arms and legs. He had seen people die on the streets many times, and they always fought it. Sidewalk surfers going for another thrill ride and panicking when they realized it was their last. This was what he needed to see back at the hospital one more time, the comfort of that sweet face. Then the air moving through the room just confirmed it. She must be one of the good ones. Not like him. Heaven had a place for her.

Her friend said the dead woman had lost a daughter, and that she had lost her place in the world. How did she find her way back? Or was she still lost until now? Well, now she was finally home. Could it be suicide? He heard the nurses talking about it just three curtains away. He sure got that. How many times had he tried to end his life and failed to do that right, like most things? But he had done right by her. When he saw the body fall toward him, he had woken from a dream about his son. Maybe her scream woke him, but it wasn't loud, more like a squeak, the way people do when they are startled, the way those damn taggers did when he used to sleep underneath the bridge, and he started to move. Like they were not really scared. As if a body moving in the dark was just another twist to the night's adventure, dipping their tiny toes into the criminal life.

He remembered her body flying down toward him and landing hard against the concrete. He held her as he had never been able to hold his three-year-old son who had fallen from a window while his crackhead daddy was screwing a strawberry. Lady of Leisure, she called herself, and her leisure was exchanging the use of her body for more drugs to numb it. He had not heard his boy fall, but only heard the ambulance sirens. It was already too late. That's how come he knew about hospital viewing rooms. His boy did not have any nice calm look on his messed-up little face. His mother tried to rip Leo apart with nail scissors in that room, but he didn't feel the cuts. Was it the drugs? No. Long after the shit was out of his system, he still felt nothing, not even the cold pavement beneath his head every night.

But earlier tonight he had felt everything. He was hurting all over, absorbing pain deep into his bones. He felt the awful hole in her head, the broken neck, the shattered ribs. Was this God's punishment? To make him feel what he had not been able to feel before? Leo believed in a vindictive God, or at least some kind of harsh disciplinary one, like his father, always sharpening his belt, keeping it ready. He still believed that God was a giant whipping hand, waiting for him to do the worst thing. Yes, the worst thing. Had he surprised God when he chose to call for help, even though that exposed him and his hiding place?

He needed a hit, really bad. But he could not go back there to get his stuff. Crime scene now. And he was the criminal, simply for having no place else to go. Even the paramedics had searched him roughly, not looking for wounds, but looking for anything he might have stolen from her. That's really why they brought him in—not to clean him up like they said, but to check his pockets.

The hurting began when he got to the hospital. The nurses had no sooner laid him out in that hospital bed, covered in blankets, when he started to bawl like a baby. He had never hurt this bad, like his legs were being scattershot, like hot pokers through his knees. This was the first time he had been able to stretch his legs out and rest them for seven years. The muscles were spastic, trying to jump out of his skin. It was like coming inside from the cold, back in Detroit where he grew up, after his hands were frostbitten. He had not felt his fingers when they were freezing, but the thawing out sure smacked him down good.

He wondered what was on the other side of thawing out, after the freezing and unfreezing of your heart. Would it be that kind of peace he saw on her face at the end? Had she finally seen some way clear of all the pain and was giving in, sinking into it? Would God forgive him enough to let him have that at the end? He would lean his life toward earning that grace now. He could try. He owed it to his boy to try to make it back home to see him again. He still had time left to try.

Burying Ground

LISA GRALEY

From *The Current That Carries* (2016)

Brammer left the undertaker sitting in the hearse and climbed the hill, feeling the steepness of the incline in his legs. The men at the top were gathered around the backhoe and stood with their backs to the road. Funny how you could recognize them after so many years. There was Wetzel and Billy, Big Chew, Carl, Squirmy, Royce, Vinton. Was it that they wore the same old coats and caps? Or was it the build of their bodies, the habit of their stances that gave them away? Brammer didn't know who was on the backhoe—one of a newer generation—maybe one of Pete's sons.

Seeing Brammer, Pete waved from the top, but then turned around to supervise the digging. Most likely it was Pete who'd let news of his daddy's death slip. Pete, who'd encouraged the men to come. In small towns, people expected a funeral, a graveside service, at the least. Probably that's what he should have scheduled. But he hadn't thought he could go through with it, having to face them all and talk about his father's last months. That spiraling down until he didn't know where he was, who Brammer was, or why there wasn't an outhouse in the backyard where there needed to be one. Though he lived with Darla and Brammer his last two years, his father couldn't forget the West Virginia farm where he'd spent the rest of his life. By then, it was too late, Brammer imagined, for his father to learn about letting go. In the end, he was like a child wanting to go home. He cried for his own mother and father, wishing they would come for him, and for that perceived abandonment, so far as Brammer could tell, there was no consolation.

Still, no one could say he hadn't done right by his daddy. He had always wondered if, when the time came, he would be able to follow through. But he and Darla had cared for his daddy up to the end. Darla, really, had treated him as if he were her own father. There was nothing to feel guilty about. No regrets. He could lay his father to rest, and they could all sleep in peace this evening when the shade crawled over the Griffith family burying ground.

At the top of the hill, Brammer paused to catch his breath. There was a loud scraping in the grave, and some of the men hunched their shoulders and winced. Rock was always a problem, Brammer knew. So much so that sometimes it took dynamite to break through. But surely, they would have tried dynamite yesterday or the day before—not now with the hearse idling in the driveway.

Brammer saw Pete shaking his head and waving his arms at the backhoe driver.

"You hit rock?" Brammer yelled toward him. "What?" Pete yelled back.

Brammer cupped his mouth and yelled louder over the machine, "I SAID DID YOU HIT ROCK?"

"WORSE," Pete yelled, then said something Brammer couldn't make out.

Pete made a short slicing motion under his throat, and the driver backed away from the grave and shut down the engine.

"It's a tractor," Pete said, a little breathless.

Brammer looked from the partially dug hole to the backhoe, trying to attach some meaning. You could call it a tractor, but technically, it was a backhoe. He felt someone's hands on his arm, turning him. It was Wetzel, shriveled up into a little old man with big ears. He nodded toward the grave, pointed to the large mound of earth still left in the wide hole.

"There's a tractor buried there," Pete said. "We been digging around it, trying to bust through the rock on the outside edges without tearing up the tractor. "But it'll take shovels to uncover it the rest of the way."

Brammer peered over the edge, straining to see into the mound of earth.

"See the top of the steering wheel?" Wetzel pointed. "And one of the fenders?"

"Whose is it?" Brammer asked.

"Whose do you think?" Big Chew asked.

Brammer glanced around at the men. He was playing catch-up—as you had to with old-timers who were always a step ahead of you. But from the tone of Big Chew's words, he knew whose tractor they thought it was.

"Dad's?"

Pete shrugged. "All my years digging graves, I never seen nothing like it."

"What makes you think it's his?"

"Don't you recognize the steering wheel?" Royce asked. Again Brammer squinted, trying to adjust his eyes to the varying degrees of earth and shadow. Had he been able to see the steering wheel, he surely would have recognized it. His father had worn the original out—worn it down to nothing—till it broke in its narrowest place, with just a hard turn one day. His father took one from an old blue Dodge they had up in the hollow, just for temporary. And then had never seen reason to replace it.

"Vinton said you reported the tractor missing a while back."

"Yeah, about a year ago," Brammer said. "I was going to have it hauled over to my place so he'd have it to tinker with." It was the truth, but Brammer said it now to win points. "Someone had already got to it," he added, then looked back down into the hole. "I don't understand why they'd bury it though."

The undertaker strode up, breathless after the climb. "What seems to be the trouble, gents?"

Pete eyed the stranger. "No trouble really. There's a tractor buried in the grave."

"Yeah, I can see it," the undertaker said.

Brammer watched him squinting his eyes, studying the earth. He wondered if he really saw it or just said he did. "They say it's my father's tractor," Brammer told him. "But I don't see how."

"Well, I'll be," the undertaker said. "That's kind of curious, ain't it? How long'll it take to dig it out?" His question fell to Wetzel, the oldest among them.

"Not long," Brammer said, cutting Wetzel off. He looked to Pete hopefully.

"There was a lot of rock around the edges," Pete said. "But we couldn't use dynamite. We had to chomp and bust it up with the backhoe. We'll have to get in there with shovels now. It's just dirt from here on."

"How'd they get the tractor down there?" Brammer asked.

"They who?" Big Chew asked.

"Whoever did it."

"Don't you know who done it?"

"How would I know?"

"You lived with him a good part of your life."

Brammer looked around at the men, their arms folded.

Brammer squinted his eyes at Pete. "Do they mean Dad?"

Pete nodded. "That's what they're claiming."

"He couldn't have done it—he wasn't able," Brammer said. "Besides, he was staying with me." By their looks, he could feel the feebleness of his protest. The jury had decided, and with them convinced against him, Brammer felt like a teenager again.

"It's been here a long time," Billy said softly. "It's all rusted out."

"So you're saying you think he buried it sometime *before* he came to live with me?" Brammer questioned. "He wasn't strong enough. It would have killed him."

"All we know, there's a tractor buried now in your daddy's plot. Been there for some time," Wetzel said. "None of us did it— or even knew about it."

"But he used that tractor for everything," Brammer said. "He didn't know he wasn't coming back—*we* didn't know. We just took him till he could get back on his feet." He felt their eyes on him. Of course, his father might have known, the way people knew things they didn't put words to. The men here might have known, too. And maybe they held it against him. In the end, when it was clear his father was going downhill, Brammer had chosen to uproot his father instead of moving himself and his wife back to the farm to care for him. He could feel the protest of the men around him. That he had a job, a life elsewhere, did not matter much. There were ways of doing things, beliefs about what things ought and ought not to be done.

Following their ears, the men turned their eyes down the drive, where the backhoe driver and another young man were already dragging shovels like sleds along the graveled ruts of the road. The shovels screeched across the quartz pebbles till the men veered off into the grass to climb the hill. When they reached the edge of the pit, they paused, looking for the best way to descend. Then they scrambled down, what seemed to Brammer, the steepest part—just what you did when you were young. They walked around the mound of dirt, studying where to start. Then one, then the other began shoveling, like they were spooning ice cream, slowly as if they meant to savor it.

Brammer tried to picture his father digging such a big hole. It would have taken him weeks—steady work at that. And how could he break through the rock? In his youth, or even in his middle years, he surely could have—he would have gotten his hands on dynamite. But at eighty-two, he wasn't able—surely he wouldn't have tried to set off an explosion—and then he would've had to do all that shoveling and lifting the rock out. When Brammer picked him up that final day, he was down to skin and bones. He trembled on the way to the car, leaning on Brammer's arm. He groaned as Brammer had never heard him groan, joints and limbs rusty in pain. At the time, Brammer wondered how his father had managed so long on his own. He regretted that he hadn't taken him sooner. And maybe he would have, if his father could have found a heart to love Darla more. But that was a sad thing that no one could do anything about.

"He couldn't have dug this hole," Brammer said. "He must have had help." He gauged the men. They met his look, then turned their gaze back to the hole.

"Brammer's probably right," Vinton said. "He must have rented a backhoe or something. A little Ditch Witch wouldn't't've done it."

"Could he even operate a big backhoe?" Brammer asked.

"Clive Griffith could operate any kind of machinery," Royce said. "You oughta know that."

"One time my old man rented a bulldozer to grade around the house," Billy said. "With Daddy on it, it was hit and miss, scrape the driveway, knock down the clothesline pole, the cats flying every which way getting out of his path. Got right up near the house—the blade stuck in midair—so that any move up or down was going to bust out the wall and my mother standing beside the mashed clothesline pole shaking her head and my daddy in such a sweat. Him debating over moving the dozer right to left or left to right, and getting more and more confused about which way the switches worked—'cause, you know, some of them work backwards—and it just got too much for him, the pressure, so he just shuts her off, sends me out to find your daddy. I remember Clive was out cutting hay, and your mother radioed him on the walky-talky. So I come back home, and he nearly beats me there, bouncing along on his tractor in high gear down the road, sitting up high and pretty. Then takes the seat in the dozer, just nudges it in reverse, pretty as you please, backs the thing away from the house. Then after he'd fiddled with the knobs a bit, goes ahead and grades the section up near the foundation—careful not to get too close—he wasn't showing off none—just looked like he'd found a new toy."

"He loved machines," Squirmy said. "He understood them."

"He liked to try out new ones," Vinton said, "but his favorite was his tractor."

"His favorite was his tractor," Brammer repeated. "I can't see him burying it."

Down in the hole, the shovelers had uncovered both big rear fenders—so that the tractor looked like a crouching cat, its hind legs poised, ready to pounce.

"It was a good tractor," Squirmy said. "Wish mine was half that good."

The undertaker seemed amused. He ran his hand over the crooked wing of his hair. "Well, now, boys, just what kind of horsepower are we talking about?"

Brammer wished he could have warned the undertaker not to get them started. No telling how long they'd be here if the men got started.

"It had a mighty force," Vinton said. "I can't count the times that ol' tractor pulled my old jeep out of that creek in front of Jim McCallister's. One time Clive give me such a jerk, the jeep went lurching forward, and I had to mash on the brakes to keep from flying into Clive."

"Sure was a good tractor," Squirmy said again, with clear nostalgia.

"Was fast, too," Royce said. "So fast he had to rig a string around his hat to keep it from blowing off. I teased him, said why didn't he get himself a bonnet."

"Yeah, it was like he was from the Old West, that hat strapped to his chin."

"Never mind the pistols."

"Oh, I forgot about them pistols," Wetzel said. "Bet you remember them, Bram?"

Brammer smiled. They were his pistols, tucked into the handholds his father had welded on the back for him to hang onto when he was little. Eventually, he found other places to hang onto and kept his toy pistols in the handholds while they bounced along. They'd go all over the farm, from one chore to the next, or to the back door for supper. They'd ride up to his cousin Denzil's, or down to Wetzel's or over to Walton's. The men would just sit around, talking from their tractors, never get down off them. Brammer remembered going through the various yards, chasing cats and dogs with his pistols.

"Stay out of Lois's flowers," his daddy would warn him. And he'd just go on as before, maybe tiptoeing through the flowers instead of tearing through them. When he heard the tractor start, he knew it was time to go. That was the end of the visit. He'd run back and get on it.

"He sure took good care of that tractor," Billy said.

"Boy, did he."

"And that tractor took care of him," Vinton said.

It was hard to tell if the men more fondly remembered his father or the tractor.

"My old man used to say if ever there was an engine charmer, he bet Clive Griffith writ the book," Pete volunteered.

"That's saying something coming from Walton," Wetzel said. "He had his way with machinery, too. And it runs in the family— you and your boy." Wetzel nodded to the backhoe operator shoveling now in the grave.

"Don't know about that." Pete looked back at the tractor. "But my daddy was good as they come." He looked like he might say more but then simply firmed his lips.

Brammer remembered the death of Pete's father. It had been an early death, a violent death—the wind felling a dead tree, just the right place, the right angle, to kill him. The randomness of the act amazed them. It happened quickly with no warning, no time to say good-bye, and Pete's daddy was young, in his prime. Pete and Brammer were just out of high school. Brammer was home on spring break, his first year of college. He remembered the way word had come, house to house, Wetzel stopping by on his tractor, getting down off his tractor—which, in a way, maybe prepared Brammer's father. He came up the porch steps, where they were sitting. Brammer was in the rocker, his father on the swing. Brammer remembered his father's face, disbelief first, then the slow settling of restrained agony—they were good friends and wouldn't he have been out there helping Walton in the woods had he not stayed home to be with Brammer? That death had come as the Bible said, like a thief in the night, took just one, left the rest standing. But it stole their peace and security.

"They sure he's dead?" Brammer's father had asked, like it was a detail someone forgot to check.

After that, Brammer's daddy took Pete under his wing—and that made Brammer and Pete more like brothers than ever. But once Brammer started spending summers away, in between his college years, that about ended it—the camaraderie. And now that they hadn't seen each other in five years, Brammer felt shy around Pete. When you left, people assumed you thought yourself better than them. But that wasn't it at all. If anything, you felt lesser. You didn't call, you didn't visit—because you had the feeling of never making the cut, of being judged by people who didn't understand why you went off in the first place—you had property here, after all, why wouldn't you stay? At some point, it was hard to bear up under that kind of censure.

"Walt's been gone a long time," Wetzel said. "I reckon him and Clive'll have some catching up to do."

"Ain't that the truth," Squirmy said.

The men grew quiet, maybe thinking of others they knew who'd gone on. When you moved away, Brammer realized, you missed this graveside talk. But you learned to live without it, the way you learned to live without many things. And it was true, too, living away, that you began to lose touch with death. You didn't know it as intimately as you once had. It wasn't part of the weekly fabric of your life. Sure, people died all around you. But you didn't know them—or hadn't known them all your life—and so death lost some of its sting. It was then you had to prod it periodically with your toe—the way you might check the pressure in your tires. But you went even further. You tipped it up and looked under—as if for lizards or fish worms—to keep it from mushrooming on you. In this way, it didn't swell, or envelop you in its surge.

"I can just picture Clive sitting on that tractor, out cutting hay or plowing or mowing—always mowing," Vinton said. "You'd see him from the road. Would wonder what he was going to mow next. Would mow great big patterns in his yard—checkerboards, big daisies, words even. You remember the time he mowed 'Hello' on the big hill in front of his house? Liked to never got him to mow it out."

"Not till someone come along one night, mowed out the 'o.'"

"He always thought that was the McComas boy."

"I figure it was. He never did amount to much."

"Where's he now?"

"Last I heard, camping down't McCorkle, collecting workers comp."

"Well, it wasn't for his daddy's lack of trying."

The men grew quiet, and Brammer imagined them thinking of their own sons and daughters, the best and worst of them, the ways they didn't measure up. For how could you measure up when the men carried such high standards?

"What I picture is ol' Clive pulling that old dog of his—what was his name?

"Eeensie-Weensie," Wetzel said.

"Pulling him around on that trailer. That dog went everywhere he did."

"I bet he's buried somewhere around here—I remember Clive chiseling a stone for him." Royce turned his head, searching.

"Where'd he get that name?"

"Was you, wasn't it, Brammer?" Billy asked.

Brammer nodded his head. He'd given him the name when he was a boy. The dog had fine lines along the ridge of his back radiating out like a spider web.

Lots of the old dogs were buried here. Pets, sure, but work dogs, too, or dogs that thought they were working, always padding along behind the tractor whether it was the hoe, the rake, fence posts, or buckets of water you were hauling on the trailer. His father would be happy to see them all again—and Brammer hoped he would, hoped that Saint Francis had been right about that, and the people of other faiths and others who believed in the souls of animals. For how could you look into their eyes and not see a soul?

Down in the hole, the hood of the tractor was visible. Brammer could make out the steering wheel now and the shape of the round seat—like a misshapen dishpan. The tractor appeared to be emerging from an ocean, the waves dropping lower and lower around it.

"Why do we have to dig it out?" Brammer asked suddenly. "Can't we just bury Dad on the other side of Mom? And leave the tractor where it is? If he put it there, he must have done it for a reason."

"The headstone would be wrong then," Pete said. He pointed

to the monument that had been dragged off to the side so the backhoe could do its work. Brammer looked at the names and dates of his parents. He forced himself to stare at the stone. It was hard to see, hard to believe. It would be up to him to have the date added to his father's side. That would be one of the final things.

"See," Pete continued. "He would be where the stone says she is, and she would be where it says he is. Unless you put it at their feet, facing the other direction. Then it would go against the direction of all the others.

Brammer couldn't see that it made much difference in the long run, but maybe it did to everyone here. He wondered what Darla would have said. She seemed distant to him now, somehow out of this orbit. He had told her it would be a short trip.

"You remember that time he was sitting on his tractor in the middle of the hay field? One of Carl Lucas's boys was coming home from Buckeye—" Vinton said.

"Was Carl's grandson, I believe," Wetzel interrupted.

"I believe you're right. Was his grandson, little bitty thing—all those boys was tiny till they got to high school and busted out. Well, Clive was sitting in the field he'd been mowing, just sitting on his tractor, engine cut off. 'What you watching?' the boy asks Clive.

"Clive puts his finger to his lips, points. He'd jumped a rabbit and her young'uns, and the rabbit and all the little ones was hopping this way and that. She was hopping ahead, trying to get them to follow, but the little ones was just hopping ever which way. When Clive sees this ole boy of Carl Lucas's—"

"His grandson—"

"—this grandson—Clive hops off his tractor to help the boy catch one. They was tiny, no bigger than your fist. So the two of them was running around and around the tractor, and Carl himself comes along, says, 'Is it hide and seek, boys?' And Clive, pretty as you please, stands up with his hat in his hand, sort of bows like, then pulls a rabbit out. Carl said in that moment, the light came on in that ol' boy's face, said you could have lit a baseball field by his face."

"Course you couldn't help getting them rabbits sometimes when you was cutting hay. That was hard on old Clive then."

"Hard on any of us—especially if they had young ones. Was like you were the grim reaper," Billy said, then turning to the undertaker, he added, "No offense."

"None taken," the undertaker said. "I done my share of mowing. Hit terrapins and ground-chucks and things like that. Makes you sick to your stomach."

"I believe that ol' rabbit lived to be fifteen or sixteen, and when he died, that ol' boy broke down and cried. You'd thought he'd lost a brother."

"Used to ride him around in a milk crate attached to the handlebars of his bicycle, didn't he?"

Brammer remembered Russell Lucas's rabbit mainly because his father had caught one for him from the same batch. Brought it home to him in the pocket of his jacket that afternoon. They'd put it in the empty hamster cage—was a tiny thing. It didn't live long, though. Died the next day. Brammer was holding it in his hand. It was squirming and struggling so much that he thought it was getting stronger, but then it just went stiff in his hand. He felt the life go out of it. He never forgot. The way the rabbit turned dead—the way its breath left it and didn't come back. Was no question. And Brammer knew it. But still begged to take it to the hospital—how ridiculous it seemed now—but his father wouldn't. He blamed his father then, and had asked didn't he love him. For years afterward, he wished he hadn't said that. It was the kind of early heartbreak you gave your father. And it left a sore spot in Brammer and in his father—something that got nettled—for Brammer could read it on his father's face, every time somebody mentioned Russell Lucas's rabbit.

"Well, look here," Brammer said before the men could start in on something else. "What're we going to do? Instead of digging the tractor out the rest of the way, why don't we just bury him on the other side of it. There's enough room. We wouldn't have to dig anymore."

"Then the tractor'll be laying between him and your mother," Pete said.

"They can reach across it," Brammer said. He felt himself in the undertow of their talk. "They was always reaching across it anyway—when he was working. Her offering him something for energy, a bottle of RC or a spoon of peanut butter."

"He sure liked his RC," Big Chew said.

The young men were shoveling dirt now that had been packed in tight around the tractor. There were flakes of red paint in the shovelfuls landing at Brammer's feet, and he was glad his father wasn't here to witness it.

"I just don't see the point of going to all this trouble to dig the tractor out—if he wanted it buried," Brammer said.

"I don't know. I don't know," Big Chew was shaking his head. "I suspect he don't care what we do with the tractor so long as we found it. I believe he buried it so we'd find it."

"Be kind of hard to miss, wouldn't it?" Squirmy said.

"It's like a proxy," Royce said.

"What d'you mean, a proxy?"

"You know, the person who can stand in to vote for you—something that stands in your place—in case you're not going to be there. A sub."

Brammer felt his face growing warm. There'd never been any question about where his father would be buried. It was nothing they had talked about, but was just a given. But maybe it had been something his father feared when he left the farm to come stay with him.

"It's more like a bookmark," Billy said, looking at Brammer. "Something to mark his place till he could get back."

216

"Well, this'll be something to tell back in Belton," the undertaker said. "It beats all I ever saw. You still hear on occasion someone taking a tractor apart, building it back in the loft or on the roof of a barn—some place unusual," the undertaker said. "But no one thinks to bury one in his grave." The undertaker seemed to be enjoying himself.

"What we could do," Pete said, "is clear out a place over on the far side of the hole like you said, Brammer, but then scoot the tractor over—all of us together—scoot it over so Clive could rest easy between your mother and the tractor."

"That all right with you, Brammer?" Wetzel asked.

"I guess," Brammer said. But he wished his father had been there to ask. What had he intended? Why hadn't he said something?

The men were down to throwing out half shovelfuls, the soil in the crevices and fine lines of the tractor. Despite the rust and so many loose paint flecks, the tractor retained some of its red color.

"That's the tractor I remember," Big Chew said. "He was always touching up the rusty spots."

"He'd sure have a job if he did it today," Wetzel said. "Would have to sand everything down to the bare metal, start from scratch."

"He didn't take much to a green tractor," Royce said.

"No, he didn't approve of John Deere. Was nothing again' the engine—but was the color that bothered him. Was like he didn't understand a green tractor."

Brammer thought of his riding lawn mower. Maybe that was his father's complaint about it. "It's not a real tractor," his father was fond of saying, in the same tone he complained that Darla's Yorkies were not real dogs. With the lawn mower, though, his father had mowed Brammer's yard every other day for nearly two years—even in the winter when snow wasn't on.

"That can't be good for the grass," Brammer had said, but his father shrugged him off. One day, Brammer found him in the neighborhood baseball field, mowing.

"How'd you get here?"

"Drove."

"On the road?" But Brammer knew the answer. That was the point when he decided to fetch his father's tractor from home. At least it would sit higher and be more visible to folks driving on the street. It had all kinds of reflective gear and flashing lights his father had rigged. But he didn't tell his father—he didn't want to get his hopes up. And it was a good thing, for when they went back to the farm and found it missing, Brammer's father had taken it hard. His father shuffled out to the barn to see for himself, then went around touching everything, putting his hands on the old logs of the barn, running his hands along the weathered planks. It was nearly more than Brammer could stand. His father stared at the rutted ground where the tractor used to sit. But he didn't say anything, just firmed his lips. Brammer thought he was blaming him, and he saw, by the light through the open door, his father's wet eyes.

But that was life, Brammer told himself at the time. You moved on—you had to. It was this ability to adapt that helped human beings survive loss—losses more awful than most of the people he knew went through. The problem with his father's generation was that they held on to everything. They couldn't let go. His mother had stored away enough leftover tin foil to cover the dome of the West Virginia capitol. And his father saved little bitty slivers of soap that were smaller than sucked candy. They had trouble throwing anything away. And it was also true, Brammer knew, with the connection they felt for each other. He understood how his father had held on and sheltered the bond with his mother for the five uneasy years after her death. Of course, that made more sense. You couldn't help but cling, the biblical word was *cleave*, to the one who shared with you your hopes and losses.

But here, in a wild—the word *ecstasy* came to Brammer—in a wild ecstasy, an uncharacteristic turn, his father had buried an old but perfectly functioning tractor. It had seen better days, sure. But what on earth would make his father do it?

"Say, what model would you say that tractor is?" the undertaker asked.

"He got it back in the sixties," Wetzel said. "How old are you, Brammer?"

"I'll be forty-eight in March."

"That's how old the tractor is," Wetzel said. "Libby was pregnant with Brammer when they bought it. Was a big deal at the time. Could they afford the payments, and the baby on the way? Was all he talked about for a while. But Clive wanted it so bad. It was Libby finally went and put a down payment on it."

"I remember him telling about that. He was scared they would lose it. Or the house one," Billy said.

"I believe it was hard for them the first years."

"Was hard for everybody."

"Always hard on anybody just getting started."

"Look," the undertaker pointed. "The big old headlights. Like frog eyes."

Even with one of the headlights broken out, the tractor had a face, and it seemed to gaze at them through its one good eye. The face was as familiar to Brammer as anyone he had ever loved.

"One time I tried to buy him a new one," Brammer said. He felt the attention of the men shift his direction. "He wouldn't hear of it. Then I was for going on and buying it behind his back. And finally Mom said, 'Even if you get him a new one, it's the old one he's going to use.' So I didn't."

"Like as not he would have warmed up to the new one," Wetzel said. "If it was from you. He'd found use for both of them. Wouldn't have wanted to hurt your feelings none. Or your mother's."

"I doubt it, boys," Big Chew said. "I give him the chance to buy my tractor at a real good price—after we quit raising a garden. He wouldn't have nothing to do with it."

"Yeah, but look at what you're talking about there," Vinton said.

Some of the men laughed. Even Brammer knew Big Chew's tractor, though bought new, was lopsided for some reason—and had a peculiar sound, when it was running, like a tea kettle. Every one of them had proposed some solution to get the whistle out—but no one, not Walt nor even Brammer's daddy could ever fix it. When Big Chew was coming to visit, everyone knew a long ways off.

"Don't much blame him myself," the undertaker said. "This is the first hearse I ever had." He pointed down the drive to where Brammer's father was lying. Brammer saw the undertaker had rolled down all the windows, and he imagined his father recognizing the breezes of home. He wondered if he minded being kept waiting. But then remembered it was by his own devising. Was that why he had done it? To keep them waiting?

"You got a son who'll take it over for you?"

"Nope. I'll be the last one. My daddy was an undertaker and his before him. But I'll be the last one. I had a boy, he got killed in a car wreck."

"That's rough," Billy said.

Brammer heard some of the men take a deep breath. He thought they were probably imagining it. For a minute, the only sounds were the slicing of the shovels, the bare metal of the shovels scraping the metal of the tractor, and the thudding of the dirt landing at their feet.

"Ain't you ever afraid of it breaking down, and you on your way to the cemetery?" Vinton asked, breaking the silence.

"Whew," Big Chew said, "and what if you were in the heat of summer? You probably ain't got no air condition."

The men recovered and laughed a little. But then, seeming to remember that one of them was lying now in the hearse, stopped short. They turned their attention to the gravediggers. The tractor had taken its old shape. The men had cleared most of the dirt away. Pete's boy brushed off a swath from the top with his forearm. It was something to see, the tractor sitting down there in the grave and, for the most part, composed. Brammer wished he had a picture of it, something to show Darla, for how could he describe to her all about it—and all that the men said, too?

"Looks like you all could use some brooms," Royce said. "Want me to get one from my truck?"

"I've got one in the back of my truck, too," Squirmy said. "Bring it, too."

With the brooms, the men made gentle sweeping motions over the tractor like they were archaeologists uncovering an ancient artifact. Brammer thought of King Tut, buried with all his treasures. So the tractor was what his father had intended to take with him? It had not been easy, he imagined, for his father to say good-bye to it. But perhaps he thought he'd be reunited with it. If his father had been on a desert island and told he could take only one thing, Brammer guessed the tractor would have been it. And why not? You used it to put out your crop and to bring in your crop. You cut your hay with it to feed your stock. On a farm, without one, you were nothing. You needed it from beginning to end.

He remembered that in the springtime, when they broke the ground, he had ridden on top of the disk behind the tractor to give it weight, so it would cut deeper. It had been, then, like a carnival ride. Around and around they'd go, the tractor pulling the disk, and Brammer laughing, his father smiling back on him, sometimes just speeding up or cutting the wheel hard, Brammer knew, to make it more fun—but not so much as to throw him off. From behind the tractor and disk would spring huge coils of earth, and out of them came fish worms hopping up, some cut in two, all of them hopping and wiggling to get back under the earth, for they were never more alive than when they'd just been uncovered. And he and his father would go along afterward, collecting them in coffee cans of dirt, saving them to go fishing.

With the tractor, his father had pulled out tree stumps, rocking back and forth, wiggling the stump, tugging it like it was a giant tooth. In the fall, they'd timbered in the woods for firewood that would serve in emergencies or on special days when you felt like having a fire. They took fallen trees mostly, ones that were seasoned—so they didn't have to cut the live ones. His father would trim off the limbs, then hook a chain around the logs and pull them down the path coming off the mountain, the logs rolling and zigzagging through the woods, ricocheting off the trunks of standing trees, jarring the leaves out of them, all the way down, and Brammer ran out in front of the tractor, in utter abandon, headlong down the hillside, heralding their coming.

On the trailer, his father had hauled buckets of water, tubs of potatoes, bales of hay. He had hauled all the dogs with all the old names—Old Skip and Rover and Billy and Tanner and Bob-Randy and Bear and Eensie-Weensie, and together with them, Brammer.

His father had taught him to drive on the tractor, then later how to plow straight rows. After he learned, his father expected it of him—even on days when Brammer wanted to be out running with Pete in the old El Camino Pete's father had fixed up. One time Brammer was supposed to plow but sneaked off with Pete. That was the time they tried smoking pot with Butch Mc-Comas under one of the big hilltop rocks up Ely, which might have made for a pleasant memory if not for what always trailed it.

When he got back to the farm, his father had lain off all the field himself, plowed it, and even sown the corn. He didn't say anything to Brammer. That was his way. He didn't say anything to him for days, just kept him locked out of his conversation. It was one of those disappointments in you your father was bound to have. And you didn't know how to make up for it. There was no way to make it up. Your father kept stubborn and locked you out. There were so many things a father would hold against you when you were just making your way in the world, when you were just seeking joy and then later, too, when you had found your own steadfast sustenance.

"Say, guess what?" one of the young men yelled from the grave of the tractor. "He left the key in it."

"Give it a try," Vinton said.

"Nah." The man frowned. "There's probably not even gas in the tank." "Like that'd be the main concern," Squirmy said.

"Let Brammer try it."

"Yeah, Brammer. You go try it."

Brammer shook his head. "It won't start," he said. "After all this time—and out in the weather, rain seeping down, rusting away." He glanced at the men to make sure they were joking, but they looked serious. That was just how they would look, leading you along. He had never really acquired the ability to read them, and he wondered if Pete had. He looked at Pete now for some sign.

"Go on," Pete said. "You may's well try before we cover her back up next to your daddy."

So Pete was one of them now. Brammer didn't like being put on the spot, but he wanted to do right by his father. He looked at the men again. Wetzel nodded toward the grave. "Go on down there," he said.

Brammer swallowed. His heart was beating hard, and he felt himself breaking into a sweat.

"It's all right," Billy encouraged him. "For old time's sake."

Sometimes the right thing was going along with them even when you knew what they were up to. Brammer started down the side of the hole and felt the loose earth slipping into the tops of his shoes. He knew very well that the tractor wouldn't start. Maybe they would laugh at his gullibility. Maybe that's what they would tell stories about at the next funeral, how he got down in the pit to start his father's tractor that had been seizing up and rusting more than two years in the grave. He knew it wouldn't start, but he didn't mind getting a closer look anyway.

He approached the tractor as if it were a strange horse, slowly, holding his hand out to it, in friendship. He could see the rusty brake pedals— pads long worn off, the clutch pedal—what was nothing but a rod, the paint worn off decades ago. All the pedals were rusty now—no boot soles to keep the rust at bay. And here was the big dent, the bent fender where Brammer had one time backed his father's truck into it because he had backed without looking in the rearview mirror. His father had been disappointed that day, too. And Brammer had cried—even though he was too old to cry—but he had felt the too-great weight of the violation.

On the tractor he saw the handholds his father had welded for him, and just barely he could make out the rust-swollen pistols—welded now, whether by his father or by time, as permanent fixtures. Brammer switched his gaze to the steering wheel, for it was too much to look at the pistols. But he would remember them and tell Darla.

When he touched the blue-vinyl steering wheel, he felt the first wave topple the flood wall. He sensed what was coming and knew there was nothing now left to stop it—it had been set in motion by the pistols and by the tractor and by the memories of the men, and now it spun closer. Most likely, the men had set him up. They had herded him into a chute where there was no place to go but straight through. He reached for the key with his right hand. The key ring was corroded and snapped in two at the touch of his fingers. But the brass key itself was firm between his forefinger and thumb. Leaning his wrist clockwise, he turned the key in the ignition and was surprised at its turning at all.

There was a click and then nothing. Nothing took hold. Nothing registered. There was no spark. No turn over. No intake. No anything. But in the silence, Brammer heard the familiar chug-chug-chug and chortle of the tractor starting. It turned over in his heart, and he felt it saturate him, the sound of the day starting, the goats waiting to be let out of the barn, the tractor puttering forward, the dogs all bounding toward it determined to go wherever it was going, the throttle increasing, and you were late to it and had to get running—ground to break, rows to plow, corn to sow, all of it starting without you, but starting, and you could run to catch it if you were fast enough.

It started in his abdomen and worked its way upward—not nausea nor faintness but heat, rushing heat, and he felt it rushing and overtaking him. He swallowed and clutched the steering wheel and blinked, trying to push it back but felt a hard sob escape, and others, lined up behind like waves on a shoreline. He knew the men were watching him, but he couldn't stop. He gripped the steering wheel tighter and leaned his head down on his arm. He longed for the comfort of Darla, the way she cradled his head, the consolation of her hand on his neck, her silent but strong presence when silence and strength was what he needed. What had they been thinking, when they decided she wouldn't come?

He heard the men mumbling and moving about. Would they leave him in the grave alone with his grief? When he looked up, he saw them climbing down, some sliding, one or two jumping into the pit. The undertaker was helping Wetzel. For just a second, Brammer thought it was the tractor they were coming for, but then he felt the solid grasps and pats of their hands on his shoulders and the circle of their arms around him.

CONTRIBUTORS

ED ALLEN is the author of two novels: *Straight through the Night* and *Mustang Sally*. His short story collection *Ate It Anyway* won the 2002 Flannery O'Connor Award for Short Fiction. His poetry collection *67 Mixed Messages* was published in 2006. He is professor emeritus of English at the University of South Dakota and now teaches in the low residency creative writing program at University of Alaska, Anchorage.

ROBERT ANDERSON, Flannery O'Connor Award winner in 1999 for *Ice Age*, is also the author of *Little Fugue* (2005). He lives in New York City and teaches writing at the Nationwide Master Institute in Flushing, Queens.

MARY CLYDE's *Survival Rates* won the Flannery O'Connor Award in 1999. Her novel *No Morning Sun* is awaiting publication. She is retired from teaching literature and creative writing and lives in Phoenix with a succession of golden retrievers.

MOLLY GILES Flannery O'Connor Award winner in 1985 for *Rough Translations*, has subsequently published a novel, *Iron Shoes*, and three other award-winning short story collections, *Creek Walk*, *All the Wrong Places*, and *Bothered*. Retired from teaching at San Francisco State University and the University of Arkansas, she lives in Woodacre, California.

JACQUELIN GORMAN, Flannery O'Connor Award winner in 2012 for *The Viewing Room*, teaches creative writing at Stevenson University in Baltimore, Maryland. She previously published a memoir, *The Seeing Glass* (1997), and is currently writing a collection of personal essays.

TONI GRAHAM, a Flannery O'Connor Award winner for *The Suicide Club* in 2015, is the author of two previous collections of short stories: *Waiting for Elvis*, winner of the John Gardner Book Award, and *The Daiquiri Girls*, winner of the Grace Paley Prize for Short Fiction. She teaches creative writing at Oklahoma State University, where she serves as editor and fiction editor for *The Cimarron Review*.

LISA GRALEY Flannery O'Connor Award winner in 2015 for *The Current That Carries*, teaches English and humanities at the University of Louisiana at Lafayette. She is also the author of a poetry collection, *Box of Blue Horses*. She has published stories in *Glimmer Train*, the *Georgia Review*, the *McNeese Review*, and *Impost: A Journal of Creative and Critical Work*. A native of West Virginia, she is currently at work on a novel.

MONICA MCFAWN is a writer, artist, and performer living in Michigan. Her short story collection *Bright Shards of Someplace Else* won the Flannery O'Connor Award for Short Fiction as well as a Michigan Notable Book award. She is also the author of an art and poetry chapbook, "A Catalogue of Rare Movements," and her drawings and animations have been shown in galleries around the country. McFawn is a recipient of an NEA Fellowship in Literature and Walter E. Dakin Fellowship from the Sewanee Writers' Conference. She is an assistant professor at Northern Michigan University, where she teaches fiction and scriptwriting. When she isn't writing, drawing, or teaching, she trains her Welsh Cob cross pony in dressage and jumping.

DIANNE NELSON OBERHANSLY's latest book is *The Madonna of Starbucks*. Her Flannery O'Connor Award–winning collection, *A Brief History of Male Nudes in America*, was published in 1993. *Downwinders: An Atomic Tale*, which she cowrote with Curtis Oberhansly, was chosen as a Utah Book of the Year. Oberhansly's fiction has appeared widely in journals, including in the *Iowa Review*, *Ploughshares*, and the *New England Review*, and her poems have been published in *Paper Nautilus*, *Canary*, *Third Wednesday*, and elsewhere. She lives in rural Utah, where she is a hiker, a slow food enthusiast, and an arts supporter and educator.

GINA OCHSNER is the author of the short story collections *The Necessary Grace to Fall* and *People I Wanted to Be*, both of which received the Oregon Book Award. She has written *The Russian Dreambook of Color and Flight* and *The Hidden Letters of Velta B.* She is the grateful recipient of an NEA fellowship award as well as a Guggenheim Fellowship and a Howard Foundation Fellowship Award. She teaches at Corban University and with Seattle Pacific's low residency MFA program.

ANNE PANNING, Flannery O'Connor Award winner in 2006 for *Super America*, is also the author of a previous short story collection and a novel. Her memoir *Dragonfly Notes: On Distance and Loss* is forthcoming from Stillhouse Press. She teaches creative writing at SUNY–Brockport, where she lives with her family.

Author of eleven books, MELISSA PRITCHARD has been a five-time winner of Pushcart and O. Henry prizes, along with numerous other national awards and fellowships. An Arizona State University emeritus professor, she lives in Columbus, Georgia, where she was a recent fellow at the Carson McCullers Center for Writers and Musicians.

ANNE RAEFF's second novel, *Winter Kept Us Warm*, was published in 2018. Her short story collection *The Jungle around Us* won the 2015 Flannery O'Connor Award for Short Fiction. The collection was also a finalist for the California Book Award and was on the *San Francisco Chronicle*'s 100 Best Books of 2017 list. *Clara Mondschein's Melancholia*, also a novel, was published in 2002. Raeff's stories and essays have appeared in *New England Review*, *ZYZZYVA*, and *Guernica*, among other places. She is proud to be a high school teacher and works primarily with recent immigrants. She lives in San Francisco with her wife and two cats.

BARBARA SUTTON's stories have appeared in *Agni*, the *Missouri Review*, the *Antioch Review*, the *Harvard Review*, *Image*, and other publications. She works as a government speechwriter in New York City and blogs at *Sketches by Baz*.

NANCY ZAFRIS is the author of two novels, *Lucky Strike* and *The Metal Shredders*. Her stories have appeared in numerous literary magazines, and she is fiction editor of the *Kenyon Review*.

THE FLANNERY O'CONNOR AWARD
FOR SHORT FICTION

DAVID WALTON, *Evening Out*

LEIGH ALLISON WILSON, *From the Bottom Up*

SANDRA THOMPSON, *Close-Ups*

SUSAN NEVILLE, *The Invention of Flight*

MARY HOOD, *How Far She Went*

FRANÇOIS CAMOIN, *Why Men Are Afraid of Women*

MOLLY GILES, *Rough Translations*

DANIEL CURLEY, *Living with Snakes*

PETER MEINKE, *The Piano Tuner*

TONY ARDIZZONE, *The Evening News*

SALVATORE LA PUMA, *The Boys of Bensonhurst*

MELISSA PRITCHARD, *Spirit Seizures*

PHILIP F. DEAVER, *Silent Retreats*

GAIL GALLOWAY ADAMS, *The Purchase of Order*

CAROLE L. GLICKFELD, *Useful Gifts*

ANTONYA NELSON, *The Expendables*

NANCY ZAFRIS, *The People I Know*

ROBERT ABEL, *Ghost Traps*

T. M. MCNALLY, *Low Flying Aircraft*

ALFRED DEPEW, *The Melancholy of Departure*

DENNIS HATHAWAY, *The Consequences of Desire*

RITA CIRESI, *Mother Rocket*

DIANNE NELSON OBERHANSLY, *A Brief History
of Male Nudes in America*

CHRISTOPHER MCILROY, *All My Relations*

CAROL LEE LORENZO, *Nervous Dancer*

C. M. MAYO, *Sky over El Nido*

WENDY BRENNER, *Large Animals in Everyday Life*

PAUL RAWLINS, *No Lie Like Love*

HARVEY GROSSINGER, *The Quarry*

HA JIN, *Under the Red Flag*

ANDY PLATTNER, *Winter Money*

FRANK SOOS, *Unified Field Theory*

MARY CLYDE, *Survival Rates*

HESTER KAPLAN, *The Edge of Marriage*

ANNIVERSARY ANTHOLOGIES

TENTH ANNIVERSARY
The Flannery O'Connor Award: Selected Stories,
EDITED BY CHARLES EAST

FIFTEENTH ANNIVERSARY
Listening to the Voices:
Stories from the Flannery O'Connor Award,
EDITED BY CHARLES EAST

THIRTIETH ANNIVERSARY
Stories from the Flannery O'Connor Award:
A 30th Anniversary Anthology: The Early Years,
EDITED BY CHARLES EAST
Stories from the Flannery O'Connor Award:
A 30th Anniversary Anthology: The Recent Years,
EDITED BY NANCY ZAFRIS

THEMATIC ANTHOLOGIES

Hold That Knowledge: Stories about Love
from the Flannery O'Connor Award for Short Fiction,
EDITED BY ETHAN LAUGHMAN
The Slow Release: Stories about Death
from the Flannery O'Connor Award for Short Fiction,
EDITED BY ETHAN LAUGHMAN